I0611867

Murder in the Tidwell Building

Murder in the Tidwell Building

JAMES D. NOGALSKI
and MARK E. BIDDLE

RESOURCE *Publications* · Eugene, Oregon

MURDER IN THE TIDWELL BUILDING

Copyright © 2025 James D. Nogalski and Mark E. Biddle. All rights reserved. Except for brief quotations in critical publications or reviews, no part of this book may be reproduced in any manner without prior written permission from the publisher. Write: Permissions, Wipf and Stock Publishers, 199 W. 8th Ave., Suite 3, Eugene, OR 97401.

Resource Publications
An Imprint of Wipf and Stock Publishers
199 W. 8th Ave., Suite 3
Eugene, OR 97401

www.wipfandstock.com

PAPERBACK ISBN: 979-8-3852-5699-0
HARDCOVER ISBN: 979-8-3852-5700-3
EBOOK ISBN: 979-8-3852-5701-0

VERSION NUMBER 08/28/25

To our partners in crime, Melanie and Priscilla.

Acknowledgements

This is the place where authors typically thank those who have helped them conduct research in order to write the book. In our case, this is not necessary because we have worked with the people who inhabit the pages of this book as characters. We should note, however, that this book is a work of fiction. Any correspondence to people living or dead is purely coincidental or used with permission. The communications professor and the story he tells about Hollywood screenwriters who appear in Chapter 23 are real, but the conversation recorded there is fictional. References to the history of Baylor University did happen, but the circumstance surrounding their references in the book did not. The building names of Baylor University (including the title character) are also real, but the scenes that take place in them are not.

There are important people we would like to acknowledge and thank. The women at the information desk in the Waco Police Department generously answered questions concerning the structure of the Department. Numerous colleagues and family members of the authors, when they learned about the book, were quite encouraging of the endeavor. Their questions and encouragement spurred us on. Drs. Carey Newman and Maura Jortner provided us with technical expertise that helped us understand the publishing world of novelists. This book represents a very different kind of book than the academic literature we Hebrew Bible professors typically produce. They helped us understand and navigate those differences.

A special word of thanks goes to our partners, Melanie Nogalski and Priscilla Lindsey Biddle. These women gave generously of their time to read a draft of the manuscript and to offer extraordinarily helpful critique. Our partners not only read a draft of the manuscript, however, they also listened as we told them about the plot as it unfolded, and about who the characters were. They engaged us as we described scenes as we thought about them. They quite literally became our partners in crime.

Finally, we would like to acknowledge all those we have known who have suffered from the ambition and bigotry of others, often in the name of religion. Their stories inspired us to write this book. May they find peace, justice, and kindness—or as the Hebrew Bible would say, *shalom*, *mishpat*, and *hesed*. Their diverse stories testify to the lives they have lived, lives that were not defined by the suffering inflicted upon them by others. Their lives are filled with joy and truth-telling, and they have touched the lives of all those who know them.

Detective Dean Piper of the Waco Police Department, known to his friends as Dino, had been waiting for his partner, Jack Farmer, to arrive for breakfast. He had finished one cup of coffee while he waited. Dino had grown up in the suburbs of three different metropolitan areas in the Midwest, but he had lived in Waco for the better part of twenty-five years. His Midwest roots taught him to be punctual. People were more laid back in Texas about starting times, and his partner was no exception.

Dino looked at his watch. Not surprisingly, Jack was late again. He usually blamed his wife, Mariposa, or his two teenage daughters for his tardiness, but Dino knows better. Jack tells everyone that he is meticulous about being on time, but that is not exactly true. Jack is selectively punctual and shows up when he wants to, whether he wants to be five minutes early or wants to saunter in fifteen minutes late. In his mind, he's on time either way.

Dino, on the other hand, is consistently punctual. He was already on his second cup of coffee, waiting for Jack to arrive before he ordered breakfast. As the server came by for the third time to see if Dino was ready to order, Dino saw Jack pull into a parking spot, so he ordered for the both of them. Jack always gets the same thing when they eat here, *huevos rancheros*. For his part, Dino always gets their biscuits and gravy that comes with a side of sausage.

"Sit down partner," Dino greeted Jack. "Let me guess. You're late because Mariposa wouldn't let you leave the house. She just had to have you with her for another ten minutes."

"What are you talking about, Dino? I'm not late. I'm right on time. My food hasn't even arrived yet. But now that you mention it, I did spend a little more time than usual with Mariposa today. What can I say? She likes my company, if you get my drift." Jack winked.

"TMI, Jack. TMI. I ordered your usual. You'll have to get your own coffee. And you are most certainly late. It's almost eight fifteen and we

1

have to be at work at nine. You know Mendoza will tear us a new one if we're late," referring to their sergeant, George Mendoza.

"Ah, he's not so bad. Yeah, he can be a little gruff and a little impatient, but I don't understand why he gets on your nerves so much."

"He's not just a little impatient. When he wants something, he wants it yesterday. It doesn't matter what you're doing at the moment. He expects you to drop everything because the next task he is going to assign you is always the most important task that takes precedence over everything. Half the time, he's pulling us off an important case to assign us to some penny-ante case that's not worth our time investigating. You remember two weeks ago when he pulled us off the home invasion case and we had to spend three days trying to track down the stolen bicycle just because the bicycle belonged to the son of some crony of the lieutenant. He is always trying to curry favor with someone up the food chain."

"Man, you really gotta lighten up or you'll have a heart attack. You gotta learn to let go."

When the food arrived, Dino and Jack began eating. Jack asked Dino, "So, how's Teri and the kids?" Dino's wife, Teri, works as a paralegal in a law firm. They have two adult daughters, Eryn and Tommi. Tommi lives in Waco, where she works as an academic counselor at Baylor University. Eryn lives in Austin, where she works from home as a financial analyst for a major corporation. Both are happily married.

"The kids are fine, I think. Eryn called last weekend to catch us up on what she's been doing. She was, as always, on her way somewhere. She calls every couple weeks as she's driving to pick up her groceries or go to her yoga class. We haven't spoken to Tommi in the better part of a month, even though she lives in town. If we want to talk with her, we're the ones who have to pick up the phone. We just assume everything is fine with her unless she tells us otherwise."

"Your house must be awfully quiet at night. I can't imagine what it would be like to be an empty nester. Sofia and Juanita run me ragged trying to take them to places they're supposed to be. Juanita is becoming more and more like a typical teenager, especially with her mom. Sofia often tells Mariposa she's ruining her life. Mariposa does not take kindly to that. Fortunately, Juanita hasn't hit that stage yet."

"She will. Both our girls went through phases when we couldn't do anything right. They both told us how we ruined their lives because we didn't know how to spell. In middle school, Eryn told us all the girls made fun of her because she spelled her name with a 'y' instead of an 'i' like 'normal' kids. It was even worse with Tommi. On the first day of eighth grade when the teacher called the roll, the teacher noticed they also had a boy in the class named Tommy. So, when she got to our daughter's name, she called out her name as 'Tommi with an i.' The whole class started calling her 'girl Tommi' after that. She came home and screamed at us that night because we gave her a boy's name."

"We've seen some of the same thing with Sofia and Juanita. The kids tease Juanita, calling her a Mexican because of her name, and she gets upset. They do the same with Sofia because she spells her name with an 'f' instead of 'ph.' They both blame the bullies, but Sofia takes it to another level and says its our fault. We've lucked out so far with Juanita, but I'm sure that's coming. For now, Juanita still likes to do things with her dad. Although, I caught hell from Mariposa last week when I missed Sofia's soccer game, so I better not miss Juanita's game today."

"And whose fault was that?"

"What you mean?"

"I mean Mendoza made you miss that game. We were just about to leave for the day when he sent us out to look for that dadgum bicycle."

"True, but what're you gonna do? He's the boss."

Dino started to say something else about sergeant Mendoza, but Jack's cell phone rang. "Speak of the devil," Jack reported as he answered the phone. He listened intently for a couple minutes, periodically muttering "Yes, sir" into the mouthpiece. When he hung up, Jack looked longingly at his plate and said, "Mendoza wants us in the office ASAP. He's got a case for us."

"What kind of case?"

"He said he'd tell us when we get there."

"Why couldn't he tell you on the phone? If it's an emergency, we should be going straight to the crime scene, but we're not, are we? No, 'his highness' summons us to appear and bow down before him. Sorry. I've not yet finished my breakfast. You can go ahead if you want, but I'm going to sit here and eat until I finish my biscuits."

Jack smiled and nodded, "I find your logic impeccable, partner. These *huevos rancheros* aren't going to eat themselves. Besides, I can eat them ASAP."

1

The Tidwell Bible Building sits majestically on the campus of Baylor University in Waco, Texas. Today, the building buzzed with activity, but not with the sound of students roaming the halls. It is not a normal semester for the Tidwell Building because the building is being renovated from top to bottom. Sledgehammers pound against concrete and metal as the historic building is taken down to the studs. Crews work on all six floors to completely redesign the classroom and office spaces. Everything else will be gutted and rebuilt.

On the first floor, workers have been demolishing the inside of Miller Chapel for days after having spent six months reducing the rest of the building to a skeleton. The chapel was originally constructed for students to attend required chapel services three times a week. First-year students at Baylor still must attend chapel as part of the university's commitment to maintain a Christian identity. Apparently, one year of required piety suffices. For decades, however, the student body had outgrown the space. Instead, the chapel had served as a large lecture hall for special events. Prior to the renovation of the Tidwell Building, the stage at the front of the long chapel looked less like a lecture hall and more like a sanctuary in a large Baptist church. It boasted a pipe organ, a piano, and a speaker's platform that looked like a pulpit, and had forty-four sets of long church pews that could seat up to five hundred people if they crammed close together.

Five modern stained-glass windows line each side of the chapel. The Miller family donated the windows, hence the name, Miller Chapel. After the renovation, the cavernous space will house three floors of faculty offices.

In the initial phase of demo, workers pried the pews from their sacred spots where they had stood since the completion of the Tidwell

4

Building in 1954. The pews were permanently affixed to the concrete floor, so removing them had taken days of hard, loud, and dirty work. A large pipe organ and a grand piano had lived on either side of the stage. Pipes for the organ rose above the choir loft. Behind the pipes, not visible to those sitting in chapel rested an entry to the back of the chapel.

Workers busied themselves by removing the stage and the choir loft. They had removed the organ and piano weeks earlier, but today workers had begun removing the pipes themselves and demolishing the offices in the second-floor hallway.

Suddenly, someone yelled, "What the hell? Who put a skeleton in the crawl space?"

Immediately, mayhem ensued. Workers in the second-story hallway behind the choir loft ran to the hatch at the end of the hall that opened into the space behind the organ pipes. A few workers ran into the space and yelled back at the others. Cell phones came out of pockets. Texts were sent. Cameras clicked. More texts went out. Two workers almost jumped down the small stairway at the other end of the hall. Within minutes, those working on the sixth floor at the other end of the building came running down five flights of stairs at breakneck speed to reach the chapel on the ground floor. A few tripped as they descended the stairs two at a time. Some cussed when they heard the news. Others mumbled to themselves. All of them left their stations fand headed to the chapel.

The empty halls of the building magnified the noise exponentially. As more crew members make their way to the chapel, a crowd formed at the bottom of the steps leading to the second floor. People spoke excitedly to one another while looking at the pictures on their phones. Like water from hoses, they streamed onto the chapel floor, and the mob moved in rivulets. They gathered in a pool near the bottom of the stage. Those in back tried to reach the steps to the second-floor hallway, but others had already packed the stairs.

Those who did reach the upstairs hallway shouted questions to those in the crawl space. Those in the crawl space yelled back in response. In turn, those in the hallway relayed information downstairs. The noise in the building became louder and continued to escalate for a full ten minutes until one lone voice asked, "Has anyone called the cops?"

Silence replaced the commotion as dozens of people simultaneously began calling 911 and texting the police station. It was not a normal day in the Tidwell Building.

2

Jack and Dino arrived at police headquarters and made their way up to the major crimes division on the fifth floor. They had barely reached their desks when Sergeant George Mendoza called them into his office with a voice loud enough to wake the dead. Dino raised an eyebrow to Jack to make sure Jack understood his frustration at the manner that his sergeant spoke to them. Jack shrugged his shoulders, signaling he knew, but he was not bothered as much as Dino.

The detectives entered Mendoza's office, spacing themselves far enough apart to follow the CDC guidelines for physical distancing in the aftermath of the COVID outbreak. Mendoza asked, "Where have you guys been? I told you to get here ASAP."

Dino responded, "We had to finish our breakfast. I figured if the case was that time sensitive, you would have told us over the phone to go straight to the scene. I just figured you meant for us to come by your office first thing we got in. I didn't think time would be all that important."

Mendoza looked as if he might bite off Dino's head. "This case is very important. That's what ASAP means. There's been a body found on Baylor's campus at the Tidwell Building. I need the two of you to go there and check it out. And do it now. Report back to me once you know what we're dealing with. This case is gonna be all over the news. Reporters are going to want to speak with me and I don't want to look like an idiot. Is that clear?"

Jack responded quickly, so Dino didn't tell the sergeant what he was obviously thinking. "We're on it, Sarge."

* * *

Dino is the senior of the two detectives by fifteen years, so he chose to drive while Jack rode shotgun. Dino goes by the nickname given him as a child. He now prefers Dino to his given name, Dean, which he considers stodgy. Now in his mid-fifties, he only uses the name Dean on formal documents, or when he introduces himself in an official capacity as detective Dean Piper of the Waco Police Department. He has served the department for nearly twenty-five years, joining as a junior patrolman before becoming a detective. Dogged and tenacious, Dino pursues his cases methodically. Piece by piece, he follows a process, eliminating suspects only after finding irrefutable evidence corroborating their alibi. He does not dazzle anyone when he enters a crime scene. On stakeouts, he works crossword puzzles and fills in Sudoku squares.

Some suspects mistake his dry demeanor for a lack of interest. They are wrong. His eyes take in a room quickly. He observes details, including the behavior of suspects as they respond to his questions. He has good instincts, but he does not rely on them principally. He has outlasted most of his peers and is now the senior detective in the department. Wizened with experience and years of interviews, he possesses an unusually keen ability to sense when someone is lying or hiding parts of their story. He closes more cases than not.

Waco is not a large city, but it is big enough to have the conveniences of city life, yet small enough to lack the traffic congestion of larger urban areas. Dino enjoys the slower pace and the ability to get around town, stopped only by traffic lights that are not well synchronized with one another. Waco is too small to have rush hour traffic, but it is large enough to have a rush half-hour in the mornings when parents drive their kids to school on the way to work, and at five o'clock when everyone in town leaves for home.

Dino's partner differs from Dino considerably in appearance, temperament, and behavior. Naturally surlier than his partner, he is more brusque than patient, Jack Farmer is cut from sturdy cloth. When he was born, his parents and both sets of grandparents lived in the mountains of northwest Georgia, close to a small papermill town, but his dad's work took them to central Florida. Jack and his parents missed home. When the right job opportunity presented itself, his father moved the family back to Georgia, where Jack finished junior high and high school. Despite his preference for the mountains, Jack always privately thanked Florida for giving him the ability to speak with the flat American accent of television news reporters and for sparking his avid interests in aeronautics and science fiction. By the time he completed high school, Jack had grown uncomfortable with his hometown. He considered it too provincial, parochial, and poor.

He left for college in the big city of Birmingham and never went back except to visit his family, which, it turned out, was more important to him than the place. Not quite as tall as Dino, he is taller than most and has the upper body strength of a horse. Never an athlete in high school, his strength came from hauling hay bales as a kid and working on road crews for the state during summer vacations as a teenager. He'd spent so much time shoveling manure as a kid, he could identify which animal had left the aroma behind purely by the smell it produced.

Jack can be as boisterous as Dino is quiet. He loves to regale people with stories of his life on the farm and will often be the center of attention at gatherings with friends because of the power of his voice and his ability to weave a yarn. Unlike Dino, Jack leads with his gut.

After college, where he'd majored in criminology, Jack went into law enforcement. He was hired as a detective by the police department in Waco, Texas. The department was expanding and needed someone with a college degree to add fresh perspective. Jack took the job with the intention of returning to the southeast as soon as a good opportunity arose. The ubiquitous brown and, above all, the heat of Waco reminded him too much of central Florida. But, shortly after joining WPD, he met and soon married Mariposa, a student at Baylor who came from an established Hispanic family with roots in Texas reaching back to Spanish colonial times. Mariposa's love for her heritage and her family meant that Jack had to become a Texan, the heat notwithstanding. She also made Jack promise that he would learn Spanish once they married but (much to the chagrin of his mother-in-law), he has not yet kept that vow—though he has recently gotten serious about doing so (without his mother-in-law's knowledge). After seventeen years on the force, his career has stalled. He is not well suited for climbing the career ladder because he does not suffer fools well and too many of the professional bureaucrats above him fall into that category.

Despite their many differences, Dino and Jack share important qualities about the things that matter most in a criminal investigation. They both believe that getting to the truth is important and that justice matters for all. The latter occasionally rankles their colleagues, most of whom think some crimes and some victims are more important than others.

As they drove to Baylor's campus after their run-in with the sergeant, Jack could sense Dino seething at the way Mendoza had treated them. Jack thought he had better do something to change the mood. He inquired nonchalantly, "Hey, we got interrupted at the restaurant. You never told me what you and Teri are up to in that quiet house of yours. We've been so busy the last couple weeks, it seems like we've not had a chance to catch up."

Dino told Jack that he and Teri had worked on an upholstering project together over the weekend and that he had worked on a little carpentry project. "What're you making now?" Jack asked.

Dino replied vaguely, "It's no big deal. I'm just tinkering with some odds and ends." Dino did not tell Jack about the project because he wanted it to be a surprise. He was making a jewelry box for Jack's older daughter, Sofia, for her fifteenth birthday celebration, her *quinceañera*. While the gift is for Sofia, Dino knew that Jack would also find the gesture moving. He did not want Jack thinking he had to reciprocate, so he changed the subject.

As they turned the corner onto James Street and made their way toward the Tidwell Building, Dino mentioned to Jack, "Keep an eye out for a spot to park." The two small parking lots on the left flank the back of the Tidwell Building, but they were completely full, so Dino turned right into yet another parking lot. This lot officially belonged to Seventh and James Baptist Church, a large historic church named for the street corner where it stands. A sign declared the lot closest to Tidwell as reserved for faculty, but the detectives were on official police business, so Dino decided he will park there anyway. Once they turned into the parking lot, they realized that all four rows of parking spaces were full.

Jack pointed to an open space, but Dino refused to park there because it was reserved for those with disabilities. Jack grimaced and opined Dino should take the space anyway. Fortunately, someone backed out of another spot at just that moment and Dino parked his police sedan in it.

The parking lot stands near the back entrance to the Tidwell Building, but the building was now a construction site, surrounded by a chain link fence. They walked around the left side of the building. They reached the front, where yellow police tape cordoned off the only gate, identifying the entire building as a crime scene. A man stood beside the gate looking agitated. He apparently recognized them as cops as they walked down the sidewalk leading up to the building.

He spoke first. "It's about damn time you got here. How long is this going to take?"

"We are detectives from the Waco PD," Dino responded as they pull out their badges for the man to see. "I'm Detective Piper, and this is Detective Farmer. Who might you be?"

"Sorry," he mumbled sheepishly. "I'm the foreman on the construction crew that found the body. I've been standing here waiting for you to show up ever since the officers who arrived on the scene kicked everyone out of the building. I've had to send my entire crew home for the day. We are on a very tight schedule. If we don't finish this renovation on time and on budget, it'll cost my company two hundred grand."

"Okay, then. It's best if you take us inside and show us where to find the body."

"Right. Of course. I just wondered how long you will keep my crew from doing its job."

Jack interjected, "We can't answer that before inspecting the crime scene. I will say that the fastest way for you to do your job is to help us do ours. Take us inside."

The man turned and ducked under the tape and stepped inside the fence. Dino paused to look up at the Tidwell Building while Jack began walking toward the steps leading up to the main entrance. When it opened, journalists touted the building as an architectural gem. It remained the tallest building on Baylor's campus and the second tallest building in Waco. The Tidwell Bible Building housed the Department of Religion, called the Bible Department at the time.

The steps lead to a wide entrance containing three sets of double doors that open outward. Each door had six glass panes on the top half. Above the front doors, the name TIDWELL BIBLE BUILDING is etched into the concrete in all capital letters each one nearly a foot tall, with BIBLE standing right in the center.

"The building," Dino thought to himself, "sure makes a statement, although it's not altogether unambiguous." The odd combination of art deco and neo-classical styles helps to make the building iconic, as if Baylor's architecture symbolizes the tension between tradition and trends of the time. The wings on either side of the tower make the exterior symmetrical. The center tower rises six stories above the entrance. A concrete mural containing panels depicting scenes from the Bible caps the tower.

The rest of the façade is constructed of brick the same color as the concrete panel that crowns the center portion of the entryway.

On the second floor, above the building's name, a concrete railing spans the width of the main tower. Four Grecian urns perch on top of the railing, giving the building a gothic feel. The tower itself sits back from the main entrance, creating an optical allusion that a large balcony lies behind the railing.

The building's exterior thus looks like two giant staircases that ascend to the middle of the seven-story tower. The center portion of the tower gives off an art deco vibe popular in the nineteen thirties. Nine windows decorate the front of the first three stories in a three-by-three pattern. These windows are twice as high as they are wide, separated only by the brick frames holding them in place.

The first floor of the building sits on a raised foundation that requires visitors to look up as they approach, and the center tower looks like it's trying to reach the heavens. Dino assumed the raised foundation meant the building also has a basement. He followed his partner and the foreman up the stairs and entered the Tidwell Building through the door on the right.

3

The contrast between the majestic structure outside and the inside of the building could not have been starker. "This looks like a war zone," Dino remarked to the foreman.

"Yeah, we've been doing demo for weeks already. We're taking the entire building down to the studs. That's how we uncovered the body."

Dino stood in the dark, dimly lit foyer, waiting for his eyes to adjust from the sunlight to the dark rotunda on the first floor. He noted to Jack, "I bet this building could hold a lot of secrets." A long hallway extended outward to his left and his right. Straight ahead lay a cavernous, empty room.

"It's this way," stated the foreman as he headed into the empty room straight ahead.

Dino asked, "What is this room?" as he walked through the doorway where the two double doors had been removed.

"This is Miller Chapel. When we started the demo, it was filled with church pews. Twenty-two rows of them on each side, with an aisle down the center. We had the devil of a time getting them out of here. They were all bolted into the concrete, and they were as long as all get out. When the place was full, you could pack ten to thirteen people into the pew on each side of the aisle. The place could hold more than five hundred people when it had to."

Dino wondered why they would fill a lecture hall with pews, but then he noticed that each side of the room had five sets of modern stained-glass windows which made the chapel seem well lit compared to the foyer. The far end of the room had a raised platform for the speakers. He saw a door to his left and asked the foreman what it was.

"They call that the small chapel. It also had church pews for seats bolted into the floor when we started. As I understand it, they originally used the small chapel for the preaching classes, so students could practice their sermons in something resembling a church sanctuary. Don't think they teach preaching that way anymore, since it looked like they tried to use it for a small meeting room." He chuckled a bit before continuing. "Our crew calls it by another name so we can keep them straight. Since this large room is called 'Miller Chapel,' we've been calling that room 'Miller Lite.'"

Dino could not help but smile at the irony of the name. Farmer retorted with a wry grin, "You may not want that to get out. Can't have a bunch of Baptist professors of religion think you're making fun of their building."

"Actually," the foreman explained, "one of them told us that was the name they used for the small chapel. We didn't invent it; we just kept using it. The body's this way." The foreman took off toward the far end of the expansive room. The detectives followed. Dino noticed that the raised stage of the chapel had huge pipes rising from the stage. Some of them looked to be fifteen feet tall. The pipes gleamed as they rose symmetrically up the wall in a row of metal spikes gently curving upwards against the chapel's back wall. "The chapel must have had a big pipe organ," Dino remarked.

"It did. It had a pipe organ on the left and a grand piano on the right side of the stage. The instruments were gone when we got here, but they had walled off spots for them that we removed. Today, we started demoing the stage itself and that's when one of our folks found the body. Follow me. The body's up on the second floor behind the organ pipes."

Dino and Farmer followed him to the far corner of the chapel, where a small staircase led up to a second-floor hallway. The hallway had three small offices along the left, originally designed as storage closets. The right-hand side was the back wall of the building. Over time, as the Religion Department grew, they had converted these closets into faculty offices.

The foreman walked past all three offices, and then Dino noticed a waist-high hatch at the end of the hallway. The foreman bent down and walked through it. Dino and Farmer did likewise and were immediately surprised by the size of the space. Once inside, the ceilings were the same height as the rest of the second floor. The foreman continued down a short hallway and turned left into a room that looked like another hallway except it had no exit.

"This room is right behind the pipes for the organ. They designed it to allow access to the pipes if they ever needed repair. I don't think they used it often. It was full of junk: old chairs and tables, and stuff like that. It had a bunch of old crates pushed all the way to the far end of the hallway. I sent someone up here this morning to haul the junk out so we could get to the pipes to take them down."

Dino and Farmer joined the foreman at the far end of the room that fills the gap between the three offices and the organ pipes. "When my guy got to the last crate here, he started to pull it out like he'd done with the others. It came apart, and that's when he found this body."

Dino and Farmer passed the foreman to peer into the crate, one end of which had pulled apart from the rest of the box. Farmer pulled it entirely off the box so they could get a better look at what was inside. "'Body' might be a bit of an overstatement. It's just a bunch of bones. And they sure ain't fresh," he blurted out. As Dino came closer, he leaned down to get a better look. "Sure enough. This thing looks like it's been here quite a while. I wonder how it got here of all places. I can't tell from here what killed him, but I'm certain he didn't climb into the crate on his own. We'll have to wait and see if forensics can give us the cause of death and narrow down a time frame."

Farmer put on a pair of gloves and bent down and to check for identification. "No wallet. No keys. Unless this guy was in the habit of leaving his keys and wallet behind, someone removed them to hide his identity."

"That's unfortunate," Dino commented, "but look at this guy's shoes. Those are solid leather, and they look expensive. This guy was not wearing tennis shoes."

Farmer ran his hand around the bones. "There's a couple plastic buttons, but not much else. Wait, here's something." He held up a ring. "Looks like a class ring from Baylor. It's got initials inside." He squinted and looked closely. "It looks like RD. I'm guessing the killer either didn't notice it or else couldn't get it off his finger."

"Is there a date on the ring?" Dino asked.

"There's a lot of writing on it, but the writing's small. Wait, there is a year on it. Let me get a better look at it." He blew on the ring to get rid of the dust around the lettering. "The date says . . . 1845. Wait, the bones have been here a while, but not that long. That's gotta be the date that Baylor was founded, not the year the guy graduated."

"Not much to go on, but it's something. Bag it up," Dino instructed the patrolman as he scanned the space. "I can understand why someone might stash a body in this room. I bet hardly anyone ever comes in here, but how did they get the body through the building without being seen, and how did they get it up those stairs? This crate barely fits, and the crate would have been terribly heavy with a dead body in it."

"Not only that," claimed Farmer, "but how did no one notice the smell? This thing would have stunk to high heaven for days on end as it rotted in the crate."

"Yeah," continued Dino, "we've gotta get forensics in here to look at these bones and see if we can get any kind of timeline for the death. We're gonna have to figure out when this guy died and who had access to this space at that time. We're gonna need DNA tests to see if we can figure out who he was. How did he get here and who is he? We'll need to look for missing persons reports from that time. We'll also need forensics to analyze the room and the box to see if the person who put him here left any evidence behind."

"I'm not optimistic about DNA tests on anything we find after this long, but we'll have to see. We'll get DNA from the bones, but unless the victim is in CODIS, or some other government database, I doubt that will tell us much. If the body's as old as I think, we're going to use a lot of shoe leather to figure out who might have been involved. If we can find a lead on the vic's identity, at least the DNA might help us confirm it."

"I'll call forensics," volunteered Dino, "You call the office and tell the sergeant what we've found."

"I guess this means you won't let my crew back into the building tomorrow," the foreman sighed with resignation.

"No," Dino confirmed. "It's gonna take a minute to put the pieces together. There may not be anything forensically valuable left, but we have to check it out just in case."

"I was afraid of that. Please do whatever you can to move things along, so I can get my crew back in as soon as possible. Let me know if there is *anything* I can do to speed up the process. We really do have a lot riding on getting this building stripped out."

"Actually, there's one thing I can think of that maybe you can help me with. Who would I contact who knows about the building? Preferably someone who's been here a while and knows the history of the last ten to twenty years."

"Most of my contacts have been with the designers and the architects for the project. I doubt they know much about the inner workings of the people who were here that long ago. They don't have much good to say about the faculty of the two departments that were in here before the renovation. Apparently, they threw quite a fit when the architect came up with what he thought was the final design. They complained that there were no classrooms in the building, only faculty and administrative offices. The architect had to produce another design that included some classroom spaces so they could teach courses in the building."

Dino replied, "All well and good, but we need someone who knows what was going on in this building for the last ten to twenty years, not last fall."

The foreman scratched his chin, "Well, there have been a few things we had to ask the designers about that they had to ask someone from the Religion Department. They copied me on the emails. I think the name was Becky Long. She's the administrative assistant to the chair of the Religion Department. Word is, she keeps things together for them. You might start with her. They moved the department chair's office to the basement of another building across the quad. I can get you her office location."

"That would be helpful. I imagine forensics will take a day or two at least to comb through the crime scene. In the meantime, though, can you give us a tour of the building, so we know what we're looking at?"

"Absolutely. It would be great if we were only out a couple of days."

"I can't make any promises right now. Forensics may have to look at other rooms in the building. Give us a minute so we can call the office to get a forensic unit out here. Then, you can give us a tour of the building. It's now one huge crime scene."

"While you do that, I will get my office to text me the office number of Becky Long."

4

After several minutes, the three men went back downstairs, through the chapel, and into the center of the foyer. "What was down these hallways before the renovation?" Dino inquired.

"To the left were three administrative office suites for the Religion Department and a large classroom that seated sixty. A stairwell was beside the classroom, with a small elevator across from it. To the right, you have an entry door to Miller Lite, I mean the small chapel, and a supply closet on one side. On the other side was the women's bathroom, a large stairwell, and another large classroom."

"No men's room?" Farmer asked.

"Nope. Apparently, the main bathroom on the first floor was for men originally. At some point, they converted it into a women's room. There were two small one-seater bathrooms at the far end of the chapel, one for men and one for women. Seems they included those so wedding parties had a place to go. I'm told they used to do a lot of weddings in the chapel."

"That elevator looks quite small," Dino commented.

"Yep. It's not up to code. They tried to get by with a much more modest renovation, but the city wouldn't grandfather the elevator. It's too small for wheelchairs, and it doesn't go all the way to the sixth floor. The ADA requires handicap access to every floor. Only one person with a wheelchair could squeeze into the elevator."

"Before they could get approval to renovate, they had to submit plans for a new elevator. As I said, the new elevator has to serve all six stories. But, since there's not room for an elevator shaft inside the tower, we'll have to add an elevator shaft on the outside of the tower to reach those last two floors. The new elevator will be a real upgrade, both in terms of size and speed."

"Man, that must've jacked up the price," Dino observed.

"It sure did," agreed the foreman. "According to the paper, the reno will cost about twenty million bucks."

Farmer whistled and added, "Seems like you could've built a brand spanking new building for that."

"Alumni and donors wouldn't stand for it. Almost every Baylor student since 1954 took required religion courses in this building." The foreman continued, "A lot of heavy hitters have strong feelings about this building. Students got engaged here and even more got married in the chapel because they wanted a big Baylor wedding. You could cram a lot of friends and family into those pews. Not to mention, the Miller family is still around, and they would not be pleased about demolishing the chapel with those beautiful stained-glass windows."

The foreman moved on to the stairwell to the right. "We'll take this one. It'll take us all the way to the fourth floor. The other one only goes to the third floor. We have four stairwells in this building, but none of them go all the way from top to bottom. It's a bit of a maze."

The foreman started up the stairs, but Dino stopped him. "What's downstairs?"

"The basement. Not much to it. It only runs under the center part of the building and the chapel. It had a couple of classrooms and faculty offices on both sides underneath the current chapel. The religion department was on one side and the history department on the other. Even though it's called the Bible Building, the religion and history departments shared the space. After the renovation, the sociology department will also be here."

"We're gutting the basement. We have to create a stairwell up to the first floor at the far end of the chapel, so people from the basement can get out in case of emergency. It'll run from the basement to the second floor where the current stairwell with the body is."

"Also, the designs call for making use of the vertical space by making two floors of offices where the chapel currently stands. We'll construct a two-story box inside the current chapel walls. The outside walls will stay, along with the stained-glass windows, but walkways around the offices will serve as hallways and provide natural light. The basement and first floor will house the Religion Department. The second floor will contain offices for the history and sociology departments."

"Actually, let me correct myself," he said. "There will no longer be a basement. Instead that floor will be called the garden-level."

Farmer smirked, "Sounds like the PR department worked overtime to come up with that one."

"I just do as I'm told," the foreman murmured.

Dino could picture the new, sleek design. "It'll sure look different," he commented, as he and Farmer follow the foreman upstairs.

"The second and third floors consist of hallways that run the length of the center section of the building. They contained conference rooms, office spaces, and classrooms. The fourth floor is considerably smaller, with only a seminar room and a faculty lounge that had just enough space for a coffee maker, a sink, and a refrigerator; not much room for lounging. The elevator was across from the stairs, and like the stairs that we came up, the elevator stopped at the fourth floor. Off to the right, a narrow spiral staircase goes to the fifth floor which had two small offices and two larger offices with a reception area."

"The sixth floor, however, contained only one spacious office with a high ceiling. When we got here, bookshelves lined the walls from floor to ceiling. The shelves went up so high that you had to roll a ladder around a track to reach the highest shelves. Metal filing cabinets filled the hallway leading from the stairs."

The office windows at the top of the tower provided an unobstructed view of the main walkway that looks out across Speight Avenue onto the Founders Mall that leads to Pat Neff Hall, where the president and provost have their offices. "Man, whoever had this office must have been the envy of everyone in the building," Farmer observed.

"Except when it rained," the foreman explained. "The windows leaked badly. Every time they tried to repair them, the leaks started again within six months. It was so bad because water seeped inside the walls at the top and worked its way down the tower into the basement, just outside the women's bathroom. After bad storms, it created a puddle so large and deep that they called it Lake Tidwell."

"Sounds like a mixed blessing," Dino remarked. "Great view with a water hazard. Where does that hatch go?" he asked pointing to an opening in the ceiling that is padlocked shut.

"That's the attic," the foreman answered. "The tower was supposed to be three stories taller originally, but when they determined they didn't have enough money to finish it, they just put a decorative cap on top. It's only seven stories high, not ten. The attic's padlocked because students would sneak in at night and climb the ladder into the attic where they would spend the night sipping and soliloquizing, if you know what I mean."

"So, they knew how to get into the building at night?" Dino summarized, suddenly fearing that his suspect pool had grown exponentially.

The foreman nodded. "I'm told that the doors were so unreliable that most nights the cleaning crews didn't even bother to lock them. Over the years, the maintenance staff started routinely issuing master keys to all new hires. It wouldn't have been difficult for students to make duplicates so they could come and go as they pleased. That's one reason that all the entry points in the renovated building will have digital access cards."

Dino and Farmer looked at one another knowing that narrowing the suspect pool would be even more difficult than they had originally thought. Farmer thanked the foreman, and added, "We should probably get back to the body. They will be here soon to collect it."

5

Minutes after the detectives returned to the room with the body, a forensics tech arrived to make an initial assessment. The mortician's van arrived several minutes later. Waco is not a big enough city to have its own medical examiner. The police department contracts with a local mortuary to transport dead bodies to Dallas for autopsies and full forensic work ups. They were fortunate, however, to have a forensic tech who graduated medical school. Dino and Farmer stood to the side as Dr. Emily Hracek carefully spread a plastic tarp beside the crate. She asked one of the police officers guarding the room to give her a hand, and they gently maneuvered the bones onto the tarp so she could get a better look.

"We'll need to send him up to Dallas to do a thorough analysis," she mused, "but I'll go over to the funeral home and examine the bones more closely before they ship him there. I'll take a preliminary look now in case I see anything that might help."

"Thanks."

"For now, we can assume the victim was male, because of his shoes."

She knelt beside the victim and peered at the torso. "I don't see any bullet markings on the rib cage to suggest he was shot in the chest, but I'll have to check this area for bullet fragments. Now, let's take a look at the skull."

She crabbed her way to the top of the skeleton and cradled the skull so she could lift it and look at the back. "No visible bullet holes in the skull. He was not shot in the head. I can see evidence of blunt force trauma on the back of the skull, though. He was hit with something. Not sure what. I'll follow the body to the mortuary and take a closer look before they ship him off. Maybe I can narrow it down somewhat."

Dino asked, "How long do you think the body has been here, Doc?"

"It's hard to say. Left in this crate, all the soft tissue would be gone after a little more than a year. Bugs would have feasted for months on the skin and organs. Anything left after that would have just turned to powder. I don't even see any evidence of the bugs, however. They are long gone. All we've got are the bones, and they're hard to date with any real certainty. I may have better luck giving you some idea of the victim's age when I analyze the teeth. Beyond that, we'll have to rely on the situational clues."

"Well," responded Farmer, "that's going to be tough. There is no identification on the victim. No wallet, no driver's license."

"Yeah, that's a tough break, but look at the shoes," Hracek added. "They are genuine leather, and they look Italian. The soles are handsewn. They look like they were custom made. I'll bag them so everything stays together. I'll send the bones to the medical examiner's office in Austin, and I'll send the shoes over to forensics. If the shoes were custom ordered, maybe there'll be something to identify the manufacturer that might help your investigation."

"Maybe we can catch a break," Dino concurred. "One of us will come and see you after you've had a more thorough look at the remains. We need to identify the victim somehow. I assume you'll run DNA on the bones. How long will that take?"

"It will take a few weeks. The lab in Dallas is backed up. This is a very cold case, so they won't prioritize it. But I doubt they'll find much that will help anyway. Unless the guy has a record, there would not be a match in CODIS."

"True," Farmer agreed, "but if we can get a name from another line of investigation, the DNA could confirm the identity."

"You're right," Hracek nodded her ascent.

"So, if you had to make a guess, how long do you think these bones have been here?"

"I can't give you anything that would hold up in court, but my gut tells me that it's been at least a decade, perhaps two."

"Doc," Dino interrupted, "do you really think the shoes could help us track the victim? Custom clothing is not really in my wheelhouse."

"Well, maybe I'm telling you more about myself than you want to know," she chuckled. "I could be wrong, but I know a little something about that world, or at least I used to. My family owns the big Ford dealership up in West, so I didn't grow up hurting for money. I went to college and medical school in Houston. First, Rice University, then Baylor

College of Medicine. I thought I had to look the part. I was especially concerned about my wardrobe. A group of us would go to a bar most Saturday nights back then. We worked our tails off during the week, but we had to take a break from studying sometime. We'd sometimes go to some really swanky clubs on the weekends. I wanted to fit in with the cool kids."

"How long ago would that have been?" asked Dino, emphasizing the words "long" and "that."

Deflecting Dino's attempted ribbing, Hracek replied straightforwardly, "Longer than I care to admit. It's been eighteen years since I started med school."

Joining in on his partner's game, Jack observed, "You're aging well, Doc. Probably helps that you're not out in this Texas sun much in your line of work."

"Well, to clarify, *Detective Farmer*, I only went to those kinds of places on special occasions, like someone's birthday or an engagement party. Some of my friends there came from real money. I am ashamed to say it now, but back then, I ordered a lot of my good clothes through a custom shop like many of my friends. We either had a fair amount of disposable income or we wanted people to think we did."

"You've never struck me as being like that," replied Farmer. "You seem like a rather average Joe. Wait, that did not come out the way I meant it."

She laughed again. "Well, I'll take that as a compliment, so thanks. It took some time, but I finally learned to look at the world differently. Besides, after I decided to go into forensic pathology, it became clear that my patients did not care what I wore."

"Well, it still helps," Farmer observed. "It gives us a place to start at least."

"Glad to help. Now, I'd better pack up these bones and get them back to the morgue."

Dr. Hracek got the police officer to help her put the remains into a body bag and zip it shut. The officer carefully cradled the bag of bones, and they returned through the hatch, then back down the hallway to the stairs. The officer took the lead as they headed down the steps and out the door. The mortician had parked his van near the back door of the chapel. He gingerly lifted the bag into the back of the van and watched it drive away.

Dino and Farmer remained behind to go over the crime scene again. "Can't see much here that helps us," Farmer noted.

"We should probably get the techs up here, though," replied Dino. "We should at least get them to dust the crate for prints and check it for bloodstains. They can also double check for bullet fragments. Who knows, maybe the killer left some trace behind. You never know."

"OK, but something tells me we won't get that lucky. This body's been here quite a while, and any forensic evidence will be compromised. You go ahead and call the forensics team. I'll find the foreman and tell him it'll be at least another day before the techs can get here and do their thing. He won't be happy about it, but it's better we tell him now. Hopefully, they can get out here over the weekend, and they can start back on Monday."

"Let's hope he doesn't uncover any more bodies during the demo," Dino remarked. "A building like this probably holds a lot of secrets. If walls could talk. Speaking of secrets, after you talk to the foreman, why don't we go and see if we can find the Religion Department chair and his administrative assistant. Maybe we can get some useful information about who was in this building ten to twenty years ago."

6

The detectives left the Tidwell Building several minutes later. They crossed Speight Avenue and headed to the sidewalk that took them to Founders Mall. At its entrance sits a larger-than-life statue of Judge Robert E. B. Baylor, one of the three founders of the university, and the one for whom it is named. His bronze likeness sits regally on a chair that is eight feet tall and made of solid concrete. At the other end of the mall stands Pat Neff Hall, a high steepled building that houses the offices of the president and provost of the university.

Walking into the mall filled with flower beds and live oak trees, they followed one of the sidewalks to the left that angles across the green space. "So, how do we want to go at this, Jack? I'd like to have a plan of some sort. I'd suggest we see if we can get a list of people who were in those offices ten to twenty years ago. Maybe someone remembers something unusual."

"Maybe, but I wouldn't hold your breath," Farmer lamented. "That's a long time ago."

"We won't know unless we try. We ask the right questions, maybe it'll jog someone's memory. The victim didn't just walk himself into that crate."

They came to the edge of the mall and crossed Seventh Street in front of Memorial Hall, then turned right toward Memorial and Alexander Halls, the female and male student dorms belonging to the Honors Residential College. At the far end of Alexander, a separate door led to a basement conference room space, temporarily remodeled to house most of the administrative offices for the Department of Religion during the renovation. The space included the chair of the department in one office, and a larger suite where bookcases had been set up to mark the space used by the director of Undergraduate Studies, as well as the director and assistant director of the Ministry Guidance Program. Three desks took up most of the space of an anteroom with a staff member sitting at each desk.

Dino and Farmer made their way across the reception area to the desk of Becky Long. Her name plate identified her as the office manager and administrative associate to the chair. "Ms. Long," said Dino, "I am Detective Dean Piper, and this is Detective Jack Farmer, special crimes detectives with the Waco Police Department. We've been given your name as the person to contact regarding a case we're working."

"A homicide case?" she exclaimed. "You can't be serious. Who was killed?"

"I can't answer that," Dino replied. "That's why we need your help. The victim was found during the renovation of the Tidwell Building, but he's likely been there for over a decade. We were told you could help us figure out who had offices in the building back then."

"That can't be right," Becky declared. "I'd have heard if one of our people had been killed."

"We don't think the deceased was necessarily a faculty member," Farmer explained, "but eventually we may need to question everyone who worked in the building ten to twenty years ago. We need a list of names of people who had offices at the time."

"I'm happy to help," she said, "but it's going to take me some time to pull that information together."

"We understand, but it's important that we know whom to contact. We'll wait a couple of days anyway to see if the medical examiner can help us narrow down the time frame. Will that give you enough time?"

"That should work," she responded. "Do you want to speak with Dr. Williams, our department chair?"

"Was he here back then?" Dino inquired.

"Yes, but he may not have been chair at the time. He's only been the chair a dozen years. Before that, he was the director of Graduate Studies for twelve years, and he's been with the department for more than thirty. He'd know more about the inner workings of the department than anyone else—the people, the power dynamics, the history. It's been said, he knows where all the bodies are buried."

As soon as she said it, she noted that both detectives raised an eyebrow as she blushed beet red. "I didn't mean it like that. I just mean he's quite knowledgeable about the department."

"If he's got a few minutes, we'd like to speak with him," Dino continued.

"I'm sure he'd like to meet with you. Just a minute." She went inside the chair's office and returned shortly. "Please go in."

"Thomas Williams," the tall, dignified man rose from his desk and greeted the detectives, shaking hands with each of them. "Ms. Long said you are investigating a murder in the Tidwell Building."

"It looks that way," Dino responded. "The remains of a male individual were found this morning by the construction crew working on the second floor behind the pipe organ. Initial estimates are that the body has been there at least ten to twenty years. We were given Ms. Long's name as the person who could possibly give us the names of the people who had offices at that time."

"I'm sure if anyone can, she's the one. Please have a seat."

The detectives seated themselves at the round conference table in front of the desk, and Dr. Williams joined them. Dino began, "What can you tell us about the department at that time?"

"What do you want to know?" Williams replied. "That's right about the time that the department really started growing. Twenty years ago, we only had about twenty faculty members. Now, we have thirty. The university really grew over that time, and the PhD program in our department really benefited from the university's decision to invest in graduate programs. We added graduate faculty and graduate students, became one of the largest PhD programs on campus."

"How many of those faculty would still be around today?" Farmer asked.

"Probably about half. Some have retired but still live in the area. Some still teach for us. Some are still at Baylor but not in our department. I can have Becky give you the contact information of those still in the area."

"We'd appreciate that. Where are the faculty during the renovation?

"Scattered all over the campus. They tried to lump us altogether in a bullpen with cubicles, but that didn't sit well with faculty. They raised quite a stink. In the end, COVID happened, and the guidelines for social distancing would not let them put everyone in such a confined space. The administration ended up sticking us in almost every empty office space on campus. Hopefully, it's a short-term problem."

Dino remarked, "Well, according to the foreman of the construction crew, they are under a lot of pressure to finish the renovation as quickly as possible. He's more than a little put out with us for slowing them down."

"I bet. Baylor has done a lot of construction over the last decade, and they almost always include incentives for the builders to finish on time. Money seems to be an effective motivator."

"What can you tell us about access to the building? The foreman said that it was rather common for the building to be left open at night."

"You heard right," Williams affirmed. "Most nights, the cleaning crew left it unlocked. Some faculty members get here early because they have eight o'clock classes. Some work late or come back after dinner. Graduate students work on their dissertations until all hours of the night. Don't even get me started on the undergraduates. I can't tell you the number of times I've come to campus before eight in the morning and find students asleep in the chapel. The pads on the pews were like an invitation to stretch out. If they'd stayed up late studying for an exam, they often decided to sleep on the pews rather than go home."

"Did any of them ever cause problems?" Farmer wondered aloud.

"There were a couple times when some of the classrooms had computer equipment stolen, but it was rare. It was more a nuisance than a danger. Late night study sessions often took place. We'd come in and find pizza boxes filling the trash cans in classrooms where groups had met to study the night before."

"Was there any way to keep track of who came and went?"

"Not a chance. The renovation will make the building a lot more secure. Doors will lock themselves automatically. Entry will require you to swipe a key card, and students will not have access to the office areas. The old building had virtually no defenses to keep people out. It was supposed to be locked at night but usually wasn't, and it had to be unlocked by seven in the morning since students and faculty would begin arriving shortly after that."

"That's unfortunate," observed Farmer. "It may make it impossible to put together a reliable suspect list."

"Well," Dino said, "we've taken up enough of your time for now. We'll be back in touch with Ms. Long in a couple days. Maybe forensics can help us narrow the time frame."

As they retraced their steps back to Tidwell, the detectives fell silent. Each was thinking this was going to be a tough case to crack. The victim had no identity. The crime happened over a decade earlier. Anyone could have gotten into the building, and from there anyone could access the room where they found the body.

As they got in the car to go back to the office, Dino broke the silence and stated the obvious: "This could take a while."

7

When the detectives got back to the station, they decided to use what remained of the day to write up their reports. There was a lot to type. They needed information from forensics to narrow down the time of the crime. The next day, Saturday, they were scheduled to be off, so they decided to start fresh on Monday. That would give the forensics team the weekend to work on the body before sending the bones to Dallas for more thorough analysis. The crime had taken over a decade to come to light. One more weekend would not make a big difference.

Besides, Farmer had household and family responsibilities. It was time to change the filter on the air conditioner, and he had some errands to run. Most importantly, though, his younger daughter Juanita had a soccer game after school, and Farmer had missed his older daughter Sofia's game last week. He would be in the doghouse with two-thirds of the most important women in his life if he missed a second game in a row. Mariposa and her mother never missed an opportunity to remind him of the importance of family—three-fourths if you counted her.

Dino's kids were out on their own, but he and his wife Teri enjoyed using their empty nest to restore old furniture. They were currently reupholstering a set of dining room chairs they bought when they first moved to Waco. Teri had picked up some fabric that suited her. Dino also liked it, but the realist in him knew it meant they would soon be repainting the dining room to match the upholstery. He did not mind the work, but it seemed to him there was always something that needed attention around the house.

Dino and Farmer finished their reports narrating Monday's events regarding how and where the body was discovered. They described the crime scene and recounted Emily Hracek's initial findings, namely that it appeared that the murder happened ten to twenty years ago. Finally, they wrote up their plans for the next steps, to get a list of those who had offices in the Tidwell Building and to begin interviewing those they could in order to figure out the victim's identity and perhaps possible suspects. For the first time in a long time, they left the office on time and agreed to meet for breakfast on Monday before proceeding with the investigation.

As Jack prepared to leave, Dino asked, "You and the family are still coming tomorrow night, right?"

"Wouldn't miss it. If you're still planning on grilling hamburgers, Mariposa said she'll bring the fixings for nachos."

"That sounds great. I'll let Teri know. We are really looking forward to seeing the Farmer women. It's okay if you come along too."

*   *   *

SATURDAY, JUNE 13

The Farmer family arrived for dinner. Since the Pipers' daughters lived with their husbands, Dino and Teri's house seemed perpetually quiet. Having dinner with the Farmers would fill the house with the sounds of youth again. The Pipers' daughters maintained they have no plans for having children, so at least for the time being, the Farmers' children remained as close to grandkids as they would likely ever get. When Teri greeted them at the door, they ran into the house and made themselves at home. They knew the Pipers well, and called them Uncle Dino and Aunt Teri, which pleased both sets of parents. Jack's parents still lived in Georgia, so he didn't see them nearly as often as he would have liked. Mariposa's parents lived in town, and they saw them frequently. Teri, in particular, not only enjoyed Mariposa's company, but she felt that having Jack around made it seem like Dino had a younger brother.

Smelling the food, Jack headed out to the back patio where Dino stood flipping burgers. They began to talk while Teri took Mariposa to the kitchen where she started assembling the mountain of nachos. "Those look great!" Teri exclaimed. "White cheese, homemade salsa, and jalapenos are my favorite way to have nachos."

As Mariposa grated the cheese, she looked out the window and saw Jack and Dino deep in conversation. "I hope they don't burn the hamburgers. I'm sure they're talking shop, and not paying attention to what's on the grill. They've caught a big case, but it's Saturday night for goodness sakes."

"I'll make sure they watch the burgers," Teri responded. Calling into the den where the Farmer teens were playing an old video game left over from when her own children where young, she said, "Girls, go out and tell your dad and uncle Dino that the nachos will be ready soon, but they won't get any if they let the hamburgers burn." The girls giggled and headed out to the patio. Their arrival broke up a conversation about the skeleton in the Tidwell building. The girls delivered their message, and Dino quickly returned to flipping the burgers, so they didn't burn.

As Mariposa smiled, Teri remarked knowingly, "Sometimes you just have to be a little creative to help them get out of their own way and have some fun."

* * *

MONDAY, JUNE 15

Breakfast at the downtown Café Cappuccino on Monday felt like a treat. The food is always good, and the restaurant was quiet enough that they could hear one another talk. Dino told Farmer that he recalled that Baylor was always in the news about something from the mid-nineties to the early part of the millennium. Assuming that this was likely the time when the crime occurred, some background might be relevant. It might help their investigation if they got a better idea of some of those details.

Farmer wanted to begin figuring out suspects. "Someone had to have killed the guy, but unless we get more information from forensics, we won't make much progress. The background you want might not even be related to the murder. It's not a good use of my time."

In the end, they decided to split up. Dino would arrange to speak with the pastor of Seventh and James Baptist Church, the church right behind Tidwell. Jack would follow up with forensics and see where that took them. They agreed to meet back at the station after lunch.

* * *

Dino made his way back to the Baylor campus, this time parking in the Seventh and James Baptist Church parking lot behind the Tidwell Building. As he looked at the church from the parking lot, Dino thought that the church layout made it look like the university had swallowed the church. Founded in 1898 just across James Street from the Tidwell Building, its main auditorium was built in 1906. At the time, James Street marked the edge of Baylor's campus. For years, the church was known as Baylor's church since most of the faculty lived in houses on campus and simply walked to church on Sunday morning. Students, as well, stumbled out of bed on Sunday morning to attend services because they were expected to be there, not necessarily because they wanted to be. The church would hold about a thousand people, making it large by Waco standards, but it was no mega-church.

The current church building is a labyrinth, having added wings to the original structure over the course of the twentieth century. With its parking lots, the church now sprawls across two city blocks. Dino finally found a sign in the inner courtyard pointing him to the church office. A receptionist, a woman in her fifties, spoke on the phone. Dino ambled up to her desk. When she finished her call, he asked to see the pastor.

"Is it an emergency?"

"No, but it is important. My name is Dean Piper, and I am a detective with the Waco Police Department. I am trying to find information about what was happening ten to twenty years ago in the religious world that might have affected Baylor."

"I'm sorry, but the pastor's not in the office today, but it sounds like you might be better off speaking to our emeritus pastor. He's in the office. I can check to see if he has some time to meet with you. He was the pastor back then. Our current pastor has only been here a couple years, and he's much younger."

"That would be great."

Dino found a chair and waited. In a matter of minutes, the receptionist returned and invited him to follow her to another part of the building where a sign beside the door identified the office of Rev. Dr. Jackson Haley, Pastor Emeritus.

They walked into an office that was much larger than Dino's "office" at the department, which consisted of his desk that butted up against Farmer's desk in the middle of a bullpen where teams of detectives worked their cases. Reverend Haley's office had a full-sized desk and a seating area containing a love seat and two upholstered chairs. As the receptionist entered, she announced, "Dr. Haley, this is Detective Dean Piper from the police department."

Jackson Haley stood, walked around his desk, and greeted Dino with a firm handshake. "Please, take a seat," he said as he pointed to a plush couch. He sat in the chair on the right, and asked, "What can I do for you?"

"I'm interested in any background information about what was going on at Baylor ten to twenty years ago. I've been around Waco long enough to remember that, back then, it seemed like Baylor was constantly in the news. I gather there was a lot of controversy, but I am short on the details."

"Is this about the body in Tidwell?"

"You know about that?"

"Look, Waco's grown a lot, but it's still very much a small town. Word gets around quickly."

"Guess you're right about that. So, what can you tell me about Baylor in the early 2000s?"

"Good thing you specified a time. Baylor has always had its share of controversy, at least since the 1920s when they sided with the modernists against the fundamentalists over the teaching of evolution. The early 2000s were no exception. Baylor had been the largest Baptist college in the world for quite a while, but the university began to grow exponentially in the last half of the 1990s. That began to be a problem."

"How so?" Dino asked. "I would think that would've been a good thing."

"You would think so, but that kind of growth comes with costs. Soon, you have more students than classroom space, and the campus housing could not keep up with the increased numbers. You also have to hire more faculty to teach those students. Baylor had gone heavy into college athletics at the Division 1 level. That created a whole new world of donors and recruitment possibilities, but these new donors wanted to give to athletics more than academics. That created controversy. At the same time, Baylor began to invest more heavily in graduate education, and that also created controversy. Baylor always prided itself on its undergraduate teaching and some faculty and alumni feared this new emphasis on research would just bring a bunch of eggheads who were not interested in undergraduates. There was a lot of controversy because things were changing. Some people wanted Baylor to remain a small college like it was when they went here. The move to become a major Division One sports program in basketball and football scared a lot of people who did not want Baylor to lose its soul to become a modern university."

Dino commented, "I know something about that. I was around when a Baylor basketball player murdered one of his teammates. That almost killed the program as I recall."

"Yes, that happened in 2003, and it did nearly kill the program. That event only added fuel to the fire for those who thought Baylor was trying to become too big for its own britches. Alumni were at odds with administrators. The faculty was polarized between those who supported the changes and those who resisted. It was not pretty."

"Were the tensions so high that foul play could have resulted?"

"There were certainly shouting matches and protests, but I can't say I remember anyone actually coming to blows. Even our church got involved, unwillingly."

"What do you mean?"

"Early one Sunday morning, I started getting calls from angry members of my congregation. Not because of anything I said in a sermon, mind you. No, the Sunday paper had come out with a story about Baylor's ten-year plan. The story included a map of the master plan. That map showed that Seventh and James Baptist Church was gone. The church property is completely surrounded by Baylor, and this map showed that Baylor University had swallowed the church hook, line, and sinker. I must have had fifteen calls before eight wondering why I had sold the church out. Every one of them pointed out that our church is named for a street corner, so how could we sell the land and move someplace else. Needless to say, I had never even had the first conversation about selling our land. I'm not that stupid."

"Obviously someone was thinking about it," Dino mused, "and it speaks volumes about someone's ambition."

"I prefer the theological term, hubris," remarked the reverend.

The two men talked a while longer before Dino decided he should return to the office. He'd gotten a refresher course on the tensions at the university and that's all he needed for now. He bid Reverend Haley goodbye but asked if he could come back if he had more questions.

Haley responded, "Certainly. At my age I have far more memories than plans, so it's good to feel useful."

"I'm getting there sooner than I care to admit," Dino sighed. They shook hands and Dino returned to his car. As he drove back through downtown, the conversation with the pastor replayed in his head, and he began to wax nostalgic. He thought about all the changes he'd seen over the last ten to twenty years. Taking on a cold case, he thought, reminds him of the changes in his own life. Back then, life buzzed with activity, getting kids to school and their after-school activities, shopping at night, preparing meals. Now, with just he and Teri in the house, life at home seemed subdued. They'd found some hobbies to fill the time, but life had changed. Life at work also seemed subdued and repetitive. This cold case offered a puzzle to solve. He hoped putting the pieces together would spice things up.

8

While Dino spoke with the former pastor of Seventh and James Baptist Church, Jack got an update from the forensics tech. Dr. Emily Hracek, in her early forties, is an attractive, single, intellectual. She pays little attention to her appearance, at least when she is at work. She wears her mid-length hair either brushed straight back or in a bun. On this morning it was in a bun, which, along with her rimless glasses, made her look like the stereotypical lab scientist in a B sci-fi film.

Jack didn't know whether to look for her in the lab or in her office. Since it was close to eleven by the time he arrived at headquarters, he decided to try her office first. Her door stood half-open, so, after a perfunctory knock, he stuck his head in and was surprised to find Emily eating an early lunch at her desk.

"Oh, hey, Jack. I came in early and have a full afternoon ahead of me so I'm grabbing a sandwich while I can. How are things with you?"

"Good. It could cool down some for my taste. I hate hot. Busy times at home."

"The *quinceañera?*"

The fifteenth birthday of Jack's first-born, Sofia, was still weeks away, but planning and preparing for her celebration was demanding more of his time and effort than he wanted to give it.

"Yeah," Jack sighed. "It's not that I don't realize how important this is to her, and more so, to her grandmother. After all these years in a Mexican family, it's still a bit foreign to me. And expensive. And, I don't dance very well. Mariposa is making me take waltz lessons. She says it would take me months to get good enough not to embarrass the whole family. She's not wrong."

"Poor Jack," she feigned sympathy. "I don't suppose that facing the fact that Sofia is growing up has anything to do with your feelings about the celebration, does it?"

Jack knew she is goading him a little, but he let it pass. They had a good relationship—professional but also cordial, even friendly. Besides, the Good Lord knew that he wouldn't pass up an opportunity to rib her, and, if he's honest, he was struggling a little with Sofia's maturation. She looked and behaved so much like her mother.

"It's mostly the expense and hassle. But I'm not here for sympathy. I'm here on business."

"The skeletonized remains from Friday?"

Jack nodded.

"I finished examining the bones yesterday. Not much to go on, I'm afraid. The structure of the pelvis is that of a mature male. A number of factors, including the size of the root canal, suggest an individual in his early to mid-twenties. He was about six feet tall, give or take, and a few tufts of dark, curly hair had not yet decomposed. Otherwise, I can only give you the manner and means of death."

She pulled up an image on her computer screen and motioned for Jack to look over her shoulder.

"You can clearly see in this photo of the skull the indentation on the right parietal bone almost at the juncture with the occipital—just behind and a little above the right ear. The shape is consistent with a range of objects. Maybe a candlestick, maybe a hatchet. Its depth indicates a forceful, but not fatal blow. There are no signs of healing, so the injury occurred perimortem."

"That's it? 'Not much to go on,' indeed."

"There is one other bit of evidence—a fractured hyoid bone. In all probability, after the killer's blow rendered the victim unconscious, he—or she—strangled the victim. Strangulation, not the blow, was the cause of death. The killer may have delivered the blow to the head in an act of passion, but the second act of strangling an unconscious person was calculated. So, I am ruling it a homicide. Your jurisdiction."

"Ok. How about time of death? Anything there?"

"Sorry. Because someone stashed the body in the open air, we can't rely on morphological changes to indicate how long ago the individual deceased. I'd guess ten or fifteen years, but that is just a guess. We can always confirm identity with dental records comparisons, but we need a likely candidate first. You may have better luck with the non-human forensics."

"Well, thanks for that much. I'll pass the information on to Dino and the sergeant. At least we have a cause of death. And it suggests a struggle occurred."

"Sorry I couldn't give you more. Listen, before you go, have you had lunch?"

"No, but Dino and I had a huge breakfast just before I came."

"Dessert, then? I brought homemade cherry kolaches."

Cherries are a favorite of Jack's. He wondered if she knew that and, if so, how. Always the detective, he chided himself. "OK. But just one," he acquiesced and sat down to enjoy it. He returned the way he had come to speak with the other forensic techs. He had just enough time to get their report before meeting Dino when he returned to the station.

9

When Dino got back to the church parking lot, he decided to call Becky Long and see if she had completed the list of people who officed in Tidwell. When she confirmed she had it, he walked across campus again to her basement office. As he walked, he thought about what he'd learned from the former pastor. On the one hand, he was impressed with Baylor's longstanding commitment to take stands that did not always sit well with their constituents, such as their early recognition of evolution. On the other hand, it struck him as odd to see how the political machinations of a president threatened an entire church complex simply because it was in the way. He'd have to remember to tell his wife that story. She would find it hilarious. Still, nothing he had learned suggested that these battles were bitter enough to cause someone to commit murder.

Dino recalled his conversation with Reverend Dr. Haley about the murdered basketball player back in 2003. What if another person was killed during that time? That date was within the possible time frame of the murder. Then Dino remembered another case where a star basketball player for Baylor was charged with aggravated assault against his girl-friend in October 2010. The woman was the mother of his three-year old son. The police took her to the hospital where the doctors said her jaw was broken. Within weeks the police arrested him. The very next day, however, the woman was quoted in newspapers denying that he had hit her or broken her jaw. Dino had always suspected someone convinced her to change her story. The athletic department initially suspended the player indefinitely, but after Baylor's internal investigation, they limited the suspension to three games against inferior competition at the begin-ning of the season. Baylor's only official statement about the incident stated that the team suspended him for violating team rules. Dino lost a lot of respect for the program when that happened. He mused to himself,

"I guess it's good to know that it's against team rules to break a woman's jaw. I can understand some of the concern of those who worried about committing to big time athletics could change to character of Baylor"

He reached the basement offices of Alexander Hall, crossed the office, and stated a thankful greeting, "Morning, Ms. Long. Thanks for pulling that list together so quickly."

"Glad to help. I don't know if it's one hundred percent accurate, but it's close. There's quite a list. I sorted them into those who still work at Baylor, those who've retired, and those who've passed away. I also included their area of specialty. Not sure if that will be of any help. There's about twenty-three people in all who were on faculty back then. Less than half of them still teach at Baylor, and some of those are no longer teaching in the department. One went on to become dean and is now the university provost. Another went to Atlanta to join a church staff as the first female minister the church had ever hired. Another one transferred to the Honors College. Four have retired permanently."

"Huh?"

"Sorry, I meant to say they've passed away."

"Oh. I get it now. There's a lot more names here than I expected. Are all the departments at Baylor this big?

"No. The size of a department depends on how many classes they teach. Our department is so large because virtually every Baylor undergraduate student must take two religion classes. We teach over three thousand first-year students every semester. That's one of the big reasons they're renovating the Tidwell Building. They had to figure out how to jam more faculty offices into the building. The only way they could do that is by turning the chapel into office space and shrinking the size of the offices."

"That's a lot of people to interview," he commented. "We're going to have to prioritize who we talk to first. Is there any way you can you tell me which of these faculty members had offices behind the pipe organ in Tidwell near where the deceased was found?"

"That's a little harder to say. I've put a star beside the names of those I could recall, but it's not easy to remember them all. Those offices were quite small, and most of our folks would rather have one of the bigger offices in the basement or in the tower. Since I'm the one who assigns the offices for the Religion Department faculty, I can remember most of the faculty whom I assigned there during that time. I usually assign those offices to younger faculty, but when someone vacates one of the larger offices by retirement or departure, the remaining faculty ask for an upgrade. Well, most of them anyway. Office space has been tight for years, so every year we play musical chairs over the summer."

"I get that. Still, this is a big help, Ms. Long. Just to have a list of all the faculty in Tidwell gives us a place to start."

"No. Not all the faculty. I just gave you the names of those in the Religion Department. The History Department was also in the building, but I couldn't begin to tell you all those names because I didn't assign their offices."

"That's right. I forgot about the History Department. Where were their offices?"

"They shared the offices in the basement, and History had all the offices on the second floor. The Religion Department had half the faculty offices in the basement of Tidwell, the three administrative office suites on the first floor, and the faculty offices in the rest of the building: the entire third floor as well as the offices at the top of the tower, the fifth and sixth floor. There were no offices on the fourth floor."

Dino whistled and marveled, "Wow, that sounds like a lot of offices."

"It's not as large as the Religion Department, but yeah, it's a fair-sized department. I didn't think to track down the names of the History Department faculty from back then. Do you need me to do that?

"That would be great, but there's no rush. We'll start with this list for now. It'll take some time to track down just the Religion Department, and they are the only ones who had those offices in the back of the chapel. Thank you, Ms. Long. I really appreciate your help. I need to be as thorough as I can. The names you've given me, however, will help me and my partner get started. It'll take days to sort through all the names you've given me. That should give you plenty of time to get me the names of faculty in the History Department."

Dino reviewed the list she had given him. Twenty-three potential suspects from the Religion Department alone. Four of the faculty members had died, so he could not interview them, but one of them could still be the murderer.

"That's a huge number of suspects," he mumbled to himself, "and it doesn't even begin to address the number of potential suspects since students could access the back offices."

Something inside him doubted it was a student, but he couldn't rule it out completely. Still, he couldn't escape the sense of irony about this case either. Not only had there been a murder in the Tidwell Bible

Building, but the odds were fairly decent that the perpetrator of the crime could have been a member of the Religion Department. Even if not, it struck him as ironic that Baylor claims to be a Christian university, so someone who committed the murder also claims to be a Christian.

"Nothing very Christian about murder," he reflected as he walked back to his car.

10

Jack walked through the door to the large room where the detectives have desks. They had spent all morning chasing down some robbery case that Mendoza insisted took priority over the cold case. When they finally returned to the station and stopped for lunch, Jack had eaten his sandwich that Mariposa had fixed him. Dino had not shown up for lunch. Jack was therefore not surprised to find Dino sitting at his desk, poring over some papers. Their desks face one another, facilitating conversation, but preserving a degree of personal space. They have been partners since Jack first made detective. To find Dino with his head down in paperwork was nothing new.

"Hey, partner, what's happening?" Jack inquired.

Dino raised his head and, typical of him, got straight to business. "Just trying to get on top of some things after Mendoza sent us out to check on something a patrolman could have done. Ok. So, what have you learned?"

Jack summarized what he had learned from Emily Hracek, most of which he and Dino had already surmised from her comments at the scene.

"So, nothing new."

"Well, there are some possibilities that something may develop from the forensic analysis at the crime lab at the Department of Public Safety."

"For example?"

"Of course, there's no telling what microscopic analysis of the debris found on the scene may yield—or not yield. But the shoes seem promising."

"How do you mean?"

"Both Hracek and the forensics guy observed that the shoes, somewhat desiccated but still largely intact, seem well above Walmart grade—perhaps even custom-made. The crime lab will try to find some identifying features or marks. Could point us to something."

"And," Dino interjected, "there's the class ring."

"Yeah, the body was found at Baylor, wearing a Baylor class ring. I think we can safely posit a Baylor connection."

Their commanding officer, Sergeant Mendoza, stepped out of his office and approached the detectives. "You guys making any progress with the Baylor skeleton?"

"Depends on what you mean by progress," Dino grunted. "You sent us out yesterday for the convenience store robbery. One of the patrolmen could have taken those statements."

Jack interrupted Dino before he could continue challenging the sergeant. "What Dino means, Sergeant. . ." and then he repeated, in short form, what he has just told Dino.

"How long before you hear from the crime lab?" the sergeant asked.

"Well. . . it's a cold case, the crime lab is swamped, they tell me, and—like everything else in this state—important functions are underfunded. . ."

Dino interrupted, "So weeks, even months."

"Weeks, even months," Jack agreed.

"So," the sergeant almost demanded, "what next?"

"Well," Dino replied, "while we're waiting on forensics, we can start interviewing faculty and staff with business in the building around the time established based on Hracek's guestimate. Who knows what someone might know that turns out to be significant?"

"I just hope that the perp isn't already dead or moved to outer Mongolia in the meantime," Jack, not usually the pessimist, sighed.

"Remember the saying," the sergeant remarked as he began to head for the door and home, "'Can't never did.' But you need to work fast. I can't give you much time on this."

As soon as Menendez was out of earshot, Dino turned his attention back to his partner, "Great. He expects us to solve a decades' old murder as though it happened yesterday. It's gonna take some time, whether he likes it or not. Right now, we've gotta take into account that the building was virtually wide open during the time in question. So, our universe of possible suspects includes Baylor faculty and employees at the time, Baylor students at the time, and someone off the streets who was aware of the easy access to the building—in short, the entire population of Waco and surroundings about ten to fifteen years ago."

"Oh, then, when you put it that way, I don't see why we can't solve this thing by the middle of next week! What are next steps, Mr. Procedure?"

Dino paused for a moment, asking himself how to account for Jack's snarkiness this afternoon. Jack can be witty, and loves banter, but he is not prone to petulance. Dino worried that it might have something to do with the pressure at home. "As it so happens," he retorted, "when you came in, I was reviewing the list of Baylor religion faculty and other employees who had regular access to the building ten to fifteen years ago that I got from Mrs. Long. I suggest that we start tomorrow morning by prioritizing and divvying up the list. We can do initial interviews separately. That way, we'll cover more ground, quicker."

"Any hope of a nibble?"

That sarcasm again, Dino thought as he answered, "Can't never did."

"Ok. Sounds like a plan. Now, I need to take a cue from the sergeant and head home. *Los suegros* are coming for dinner tonight to celebrate Juanita's Most Valuable Player award."

"Congratulate her for me. I think I'll hang on here for a little longer. I want to study this list a bit more." To himself, Dino thought, "*Los suegros. . .* That explains Jack's mood. He's not always on the best of terms with his in-laws."

11

As a rule, Jack prefers to dash through the shower, grab a cup of coffee and a pastry if they have any, and head out for the day. Mariposa usually insists on preparing him a proper breakfast, which she had done this Thursday morning. "You can't face the demands of the day on and caffeine and carbs," she often said. To Jack, when she repeated her admonition this morning, it sounded like a rebuke, especially after forgetting to tell her he was having breakfast with Dino yesterday. Anyway, she is a good cook, so he usually offers little resistance, most mornings. This day she served him *huevos rancheros* garnished with *salsa casera*, his mother-in-law's homemade salsa. He and Mariposa used the opportunity to check in with each other about the girls' lives, which sometimes seemed to Jack to be more complicated than his own.

Dino was already at his desk when Jack got to the office that morning. As he entered, he set his coffee mug down, took off his jacket, and put it on the back of his desk chair. Dino looked up from his list of Religion Department faculty and asked, "How were things at home last night?"

"Well, it helped that I came home on time and that I made it to Juanita's game, but Mariposa reminded me several times to remind her when I'm meeting you for breakfast. She wasn't happy about that. I can tell I'm not completely off the hook just yet. How was your night?"

"Sounds like it was much less eventful than yours. Teri and I finished up our upholstering project, so we have our dining room together again. I called it right, though, about the wall colors. Once we brought the chairs back in from the garage and put them around the table, Teri made a comment that the new coverings on the seats did not look quite right. I told her she might be right, but I was not too concerned since the seats would either be under the table or covered by someone's behind. No one really cares whether chair seats match the wall or not."

"Did she buy your reasoning?"

"Not likely. Oh, she pretended like she would think about it. She said, 'Maybe you're right,' but mark my words. Before next weekend, she'll have paint samples taped to the wall, and I'll be expected to get up on the ladder to paint the high parts once she decides which shade of sand is the best fit."

"Sounds like you're using a little bit of hyperbole, aren't you?"

"I wish. The last time we painted the dining room, I spent a full hour at Home Depot waiting for her to pick out the color. I figured she would pick it out and we'd leave the store with the paint in hand. But no. Instead, we left the store with five cards of paint colors so she could see them on the wall and check them at different times of the day. But the kicker is that the paint samples were all called 'Sand.' There was Sand #1, Sand #2, Sand #3, Sand #4, and Sand #5."

"You are kidding, right?"

"I wish. I will give her credit, though. The colors did look different depending on whether it was daytime or nighttime. Still, it was hard to tell one shade of sand from the next. Of course, she doesn't think so. She tells me I just don't have a discerning eye."

"Man, that's hilarious. Let me know when you paint the room. I'm sure Mariposa will want to have you guys over for dinner while your dining room's out of commission."

"Looking forward to it already. Just promise me that Mariposa'll be doing the cooking. That steak you grilled for me last time could easily have been mistaken for the leather from our vic's shoes."

It wasn't true, but that doesn't matter, Dino thought. It's funny.

Jack didn't take the bait. Without missing a beat, he turned to business. "So, I saw you pouring over your list of names. What are you thinking?"

"It's not easy. We don't have a name for the victim. We know he was murdered, but not when. We don't have a picture of him since he's just a skeleton now. If we're gonna figure this out, we're gonna to have to do this systematically, step by step."

"Why am I not surprised? Coming from you, I would expect nothing less."

"Well," Dino insisted while ignoring the jab, "we're gonna have to make some assumptions based on probabilities if we're gonna narrow down the list and eliminate as many suspects as possible. Let's hope we catch a break on the ID from these interviews as well. Maybe someone will remember a young man who disappeared. It'll take at least three months to get the DNA results back from the crime lab about. If we can't identify the victim from these interviews or from the skeleton's DNA, we'll really need some luck to narrow down the list of suspects. But if we have to wait for the DNA results, Mendoza will decide the case is too cold to continue."

"So, we're talking standard investigational procedure. Who had the means, motive, and opportunity to commit the crime? MMO, right?"

"I'd say so, but we also have too big a list of potential suspects. We need to improve the odds of identifying the victim somehow. I want to run an idea by you."

"Shoot."

"I think we start with the question of opportunity. Which of those faculty in Tidwell were most likely to have had access to the victim at the back of the chapel? There were only three offices back there."

"I think I see where you're heading. How many faculty members did you say had those offices?"

"Only four, probably, during the time we're looking at. This means we start with these four people and see where that takes us. If that doesn't yield anything, we move on to the other faculty in the Religion Department next. They used the chapel more often than the History Department. So, we can progress in stages."

"Sounds like a plan to me. How do you want to begin?"

"Let's divide and conquer on the initial interviews. I'll take two and you take the other two. There's three men and a woman."

"I'm happy to take the woman," Jack exclaimed.

"Why am I not surprised? You and Dr. Hracek seemed kinda chummy."

"Not in the sense you seem to be implying, partner. I would never cheat on Mariposa. I'd be too afraid of what she'd do to me if she ever got wind of it. You'd end up investigating my murder."

"True enough. So, you take her and Glen Cheatham. The woman's name is DelRae Fontenot. According to Becky Long's list, she teaches New Testament and Cheatham teaches ethics. I'll take the provost, Larry Pridwell, who also teaches Systematic Theology, whatever that is. And I'll also take Marvin Peake who teaches Old Testament. That way, we each take one part of the Bible."

"Great, I'll speak with the female New Testament professor and the ethics professor. By the way, is it just me, or does it seem odd to you that he teaches ethics when his name is Cheatham."

Dino smirked. "It'll be even weirder if he turns out to be the killer and teaches ethics. Anyway, I created a spread sheet with the names of the Religion Department faculty and their current office locations. Because of COVID, be sure to wear a mask. My daughter Tommi tells me Baylor is big on social distancing and wearing masks. They apparently listen to different scientists than our governor who refuses to require state employees to wear masks."

Jack nodded as he stood. They decided to take two cars because it was hotter than normal for a day in mid-June. They figured that they will be going to different parts of campus, and neither of them particularly wanted to walk far in the heat.

Dino continued, "Before you go, should we discuss the specific questions we're gonna ask?"

"No need." Farmer insisted, "I'm just gonna wing it. Something will come up as we talk that will help us rule someone out or not."

As Farmer left, Dino remained in his seat, making a mental list of what he wants to find out from each person. Which office did they have? How long were they in that office? What years did that cover? What courses did they teach? Do you ever bring in guest speakers while you're away who might have used your office? When did they typically work in their offices (early mornings, late nights, only in the middle of the day)? What do they remember about things going on in the department back then? What can they remember about the other people who had those offices? Do they remember anyone being around the offices who was not a member of the Religion Department?

These interviews, he knew, were something of a long shot since they could not yet identify the victim. In some ways, he agreed with Farmer. Something usually comes up in the initial interviews that raises questions for the detectives or that reveal discrepancies between two or more accounts. "That's when the real detective work begins," he admitted to himself. "But Jack's wrong that we should just wing it. We really should have a plan for the questions we want to ask to increase the odds of something coming up. At least, that's what I have to do. Approach the interviews methodically."

Dino then left the office with plans to drive to Baylor and interview his first suspect, Dr. Marvin Peake. Peake teaches Old Testament, which

Dino found interesting because there's so much violence in that part of the Bible. He wondered if it was like the old saying, you are what you eat, with a slight modification, you are what you teach. Could Marvin Peake have a violent streak?

12

Jack paused in the parking lot to use his cellphone to call Dr. DelRae Fontenot, a vice provost at the university, to determine her availability. She was first on his list to interview. He remembered that Ms. Long had warned Dino that academics can be hard to find in their offices. If they aren't in class, they can be in a committee meeting, researching in the library, or visiting with a colleague. Her voicemail answered and he left a message. Within minutes, she called him back. "I'm sorry, detective, I'm not currently in my office, but I got your voice mail on my email."

"On your email?"

"Yes. Baylor's phone system automatically converts voicemail messages into text and sends a transcription to our emails. According to the email, you'd like to speak with me. I can give you thirty minutes, maximum, at 9:30."

"Perfect. That'll give me just enough time to get there and find a parking spot after I meet up with my partner."

When Dino got to the parking lot, he was surprised to find Jack still there consulting Ms. Long's list. Jack noted that DelRae Fontenot's office is located on the second floor of Pat Neff Building at the opposite end of Founders Mall from the Tidwell Building. When Jack saw Dino coming, he checked his list again and told Dino that Marvin Peake's office is located on the second floor of Morrison Hall during the renovation. Jack pulled up a map of Baylor on his phone. Since the parking lot behind Morrison Hall was relatively close to both offices, Jack suggested they ride together after all. On the drive over Dino once again tried to convince his partner to come up with a set of questions for each professor.

"Come on, Jack. This case is hard enough given how long ago the crime took place. We have to be strategic. We need to know which office each person had and when they were there. We need to know their work patterns, their teaching styles, and what courses they taught. We need to probe their memories of what life was like back and whether anyone else was around on a regular basis that had access to those offices."

"I get it Dino," Jack conceded. "You not only like to go by the book, you also like to work from a script. That is just not me. I do not disagree with most of the things you just mentioned. They are fine questions, but if I have to remember to make sure I ask exactly the same things as you, I'd come across as a poor actor trying to play a detective. I do not, however, have the slightest idea of what you mean by their work pattern. I have absolutely no interest in what courses they taught, and even less interest in their teaching style for God's sake. Why would I care about any of that?"

"What I mean by work pattern is when were they in their office? Did they come in early in the morning or stay late at night? That might be important because we still don't have any idea how that body ended up in that room. It seems to me that someone working late would have the advantage of not being interrupted. Maybe they remember hearing something one night. The same could be true for someone working early in the morning."

"Okay. I will give you that one, but their courses or their teaching style? What is that about? Why would I care whether they stand while they lecture or sit behind a desk?"

"Listen, from what pastor Jackson told me, a lot of the students at Baylor come from very conservative backgrounds, and some of the courses they teach in the Religion Department really upset those students. What if one of these students attacked a professor and ended up the worse for it? As for teaching style, it is not about standing or sitting. I had professors in college who really liked to get in students' faces. Some students may have gotten angry enough to lash out physically at someone. I had another professor who really was not a very good lecturer, but his classes were interesting because he brought in a lot of guest speakers who knew what they were talking about. Most importantly, we need to know whether there were other people up in that hallway. The question about guest lecturers could be relevant for identifying the victim."

"Okay. Okay. I see what you are getting at. I'll try to get that information. Just do not try to make me write the questions down."

"You do you. I am not trying to hamstring you. I just think it helps to have a plan. I will remind you, however, that Mendoza will also want to know if we find any reasons to continue this investigation in the reports we submit to him. I fear he won't give us much time to work this case if *he* decides something else is more important."

The two rode the rest of the way in silence. Dino was happy he made his point. He felt like he won the argument. Jack, on the other hand, felt vindicated. He did not want to pull out his notebook to make sure he remembered to ask all the same questions. They arrived at the parking lot and decided they would meet back at the car once they had each completed the initial interviews. When they reachd the front of Morrison Hall, Jack crossed the road while Dino turned and headed up the steps to the main entrance of Morrison Hall.

*   *   *

Once inside, Dino was stymied. The door brought him into a foyer with stairwells on either side. To the left, he saw signs taped to the wall. One had an arrow pointing straight ahead to the Honors College and the other pointing at an angle to something called BIC, which he assumed meant upstairs. To the right, he saw a hallway leading to what looked like classrooms. As he turned to the right, he saw that the two stairwells joined on the landing and then became one leading up to the second floor. On that wall he saw a third sign pointing up to the Graduate School. There were three signs, but they seemed to point in four different directions. This building looked like it had been put together in stages, not with a coordinated plan. Tidwell was being brought into the twenty-first century. It looked like Morrison Hall needed a face lift as well.

Turning around again, he saw a very old elevator directly in front of him. To the right of the elevator, he saw a black board with white letters pushed into little slots to hold them in place. It looked like something you would see at a sandwich shop announcing the special of the day. On one of the lines, once he got close enough, he could read that the Classics Department was located on the third floor, but there was no sign tell him which way to go to the Classics Department. He was now not only confused about which direction to take, but the signage taped to the walls only points to three departments, while the sign permanently affixed to the wall mentions four. None of the signs told him where Marvin Peake's office was located. He pulled out the spreadsheet and read that Peake's office was on the third floor. Since the stairwell only goes to the second floor, he decided, with some trepidation, to step into the elevator that opened just at that moment. Once several students departed the cabin, he stepped inside and pushed the button for the third floor. He had a new appreciation for how the construction foreman had described the Tidwell building as something of a maize. He thought, "It's a wonder anyone can find their way to classes in buildings like these."

As the doors started to close, he heard someone say, "Hold that door." Dino instinctively put out his hand, assuming that the elevator's sensor would recognize that the door was blocked and would open the doors. Instead, the doors kept pushing, and he had to push back with considerable force to stop the elevator from taking off with his arm sticking through the door.

A student rushed inside looking like he just got off the playground. He wore black shorts and a yellow T-shirt with the words "Jesus Saves" emblazoned on the front in bright red letters. He had no books with him, only a skateboard that looked to be nearly half as tall as he is.

"Thanks, dude. I really thought I was gonna be late. The prof will give me grief if I'm late again," he huffs as the door starts to close.

"No problem. Glad I could help. What floor?"

"Third. I've got a class on Roman literature."

When the door finally closed, Dino became disconcerted by the sounds gurgling from the elevator as it protested heavily against having to make the trip yet again. Even more disconcerting, Dino could see into the elevator shaft where the doors did not quite close. As he stood there looking into the shaft, he could see how slowly the elevator was moving as they approached the second floor. "I should have taken the stairs," Dino thought. "I could've gone up the stairs to the third floor and back again by the time we finally get there in this elevator. At this rate, the kid may still be late to class."

Once he finally got out of the elevator, he saw signs pointing him to the Classics Department. He had to make several turns, but fortunately there were signs taped to the walls indicating which direction to go. Dino felt like he'd gone deep into the belly of the building. He finally found the office number on his list. He paused briefly and knocked on the heavy wooden door, hoping his knock was loud enough to be heard.

"Come in," said a strong baritone voice.

"Are you Dr. Peake?"

The man sitting at the desk looked slightly surprised as he raised his head and peered over his reading glasses.

"I am," he affirmed, "but who are you? I don't get many grown-ups showing up here."

"My name is Dean Piper. I am a detective in the Waco Police Department, and I would like to ask you a few questions if you don't mind."

"Should I call a lawyer?"

"Do you need one?"

"Nah, I just always wanted to say that."

Dino looked at the professor more closely and saw a mischievous twinkle in his eye. Instinctively, Dino liked the guy. He was a sucker for subtle humor.

"Well, I would have been here sooner if the elevator in this building wasn't so slow. It felt like it took me half an hour to get to your office from the front door."

"That's nothing. This elevator runs like a speed demon compared to the one they're tearing out of the Tidwell Building. That thing was so small you could barely fit three people in it, and I could *literally* walk down from the fourth floor faster than I could take the elevator."

Dino grinned and said, "I like your hyperbole."

"Unfortunately, that one's not a joke. That's why they're spending so much money on the renovation. The elevator wasn't up to code, so the city would not permit the renovation unless Baylor brought the elevator into compliance. It's one of the few things that I like about the renovation. I look forward to having an up-to-date elevator. Being here on the third floor, I'd kill for that."

When Dino arched an eyebrow involuntarily, Professor Peake lamented, "Sorry. Poor choice of words."

13

Smiling, Marvin Peake stood up, walked around his desk, and held out his hand to Dino. As they shook hands, the professor pointed with his left hand to the chair that sat in front of the desk.

"Have a seat. How can I help you?"

"From your reaction a moment ago, I assume you've heard that the construction crew renovating the Tidwell Building found the skeletal remains of someone when they were getting ready to tear out the organ pipes in the chapel."

"Yeah, it's kinda hard to keep something like that secret for long."

"Well, it might've been easier than you think. Preliminary examinations suggest that someone managed to hide that body ten to twenty years before the demo crew found it."

"I assume you're here because you suspect the person was murdered."

"Due to things that we found at the scene concerning the body and its location, we assumed from the get-go that the victim didn't die of natural causes. The initial forensic exam confirmed it was a homicide and suggested a tentative timeline."

"So, you think I am involved somehow?"

"Well, as I said, the body was found in a really unusual place. We are just beginning our investigation. We're starting by speaking with faculty members who had one of those three offices on the second floor of the chapel during the period in question. Your department chair's administrative assistant, Ms. Long, prepared a list of people based on her recollections and records. You were on her list. We're just trying to get a sense from those still around what might have been going on about fifteen years ago."

"Well, I'm not particularly good with higher math, but the time frame fits. I came to Baylor as a junior professor. Since I was low man on the totem pole, I was given one of those chapel offices when I first started, and I had it for six years, the entire time I was on tenure-track. I was only upgraded to one of the larger offices after I was granted tenure and promoted to Associate Professor."

"When was that exactly?"

"Let's see, I began at Baylor in the fall of 2006. I applied for tenure in my sixth year, which would have been the academic year 2011–2012. I was granted tenure and promotion, so I started as Associate Professor in the fall of 2012. That summer, they moved my office out of the back of the chapel into one of the larger offices on the fifth floor. That one had a really good view of campus from the tower of Tidwell, but I had to be careful what I put on some of the bookshelves. Every time we had a big thunderstorm, water came through the cracks in the walls. I lost a bunch of student papers and a few books the first time that happened. They say they're gonna fix that in the renovation, but I'll believe it when I see it."

"That means you were in the office at the back of the chapel from fall 2006 until summer 2012. That is right in the sweet spot of our timeline. What can you tell me about what things were like back then?"

"You'll have to be more specific, I'm afraid. Those years are a blur to me now. When I arrived here, I was one of the lucky ones to benefit from Baylor's new emphasis upon research and writing. Most people who came before me taught four classes a semester. I was only asked to teach three courses a semester. In return, I was expected to be more productive in terms of my writing. Just a few years after I came, those who came in to do research and writing only had to teach two courses a semester. By then I was almost at the end of my time as a tenure track professor. I can tell you there was a lot of stress trying to produce scholarly books and articles while teaching over a hundred students every semester. I got through it, but I kept my head down, worked long hours, and tried to do what was expected of me, but not always much else."

"Got it. What can you tell me about who else had the offices while you were there? Our records are incomplete. Apparently, there was quite a bit of turnover in those offices since they were not as large as some of the others."

"Not so much in the early years, but that certainly became more pronounced as time went by. Let's see, when I first got there, Glen Cheatham was already there, and he was still in that office when I left. He was even lower on the priority list than I was. He was never transitioned to a research faculty position. He was classified as a lecturer and continued to teach four classes a semester. I think for the most part that suited him, though his pride was probably hurt a bit. He did not seem to hold it against me when I moved out."

"Who else do you remember?"

"The first couple years I was there, there was another junior faculty person. Not sure whatever happened to him, though. He was there in the spring semester, but then he never came back that third fall. It's like he just disappeared."

"Which fall was that?"

"That would have been fall 2008. He seemed like a nice enough guy if you got him talking about things that interested him. I don't think he connected with students all that well, or his colleagues for that matter. He was quite aloof."

"What was his name? We'll need to follow up with him."

"Oh gosh. Let me think. His name was something like . . . Danforth, that's it. Richard Danforth."

"RD," Dino blurted out, though he immediately wished he hadn't.

"What?"

"Nothing, sorry. Among other things we are still trying to identify our victim. All we've got to go on so far is a Baylor class ring inscribed with the initials, RD."

"That's quite a coincidence. Do you think it could be him?"

"No way to say. I'll have to investigate further to figure that out. Anyway, continue with your story. Who else had one of those offices while you were there?"

"Well, I had the middle office, and Glen Cheatham had the first office when you came up the stairs. When I first got there, Larry Pridwell had the last office, but he left at the end of the year. He was a real go-getter. When he came to Baylor, he negotiated a three-year credit toward tenure because he'd had a position somewhere else. He only spent one year in the back of the chapel, my first year. Then he moved up to a larger office, but not very long after that, he moved over to the dean's office. He started as Assistant Dean but somehow managed to be named Dean when the last one retired. There were a lot of eyebrows raised when that happened."

"How so?"

"Most faculty didn't know him. Those that did know him, didn't really like him."

"Why's that?

"Arrogance, plain and simple. He's quite condescending and does not know how to hide that well."

"Why did the department hire him then? I would have thought something like that would have shown up when he interviewed for the job."

"Hiring new faculty is a tricky business. It takes months to advertise the position, read the applications and then bring the three best candidates to campus. Ideally, the faculty then votes which one they like. Then, that recommendation is passed up the line into the dark hole known as the administration. The dean, provost, and president then actually approve which one is offered the position."

"I gather you're saying that that didn't happen in this case."

"Not really, no. From the outset, the administration signaled to the search committee that they wanted a 'star' for this position. Someone who would 'be somebody' in the Baptist world. That in and of itself was not all that unusual. Every search has a profile. With Baylor's push to become known as a Christian university that is also recognized as a top-tier research institution, faculty were under no illusions that they could just hire anybody. According to several people, when we spoke around the copy machine, the upper administration had an agenda for this search. They clearly had a different idea of what being a 'star' meant. They wanted someone conservative, and they wanted someone who thought that Baptists were evangelicals. Our department does not see itself as a conservative evangelical group. We're what they call moderate theologically, and mainstream academically. Back then, we also had a strong sense that Baptists were not conservative evangelicals, and all that goes with that label."

"Sorry, Doc. You've lost me now. I don't know all the theological jargon. I'm just trying to focus on the interpersonal dynamics of the department. Can you cut to the chase?"

"My bad. I've been told I tend to ramble when I tell a story. The upshot of it is we brought three people to campus for interviews. The faculty voted unanimously for one candidate, but the administration chose the candidate who was third on our list."

"Got it. So, in addition to being arrogant, he was essentially forced onto the department against its will."

"That sums it up well. My take was that the president at the time was trying to take the university, and especially the Religion Department, in a different direction. Either the president, the provost, or both simply looked at that recommendation and said, 'Unanimous? Then, no.' In retrospect, I'll give him some credit as an administrator. As the bees go, he's been fairly effective, even if he is a bit pompous."

"I'm sorry. You've lost me again. Who are the bees?"

"That's my own inside joke. I call administrators the bees because they're always buzzing about, making life difficult for faculty. They just keep multiplying, too. Every time they create a new administrative position, the new person has to create their own little hive. Baylor has grown by leaps and bounds but the administrative apparatus has grown even faster. Some of my colleagues are cruder and refer to all male and female administrators as 'B's,' spelled 'B-apostrophe s.' They use the letter as an acronym for male and female dogs of questionable familial lineage. I can't quite go that far. In my mind administration is a necessary evil, so I divide the bees into groups that describe them and their motives for being an administrator."

As Dino watched and listened, he noted a glint in Marvin Peake's eyes. He had a strong sense that the professor wanted to say more. The professor had hooked him. Dino also had a sense that these groupings might help him understand the culture here. Even if not, the look in the professor's eyes told him it will make a great story to tell Jack. Dino invited him to continue.

"Well, let's just call it my typology of bees. You've got your worker bees and your queen bees, of course. Then you got your wanna bees, your hasta bees, and your never bees. Every hive has to have a queen bee, but there's only room for one queen in a hive. Everybody else serves the queen. Most bees in a hive are the worker bees. The vast majority of them take the job very seriously. They are the ones who get the administrative work of the university done. But then you've got your wanna bees. Those are the administrators who are always angling to climb their way up the administrative ladder. They're interested in getting the work done because it helps their career. They're never satisfied with the position they've got. By contrast, the hasta bees are those administrators who have a particular skill set that everyone agrees means that person 'has to be' appointed. Finally, you've got your never bees. That's a group that will never become part of the hive, either by their own choice or someone else's. Some faculty members don't have a clue what an administrator does and wouldn't have the skill set to do it if they did. Some of them want to be an administrator, but someone has to tell them they will never be one. Others, like me, have absolutely no interest in becoming an administrator and tell anyone who will listen that they will 'never be' an administrator."

"That's hilarious," Dino exclaimed. "It's about the same in the police department, I must say. Most of us are worker bees. We report up the chain of command. Some of our bosses got there because they were excellent police officers, and now they help train those below them. Some of them, however, can be quite full of themselves. And some of them have worked the system to climb the ladder."

"That's why I call it a typology. It's applicable for most any institution that has a corporate ladder. People are people, you know."

"That's true enough. Before I leave, can you remember anyone else in those offices during those years?"

"Only DelRae. DelRae Fontenot. She came into the department as a junior professor in New Testament the fall that Pridwell moved out of the chapel office."

"Yes, we have her name. My partner's going to interview her this morning. Can you remember anyone else who might've been there on a regular basis? For example, do you bring guest lecturers in to teach a class for you?"

"No. I don't. It's too much of a hassle. It's hard to find someone in Waco who knows enough about the Old Testament to teach my courses. Especially back then. Now, I have a PhD student every semester as my graduate assistant. In theory, I could assign him or her to teach my class if I am out of town. The problem is if I'm away, it's usually for a professional conference and our doctoral students are probably presenting at the same conference. Add to that all the time it takes to get approval to pay guest speakers and to get all the forms to them that they have to fill out order to pay them, it's just not cost-effective for me. It takes too much time to arrange a guest speaker. Normally, I just cancel a couple of classes if I'm gone and try to make up the material when I get back."

"Thanks very much, Professor Peake. You've given me a lot of insight. I may need to come back and talk to you again if that's all right."

"You're quite welcome and I'm happy to help, but just call me Marvin or Marv. I'll answer to either."

"Thanks Marvin, and please call me Dino. My name is Dean, but that seems too formal for me. I'll probably talk to you again at some point. See you then."

14

Dr. Fontenot's office was one of several in the provost's suite on the first floor of Pat Neff Hall. Situated at the opposite end of Founders Mall from the Tidwell Building, the Pat Neff Building was named after a former president of Baylor, who coincidentally had also been the governor of Texas in the early 1920s. It fit Baylor's image of itself to have a former governor and a lifelong Baptist promoted to serve as its president from 1932–1947. Neff had also served as president of the Southern Baptist Convention from 1944–1946 and as Grand Master of the Masons in 1946. Less well-publicized was the criticism he received in the 1920s for his hands-off approach to the rise of the Ku Klux Klan in Texas.

As he entered the provost's suite of offices, the receptionist invited Jack to take a seat and told him Vice Provost Fontenot was still meeting with the provost, but should be available soon. Five minutes later, a woman emerged from what must be the provost's office and strode straight toward Jack, her hand extended in greeting. Jack was struck by her appearance. He estimated she was probably in her early forties, dressed professionally in skirt, blouse, and lightweight blazer. Her chestnut-highlighted brunette medium-length hair was tied in an elegant French braid, and her light brown complexion attested to her Creole-Cajun origins, with dark-rimmed glasses poised on her head for ease of access.

"Detective Farmer?" she asked as though she already knows the answer. Jack nodded as he shook her hand, noting her surprisingly firm and rigorous handshake. She is accustomed to standing her ground, Jack concluded. "Let's go into my office," she said turning immediately to another door. Her gait was energetic and purposeful. ("She gets things done," Jack noted to himself). She opened the already unlocked door, motioned for Jack to follow. She left the door slightly ajar after he entered. She walked to the large, wooden desk against the back wall, and deposited the papers and folders she was carrying.

Jack surveyed the office quickly. In addition to the desk and the bookshelves that lined three of the four walls ("Has she really read all those books," Jack wondered, "or are they props to project her competent persona?"). A small seating area with a small round table and three upholstered Bergère-style armchairs faced the table. ("Leather, real or simulated?" Jack wondered. In either case, they added to his estimation of Fontenot as a person of power).

"Please, sit down," she said as she took the chair nearest her desk. The effect, with the small table semi-separating them, artfully suggested professionalism yet intimacy. "I apologize for the delay. The provost's claim to my time outweighs any other. I also apologize that my time is so limited. I have another meeting halfway across campus so I must leave here by ten. So, let's get straight to business." She shifted slightly forward. "I assume from your message that you are investigating the incident involving the body found in Tidwell. I must say that I am not sure how helpful I can be. I was only in the chapel office in Tidwell for three years, when I was still a newly minted assistant professor."

"I'm not sure whether or how you can help, either. Especially since we don't yet know precisely when the murder was committed or even who the victim was, for that matter. I'm here to find out. You'd be surprised how what might seem insignificant to you could become crucial in the context of a murder investigation. Let me start by asking whether you remember any odd occurrence or any person who stood out at that time because of their unusual behavior. Maybe an intruder from outside the campus?"

"Well, I remember the upheaval caused by all the office-shuffling in my early days on the faculty. I don't remember anything odd along the lines of what you are suggesting. Besides, that office was tucked in the very back of the chapel, well out of the way of normal traffic. It almost felt like being in exile, at times."

"You have to understand, though, that I wasn't tenured yet in those days. If you want tenure, and you're smart, you concentrate on the basics: you teach your classes well enough to get good student reviews; you publish something; you demonstrate involvement in your professional guild; you pay attention to your committee assignments; and, above all else, you keep your head down in faculty politics—at least until you figure out where the power centers are, who your friends are, and, especially, who your enemies are."

"See, that's precisely the kind of thing that I'm interested in, Dr. Fontenot. While you were in that observer mode, you must have identified some fault lines in the faculty, some jealousies, for example."

Fontenot leaned back in her chair perceptibly. "Well, I didn't come to this office by virtue of naiveté, that's for sure. At the same, time, however, I didn't get here by talking trash, as our students would say, about my colleagues. In fact, I am uncomfortable with the question, detective."

"I'm not asking you to gossip, but this is a murder investigation. I need to know anything that might point us in the right direction. You imply that there is a story associated with your advancement in administration. As you say, you've had to avoid some enemies and cultivate some allies," Jack prompted her, with a slightly impatient tone.

"She keeps her cards close to her chest," he added to his mental profile of her. He also thought she'd probably been in some difficult negotiations. Probably a formidable opponent. "Maybe the insinuation that she had help with her career would touch a nerve, since she obviously prizes her own ability."

"How did you come to be in this office?"

Jack's gambit worked to a degree, but it also ended the interview. "If you are asking whether I earned my position through favoritism. . ." She paused a moment, seeking to remain dispassionate. ("Strong emotion leads to mistakes," she reminded herself.) "As I said, I kept my head down in those days. Still do, basically. As I see it, my job is to make Provost Pridwell look good. He gave me this position, I believe, because he recognized that that would be my priority. Now, unless you have specific questions for me, Detective Farmer," she declared dismissively as she stood up, "I should be preparing for my next meeting."

Jack stood as well. "Thank you for your time, Dr. Fontenot."

On the way back to the car, Jack felt disappointed. He had not learned anything of immediate consequence. On the other hand, he was confident that if he or Dino uncover any leads that point to a Baylor faculty member, Dr. Fontenot probably knew things that could help them develop those leads. They'll just need to figure out how to get information from her, they'll need some "specific questions" to ask. "She's not one to chew the fat," he thought, "but she knows plenty."

15

Dino left Morrison Hall and headed southwest around the quad to Pat Neff Hall to interview Larry Pridwell, the provost. Unnoticed by him, Jack had left the same building moments earlier and headed northeast after interviewing DelRae Fontenot. Jack was on his way to the Marrs-Mclean Science Building to interview Glen Cheatham. Their paths crossed one another but they were on parallel sidewalks heading in different directions, obscured from one another by buildings and foliage.

Dino entered the provost's suite of offices, which had a conference room off the hallway that led into an inner bullpen where several associate provosts had their offices, along with the provost himself. Dino introduced himself to the provost's administrative assistant. She looked at him quizzically, "Another one? Your colleague just left after speaking to Dr. Fontenot. Just a moment. I'll see if he has time to fit you in." She retreated further into the suite. Dino stood waiting while she checked to see whether the provost was available. He realized he and Jack had not thought about the logistics of these interviews.

"Provost Pridwell will be with you shortly," she stated as she returned. "He's got an important call that he needs to make first. Please have a seat and wait for him."

Dino could not help but think this "important call" was a ploy. By making him wait, the provost projected the power of his office. The provost was the chief academic officer for the university, ranking behind only the president in the hierarchy of power. Pat Neff Hall, with its high steeple that can be seen from the interstate, is arguably the most iconic building on Baylor's campus, even more so than the Tidwell Building. Because it houses both the president and the provost, as well as their respective staffs, people often refer to it as the tower of power.

Dino decided not to follow suit by pulling his badge out and demanding to see the provost immediately. Rather, he let the provost invite him into a meeting on his terms. No need to start out being confrontational. The interview would go better if the provost felt he was in control.

As he waited, Dino thought about what he had learned from his interview with Marvin Peake. He knew that Pridwell had one of the chapel offices for a brief period of time, but he needed to lock down the timeline. He also knew that Pridwell had the office at the far end of the hall, the one closest to the hatch that led to the room behind the pipe organ. Perhaps Pridwell could remember someone else who hung around the back of the chapel in those days. Maybe he could shed some light on what happened to Robert Danforth.

He was still lost in thought when the provost's administrative assistant told him that the provost would see him now. He followed her back to the provost's office and she introduced him formally to Provost Pridwell. She waited dutifully at the door as the provost stood and shook Dino's hand.

"Thank you for waiting. May I offer you a beverage? We have coffee, tea, soft drinks, or water should you wish to partake."

Dino noted that even the provost's offer sounds quite formal and somewhat pretentious. "No thank you. I don't want to take up much of your time. I know you're terribly busy."

"That will be all, Ms. Prescott. You may go."

Clearly, someone had trained Ms. Prescott in office etiquette quite well. Had Dino accepted the provost's offer to provide him with a beverage, no doubt she would have been the one to serve it, probably in porcelain coffee cups. The provost walked around the desk, and pointed to the small sofa to Dino's left, inviting him to have a seat. As he sat, Dino noted how close to the ground he felt as he sank into the plush cushions. The provost, he observed, sat in the much taller upright chair, meaning that the provost literally looked down on him.

"Yes, I'm afraid a busy schedule comes with the territory. Not only do I supervise the deans of the colleges, who in turn supervise the faculty, I also sit on the President's Council and devise strategic initiatives for the university's academic units. There certainly is much to do. So, how can I help you?"

"As you've probably heard by now, the renovation in the Tidwell Building uncovered a body in the back of the Tidwell building, behind the pipes for the pipe organ."

"Yes. I heard something to that effect. I am not sure what it has to do with me, however."

"Well, we've learned from our forensic unit that someone murdered our victim around fifteen years ago. We are operating on the assumption that someone killed him in the back of the chapel as well, since it's hard to imagine someone dragging a dead body across campus without someone noticing. So, according to our information, you had one of the three offices at the back of the chapel around that time. I'm just trying to pin down timelines. Who had which offices and in which years were they there?"

"I see. Well, let me think. I was only in that office for three years. I received tenure on a fast-track because of my teaching experience. I only spent three years here as an assistant professor. When I was promoted to associate professor, they gave me a bigger office in Tidwell. I was only in that office for a year before I became assistant dean, at which point my office moved to Burleson Hall."

"So, what years were those specifically when your office was in the back of Tidwell?"

"Oh, my goodness. Now you're making me do higher math. Well, I have been Provost for eight years. Before that, I was dean of the College of Arts and Sciences for five years, after serving as assistant dean for two years. That means I was a faculty member of the Religion Department for four years. Yes, I believe that is correct. I came to Baylor in 2003, so that means I would've been in that office until the spring of 2006. I remained in Tidwell, in the larger office, for the academic year 2006–2007 but moved up to Burleson Hall in 2007 when I became assistant dean."

"So, that means you would have had that office in the back of the chapel during the time we think the victim was most likely murdered. Do you remember anything unusual from that time?"

"I can't say that I do."

"Do you remember anyone else in those offices from that time?"

"Well, Marvin Peake was there when I got there, as was Glen Cheatham. Both were still in those offices when I was promoted. I remember that DelRae Fontenot was assigned that office when I moved out. She's now a vice provost, and a good one. I take credit for that."

"How so?"

"I saw that she has a real gift for administration. I hired her as an assistant dean once I became the dean. Any project I gave her to do, she would do. And she would do it well. She's one of the reasons why my office functioned so well while I was dean of the college. I hired good people. That was my secret. Some might say that they did all the work, and I took all the credit, but they would be wrong. I was the strategist, the leader of the team, the one who kept the balls rolling in the right direction. The president of the university saw that clearly. That's why he made me provost."

"Getting back to the offices at the back of the chapel, do you remember anyone else coming around those offices?"

"Not anyone in particular. I mean, students would sometimes make appointments to see me or one of the other professors, especially if they were doing poorly in class. I can't remember any of their names though. That's a long time ago. Can you remember the names of people you interviewed fifteen or sixteen years ago?"

"That's a fair point. I have to ask, though. I've gotta try to figure out who might've had access to the room behind the pipe organ."

"That's easy. Anyone. The doors to the chapel often remained unlocked at night. Anyone off the street could just walk right in. I can't tell you how many times I left the building late at night and found students studying in the chapel. Maybe something got out of hand one night and a couple of students got in a fight."

"Perhaps. But how many students would know about the room behind the pipe organ?"

"More than you think. As I mentioned, students came to our offices on a fairly regular basis. Any of them could have seen the door at the end of the hall that led into that room."

"Maybe so, but they would have to be strong enough to pull a body up a flight of steps."

"Well, I certainly can't imagine any of my colleagues at the time being involved in a murder. I mean, Glen Cheatham has a bit of a temper, and a short fuse,but he's not violent. We used to call him 'pop' behind his back, not because of his age, but because he's likely to explode like a firecracker. He also likes to rant, but he is like Don Quixote flailing at the windmills. He's not much of a threat to anyone. Who was the victim, by the way? I don't think you said."

"I didn't. That's one of the reasons why we're conducting these interviews. We don't yet know who he was. We are hoping that forensics will turn up something that will help us identify him. That reminds me, do you remember a faculty member by the name of Richard Danforth?"

"The name rings a bell. I have a vague recollection of someone by the name Danforth. Why do you ask? Do you think he might be the victim?"

"We're not sure yet. Marvin Peake mentioned his name as someone who was there one spring but gone in the fall. You don't remember him?"

"Now that you mention it, I think he may be the one who had the chapel office before me. People were always a little bit vague about why he left. I gathered he left suddenly, though, because they weren't sure they were going to have an office in Tidwell to put me in when they first hired me. His departure meant that they suddenly had a place for me in the building. Wow. I had not thought about him in years."

"Do you happen to remember whether he was a Baylor alum?"

"No, I don't remember very much at all about him. On your way out, we'll ask Mrs. Prescott to check on that for you. The information will be in his personnel files or with the Alumni Office."

"Thanks. I'll do that. So, you mentioned that you often left in the evening after the building was supposed to be locked. How late were you there?"

"It depends. I was an assistant professor, which means I was teaching new courses every year for most of the time I was in the department. I think most professors when they're starting out will tell you that they worked on their lecture for that day right up until the point where they had to go to class. You must remain one step ahead of the students. I've heard some say the ink on the page was still wet when they started reading their lecture. I didn't like to work that way. If you're writing a lecture right up to the last minute, you get sloppy. You make mistakes. You don't present things in the right order. So, knowing that it takes time to prepare those lectures, I would stay as long as it took for me to finish the next day's lectures. Some days I might be here till seven or seven thirty. Some nights I might not leave until ten or ten thirty. Those are long days, but it's part of what made my lectures so good. They were meticulously organized."

"Do you remember seeing anyone else up there at night?"

"Occasionally. Marvin Peake would sometimes come back to the office after dinner. Can't say I ever remember Glen Cheatham here in the evening. I don't think he really spent much time prepping for his lectures. Oh, he is popular as a lecturer, but that's because he is a performer more than a true academic. He'll walk up and down the aisles and get students excited. When he talks about Moses, he raises his fist to the sky like he is holding a staff in his hand as the Israelites parted through the Red Sea. It's great theater, but it's hogwash. In my opinion, that's not how one should deliver a proper lecture."

"Okay, Dr. Pridwell, I think that's all I need for now. If you think of anything else, please don't hesitate to give me a call." Dino handed the provost his card.

"I will, but please call me Provost Pridwell, or Mr. Provost. I realize you are not trained in the proper etiquette of addressing people in academic institutions. Still, you should use the title Dean, Provost, or President when addressing those in higher administrative posts. They have earned that respect."

"Thank you, Provost Pridwell. I will try to remember that."

"You're welcome. Have a good day, Detective Piper."

Dino seethed as he left the provost's office. The encounter reminded him of his time as a boy and young teenager growing up in the Midwest. Dino's own father had been a bully who thought boys needed discipline to teach them right from wrong. His idea of discipline involved angry tirades and a belt to the back side. Dino knew instinctively that Pridwell is also a bully. He berates people to get his own way. The provost's condescending admonishment of Dino stirred up old memories that Dino had worked hard to keep buried. The only thing his father's discipline had taught him was that he did not want to be that kind of parent, or that kind of person. The provost had done nothing to earn his respect, and Dino resented Pridwell reminding him about that part of his childhood.

16

After decorously escorting Detective Farmer out of his office, Pridwell paused briefly at Mrs. Prescott's desk to ask her to get Dino information on Richard Danforth's situation and to tell her that he wants to be undisturbed until further notice. He returned to his office, closing the door firmly and taking his seat behind his desk in his very comfortable, very expensive, leather chair.

Although he concealed it well behind the officious façade of the provost instructing the police detective in academic protocol, the interview he had just completed disturbed him for several reasons. The situation could potentially bring negative publicity for the university and, by extension, for him at a time when such publicity could impact his prospects for advancement. A head-hunter group from the east coast had contacted him late in the previous semester to inquire about his interest in the presidency at a Baptist university in the east. It is admittedly a smaller pond than Baylor, but he would be the biggest fish in it, so he entered into conversations with the firm. After only a couple of in-depth interviews with the committee, they put him on a short list of candidates who would visit the university to speak with the search committee directly. The Waco detective's interest in details about his occupancy of the old Tidwell office reminded him that police investigations can take unexpected turns. Like everyone else, after all, he would rather keep certain aspects of his personal life personal.

He sat quietly for perhaps three minutes, gazing at his portrait, a gift from his mother when he became provost, before reaching for the phone to call the head of campus police to ask that they cooperate fully with WPD. He also requested that he receive bi-weekly situation reports from the chief of police personally. Verbal reports would be fine, no need for formal paperwork. In response to the chief's objection that he did not usually report to the provost, Pridwell reminded the chief that, while the provost is only one of several vice-presidential positions at Baylor, it is widely recognized that the office is *prima inter pares*. Remembering he was talking to the police chief, Pridwell condescendingly translated for him, "That means first among equals." Furthermore, he implied, without expressly stating so, that the president had asked him to monitor the situation directly given its delicacy and possible public relations downside. Pridwell kept his remarks polite, but his tone unmistakably asserted his authority. The conversation lasted no more than five minutes.

Immediately, Pridwell placed another phone call—to his younger brother, state senator Jack Pridwell, at his senate office. To Larry's surprise, Jack himself answered on the second ring.

"Is something wrong?"

"That was quick. I expected to get the receptionist. By the way, that's an unusual greeting. What about, 'Hello, beloved brother. Good to hear from you.'"

"You lucked out. I have been making fund-raising calls all morning. When I saw your number, I picked up myself. You and I both know that you only call me for one of two reasons. Either you have bad news, or you want to ask me for a favor. Judging from your tone of voice, it must be the latter today."

"Well, I guess I can dispense with the good-natured fraternal pleasantries. You are, indeed, correct. I need a favor from you in your official capacity, but I need you to be sure to do it discreetly."

"Let's hear it. Remember, though, I can't fix traffic tickets, Larry."

"It's not for me personally. You have surely heard about Baylor's skeleton in the chapel problem."

"Everyone has. Go on."

"It's bad for Baylor's reputation. We have already begun to get calls from parents of students and prospective students about safety at the university. We need to get this off the front page. I hope that you can drop some hints, at least, with some Waco officials."

"Waco is not in my district and I'm not sure that Waco folks are going to be persuaded to stifle or neglect a murder investigation for the sake of Baylor's reputation."

"Listen, Jack, you have more influence than you admit. Besides, this is more than a town and gown thing. I want it to go away for the university's sake, of course, but it is not good for the WPD, either. It is well known that they are short-staffed. It seems to me that devoting time to tracking down a fifteen-year-old John Doe is probably not the best use of departmental resources. If they cannot show progress soon, they should create a dead-case file and let it go. That would be a win-win for everyone."

"OK. I'll see what I can do. Place a couple of low-key phone calls, at least. Meanwhile, you can do me a couple of favors."

"Oh. Put a thumb on the admissions scale for a colleague's kid?"

"No. No. Something more personal. First, would you please call Mama soon? I am tired of her grilling me about you and your family every time we talk."

"OK. I'll call Mother soon. You said a couple of favors."

"Yes. If you don't want to cause a family ruckus, please remember Daddy's birthday next month. Maybe even go home for the occasion. It won't kill you."

"Maybe not. But I would argue that not being in the same room as Dad is the best way to *avoid* a family ruckus." The provost paused a moment. "I'll think about it."

"I guess that's something."

"Now, I imagine you need to get back to fundraising. I'm counting on your help with this murder thing. Say hello to the family for me."

Pridwell hung up the phone, removed his glasses, massaged his forehead for a few moments, and sighed. He then placed a third call to Mrs. Prescott, announcing that he was ready to resume the day's schedule.

17

After Jack finished his conversation with DelRae Fontenot, he circled back across campus to the Sid Rich building to visit Glen Cheatham. Farmer still could not shake off the irony that an ethics professor might be a murderer. Still, he knew there was nothing so far to implicate any of the professors with whom they were talking as the murderer. They did not even know the identity of the victim. Jack realized that the victim's identity is the key to unlocking the crime.

Jack found Cheatham's office on the second floor, and he knocked on the door. There was no answer, but a man approached the door of the office next door and put his key in the door. "He's in class right now," he offered, "but you can probably catch him if you go down the hall to the big lecture room."

Jack thanked him and went to look for the large lecture hall. He heard a booming voice coming from the end of the hallway, so he sauntered up to the door and opened it quietly. He stepped inside the classroom and realized he was on the top level of a theater-shaped classroom with the professor on a stage at the bottom. Even though the professor had no microphone, his voice filled the room. He paced animatedly across the stage, stopping only to raise his arm with his finger pointed upward to emphasize the point he was making dramatically. Farmer was fascinated by his energy and his passion. He conveyed the impression that what he had to say was, perhaps, the most important thing a student would ever learn.

Jack noted several students looking at their watches, politely signaling to the professor that the class was over and they had to go to their next class somewhere else on campus. One young student made the mistake of standing up with his backpack, ready to walk out.

"Sit down this instant, young man. I am not finished with what I have to say. I'll tell you when it's time to go."

Sheepishly, the boy sat down but did not take out his notebook. The professor immediately returned to lecture mode. He completed two more sentences, and then he paused for effect before announcing, "That, students, concludes the lecture for today." He then turned and looked directly at the student who had stood prematurely, "So, *now* you may leave."

The student, Jack thought, looks utterly chastised and humiliated as he walks past Farmer and slinks out the door. He felt sorry for the boy. Sure, some might consider it poor etiquette to walk out of the classroom while the professor's talking, but Cheatham's anger seemed out of proportion. Jack noted to himself, "This guy's got a real temper."

The other students filed out quietly as the professor gathered up his notes and began walking up the stairs to the top of the room where Farmer stood.

"Professor Cheatham?"

"Yes. Who are you?"

Jack introduced himself and asked if he they can speak in the professor's office. Cheatham nodded, "Sure. Follow me."

When they reached the office, Cheatham sat in the chair behind his desk and Farmer took one of the chairs that filled most of the rest of the space in the small office.

Before Jack could say a word, Cheatham began to speak, obviously still worked up over the recent events. "Can you believe the nerve of that kid, the little snit? This younger generation has no respect for its elders. In my day, no student would have dared to leave class while a professor was still speaking. This generation is going to the dogs. I'm sorry you had to witness that, but he had it coming."

"Well, actually I'm here on a different matter. You may have heard that a body was found in the back of the chapel while they were renovating the Tidwell building. I would like to ask you some questions if you don't mind."

"Why me?" he asked rather defensively.

"As we understand it, you had one of those offices during the time we think that the victim may have been murdered."

"Does that make me a suspect? A lot of people had those offices through the years. It's not my fault I had one longer than most."

Cheatham's response, Jack noted, had an edge to it, but he could not tell whether that was due to anger or indignation. "Actually, at this point we're talking to everyone who had one of those offices around the time we think the murder took place. We are interested in trying to figure out who the victim might be."

"How long ago are you talking about?"

"Probably about fifteen years ago, give or take a few years on either side."

"Well, it's no secret I would've had one of the chapel offices then. In fact, I had that office the whole time I was in the Religion Department."

"Really? I was under the impression that people rotated out of those offices after they have been here a while because they were smaller than other offices."

"That's true as a general rule, but my case was complicated. For one thing, I'm classified as a lecturer, not a tenured or tenure-track professor. In some ways, it's like being a second-class citizen. I teach a lot more students because lecturers teach four courses each semester while tenured and tenure-track faculty only teach two. Also, the bulk of my teaching involves teaching the required religion classes, and those classes have up to sixty students in each class. By contrast, tenured and tenure-track faculty teach the upper-level religion courses that are limited to twenty students. That means most semesters they teach forty students, and I teach up to two hundred and forty."

"That's a big difference," Jack responded sympathetically, hoping to remain in Cheatham's good graces.

"You got that right," Cheatham agreed. "Lecturers are also on the lower rungs of the ladder when it comes to requests for office space. Even after I had been at Baylor for ten years, a new tenure-track faculty member just out of graduate school would qualify for a better office than I would because I'm just a lecturer. I eventually transferred out of the Religion Department to the Honors College so I could manage my teaching load better. I teach honors courses for half my load, which are also limited to twenty students. I still teach one or two sections a year of these large, required courses like the one you just saw, but at least the Religion Department provides me with a graduate assistant who helps me with my grading for those courses. Until fairly recently, I kept that small office at the back of the chapel so I'd have a place to meet students after class and so I wouldn't have to move all my books. Eventually, though, they decided to kick me out of that office because the department got so big that they needed all the space for their full-time people. The Honors College also didn't have enough office space for everyone, so now the powers-that-be have shipped me even further away from Tidwell into Sid Rich, where I teach the honors classes."

"Wow. That sounds tough."

"Tough? It's downright unjust and almost certainly unethical."

"You said something about a graduate assistant. Does he or she work in your office?"

"No, before the renovation, some of the larger offices in Tidwell were actually suites, and they had desks where graduate assistants and student workers could work while they're on duty. My office in the back of Tidwell was far too small, however, to hold a second desk."

"What's the difference between a graduate assistant and a student worker?"

"A student worker is an undergraduate student who works ten hours a week for the department. They do photocopying, run errands, that sort of thing, and sometimes work on special projects. Graduate assistants are PhD students who help with grading classes, proctoring exams, or substituting for professors who are away at a conference."

"So where did you meet with your graduate assistants and student workers? Did they ever spend time in your office?"

"Not on a regular basis. My graduate assistant would come to my office and sit in the chair when we had to go over the exams he had graded, or if I had to explain to him what I was looking for in a specific assignment. Student workers are different. They are assigned tasks by the office manager. You contact her if you need the student worker to do something. Sometimes people have an ongoing project, so they may request a particular student to work for them on a regular basis, but for the most part you get a different person for each task you need help with."

"Did all the faculty get graduate assistants or was it just the lecturers because you teach more students?"

"They certainly wouldn't give lecturers that kind of help and not give it to tenured faculty. All the full-time members of the Religion Department are assigned a graduate student every year to work for them. Come to think of it, though, Larry Pridwell had a student worker back then working on a project of some sort. He came to the office on a fairly regular basis. In fact, I think that student went into the graduate program when he graduated. I believe he even worked for Larry as a graduate assistant for a while"

"That's the provost, correct?"

"Yes, that's him, though he wasn't provost at the time."

"Do you remember the student's name?"

"Larry should be able to tell you his name. They seemed to have had a close relationship. He's something of a stuffed shirt, you know. All prim and proper. Of course, back then, he was just a junior professor teaching systematic theology. It was clear, though, he was always angling for something higher up the food chain."

"My partner is interviewing him as we speak. I'm sure he'll get the name from him. Do you happen to remember the names of any of the other graduate assistants from back then?"

"Oh heavens no. If you gave me a name, I might remember whether that person had ever been a graduate assistant for me, but it was a different person every year. There would be too many for me to remember. Maybe the director of Graduate Studies would have lists of who worked for whom, but I'd be surprised if they kept those liststhat long."

"Thanks for the suggestion. We'll follow up on that. Can you think of anyone else who came around those offices. We know about Pridwell, and I believe his office was given to Dr. Fontenot when he moved into a larger office. My partner is also interviewing Dr. Peake."

"I can't say I do. It's been too long."

"Were there any problems that you can recall? Do you remember any issues with students or staff that stood out. Anything or anyone who made you angry, for example."

"Me? No. I get along with everyone. I have strong opinions, but so do most of my colleagues."

"OK. Thanks. I'll be back in touch if I think of anything else."

"No problem."

As Jack walked away, he reflected upon the interviews he had conducted. There wasn't much chance that DelRae Fontenot could have killed the victim. She was so petite, it's hard to imagine her having the strength to overpower anyone. He was not inclined to see Glen Cheatham as a murderer, but he could not entirely rule him out. Farmer had seen firsthand how angry Cheatham got at a student for something as minor as leaving class while he was still lecturing. Anyone capable of that kind of rage would be capable of inflicting pain on someone. They would need more information before ruling him out. Larry Pridwell seemed all too proper to imagine him killing someone.

As he was about to leave the building, someone called his name. He turned around and recognized Tommi Piper, Dino's youngest daughter. "Tommi, how are you? I haven't seen you in ages."

"I'm good, Mr. Farmer. What are you doing on Baylor's campus?"

"Call me Jack. Mr. Farmer makes me sound old. Your dad and I are investigating the identity of the body they found in the back of the Tidwell building. He's in another building interviewing someone else. I'm here speaking with Dr. Cheatham. Do you know him?"

"Only by reputation, Mr. Farmer. Sorry, my dad drilled into us that we call our elders Mr. and Mrs."

"Like I said, that just makes me feel old. You're not a child anymore. What can you tell me about Cheatham's reputation?"

"Students love him. He's supposedly really entertaining in class."

"I'm sensing a 'but.' What about him outside of class?"

"Honestly, I've not had dealings with him directly, but some of my colleagues have born the brunt of his anger. He called one of my colleagues and chewed her out for advising one of his students improperly. She pointed out that her advice was precisely what the student was supposed to take. When she challenged him, he got very huffy, but he backed down with her and said he would take it up with the dean's office."

"I'd better get back to meet your father. You're welcome to join me and say hello."

"No can do, but tell him I'll see him this weekend. We're supposed to have dinner with mom and him. Great to see you again, Mr. Farmer."

"Jack, please." Jack felt old as she's leaving. Then he remembered his oldest daughter is turning fifteen. "I am getting old."

18

Glen Cheatham was altogether displeased that the Waco police had any interest whatsoever in his professional or personal life, and he wanted someone in authority at Baylor, someone with the right connections, to make the police go away. He called the provost's office and was put on hold, before the administrative assistant told him that the provost was unavailable. So, at his first opportunity, he marched over to see the provost in person.

Mrs. Prescott played her appointed role as the administrative assistant to the provost impeccably. Did Dr. Cheatham have an appointment? Yes, the provost was in, but he had asked that I not disturb him. If the purpose of this visit was professional, could you please make an appointment to handle it by phone, say tomorrow morning at ten when the provost's schedule would be clear? Cheatham explained that he considered the matter urgent but promised to keep his conversation with the provost brief. In the end, Mrs. Prescott relented and called the provost, "Dr. Pridwell, Dr. Cheatham is here to see you. I know that he doesn't have an appointment, but he says the matter is important and promises to be brief."

After a moment of silence from Mrs. Prescott—when Pridwell was obviously complaining about the intrusion—she told Cheatham, "He can give you ten minutes."

"I only need five," Cheatham said as Mrs. Prescott ushered him into Pridwell's office.

"Still the same impetuous Glen Cheatham, I see. I know that you are familiar with the courtesy of making appointments to see the provost. What is so urgent?"

Pridwell did not move from his seat behind his desk, and he did not invite Cheatham to sit. Cheatham would not have accepted if Pridwell had extended the offer anyway. He preferred to stand, looking down on Pridwell for the duration of what he intended to be a brief, mostly one-way, conversation.

"Yes. I understand how important it is to you that you preserve every appearance of the dignity of your office, but I knew you before you got tenure. You will always be Larry to me, your title notwithstanding. I mean no disrespect for you or the office. I merely have no interest in the game of status."

"I see. Let me repeat then, what is so urgent?"

"You may or may not know that Waco PD has been interviewing religion department faculty, me included. I am here to strongly encourage you to use your office to curb their inquisitiveness."

"Well, first off, I don't know that a police investigation should concern the chief academic officer of this university. Nor am I confident that, even if the provost were to have an interest, he could be effective. Mostly, however, I do wonder why you are so vexed over the matter. You surely know the cliché about not fearing interactions with the police if you have nothing to hide." Pridwell paused a few seconds and, looking Cheatham directly in the eye, added, "Do you have something to hide, *Glen*?"

"That's a ridiculous, even offensive, question, *Larry*. Of course not! It's just that it doesn't look good for any of us, and naturally I care that it may not look good for me. Appearances matter. The police won't hesitate to dig up things like old student complaints and long forgotten disagreements among the faculty in their search for trouble. I want, no I expect, to be left alone to do my work. I expect you to do what you can to make that happen. It is a responsibility of the office you hold to protect your faculty from unnecessary nuisance."

"You haven't changed, that much is clear. Always something of a hot head. I imagine that you would rather the police not see you in that light, correct? Well, I regret to inform you that you have wasted your time paying me this visit. I do not see it as my duty to protect you, not at all. But I am concerned about the university's public reputation. I was concerned even before you barged in here making demands. I will take *appropriate* steps to protect Baylor, but let me remind you again of the adage: if you have nothing to hide. . ."

Cheatham's face reddened noticeably. He stretched himself to his full stature, took a deep breath, and angrily whispered loudly enough to be heard, "Good day, *Dr.* Pridwell," before turning and brusquely leaving Pridwell's office.

19

Having completed interviews with the four faculty members who had offices at the back of the chapel fifteen years earlier, Dino and Jack met back at the office to compare notes and decide how to proceed. Dino began by summarizing his interviews. He told Jack that Marvin Peake would make an excellent resource as they continued their investigation. Peake, he believed, had keen insight into the culture of the university then and now. Dino recounted to Jack the details of Marvin Peake's typology of bees as an example. Jack smiled a crooked grin, especially when Dino explained the wanna bees and the never bees.

Dino was far less effusive regarding his conversation with Larry Pridwell. As he told Jack, the provost's pomposity almost oozed with every word he spoke. He came across as arrogant, condescending, and dismissive. "That being said," Dino admitted, "disliking someone isn't evidence that they've committed a crime. Nevertheless, something seems off with him. He comes across like he's holding something back most of the time, but on the other hand he's not shy about dropping hints about the problems of others."

"Interesting," Jack commented. "I had the same impression when I interviewed DelRae Fontenot. She's very tightlipped and plays her cards very close to the vest. In her case, however, I couldn't get anything from her about her colleagues. Somehow, I managed to offend her by pointing out that she had worked for Pridwell in two different offices, first as an assistant dean and now as vice provost. Still, I can't imagine her pulling off a murder like this. For one thing, she's awfully small. I can't imagine her having the strength to haul a body around the back of the chapel."

"What about Cheatham?" Dino asked.

"That's another story. He's an open book. He says what he thinks, even when he shouldn't. In that sense, the interview with him was more helpful than the interview with Fontenot. On the other hand, the guy needs some anger management training. He went off on a student like I've never seen. He came across as a bully. Like most bullies, he's defensive. He's also very opinionated and, not surprisingly, thinks very highly of his own opinions."

"Is he violent do you think?"

"In my mind anyone with a temper like that could hurt someone under the right conditions. At the same time, I didn't get the sense that he was hiding anything."

"So, it sounds like we'd like to get some more information about Pridwell and Cheatham. What you say about Cheatham lines up well with what Marvin Peake said about him. Speaking of Peake, I picked up one interesting tidbit from him. He remembered that back at that time there was a faculty member who disappeared rather mysteriously. Seems like he vanished quickly and quietly. Even more interesting, his name was Richard Danforth, meaning. . ."

"Meaning he had the initials R.D. and could've possibly owned that ring. Well, we should at least check it out."

"Speaking of follow-up, do you think it's worth our time trying to track down the graduate assistants and student workers?"

"What are you talking about? What are graduate assistants and student workers?"

"Cheatham told me about them. Student workers are undergraduates on work-study who perform tasks for the department. The department also assigns graduate students to faculty members to help them with grading and other things."

"Neither one of the people I interviewed said anything about that when I asked them if there were other people around at the time."

"Well, that's interesting. At least according to Cheatham, Pridwell had an undergraduate student worker assigned to him to help him with special projects he was working on. That same student worker, at least according to Cheatham, went on to become his graduate assistant. They worked together quite a bit."

"That's very interesting, indeed," Dino chimed in. "I specifically pressed Pridwell regarding whether anyone else would have been around during that time. You'd think he would've mentioned this student."

"Maybe, but not necessarily. When I asked Cheatham for the names of some of these students, he drew a blank. He had a different graduate student assigned to him every year."

"OK, but let's check it out anyway. It sounds like at least this one student worked closely with Pridwell for more than a year. We should at least ask him about his time with Pridwell."

Jack got a rather surprised look on his face while Dino finished his last statement. Jack held up his left hand and reached into his pocket with his right. When he pulled out the phone, Dino realized that Jack had set his phone to vibrate. Jack punched in his password and cocked an eyebrow.

"I just got a text from forensics. They think they might've found something that might be useful to us. They want me to swing by their office."

"Now things are starting to get interesting," Dino said. "Why don't you go ahead and run over there and find out what they've got. I'm gonna see what I can find out about this Richard Danforth. I'll probably have to go personally to Baylor's HR department. I doubt they'll give me what I want over the phone."

"Sounds good, but have you had lunch? There's a new Mexican fusion place that opened just a couple of weeks ago. Word is that the food is not like anything you've ever eaten before. Mexican meets Malaysian."

"You're just hoping this counts as practicing your Spanish, right?"

"No way. I can already say taco in four languages. I am studying, though. I figure if I'm going to learn to dance with my wife and daughter at the *quinceañera*, I should probably do a toast in Spanish for my mother-in-law."

"You're a good son-in-law, Jack. Don't let anybody tell you any different. Let's go grab lunch."

"Tell that to my mother-in-law."

* * *

"Piper. Farmer. My office."

Dino and Jack looked at one another, and Dino complained, "It's too soon after lunch for this."

The voice came from Sergeant George Mendoza. It's never a good sign to be hauled into your boss's office, but even less so with this sergeant. Mendoza had the political skills necessary for success on a modern urban police force, but he did not usually concern himself with individual cases. His ability to anticipate how bureaucrats would respond had helped him advance to his current post. He was sensitive to clashes of culture in Waco, in part because he was the son of a legal immigrant from Argentina. His father came from a wealthy family who ran a famous winery in Argentina, but as the third son, he knew he would never inherit any of the land needed to succeed in that profession, so he decided to try his luck in the States. The sergeant's father had thus emigrated to the United States in the seventies, and with the help of his family connections he got a decent job working for a wine distributor. He married a US citizen, and they had three children. George was the eldest, and he was quintessentially Texan, but he still carried himself with a bit of the aristocratic bearing he had inherited from his father. He had excelled at sports in high school, where he was captain of his baseball team as well as cornerback for his high school football team (American football, not soccer). He was not interested in academics, but he was quite smart. He had gone to the police academy instead of college and had spent more than thirteen years on the force. After five years (two as a detective), he had applied for and received a promotion to sergeant. He had been assigned to two smaller units previously and had only been assigned to the special crimes unit a little over a year earlier. It was an open secret that he was angling to make lieutenant when his boss retired, but the Waco Police Department does not have that many lieutenants. Rumor had it that he had managed to move to more important units because of his ability to schmooze with the administrators above him. He reveled in the knowledge that they promoted him over more experienced officers. He was therefore considerably younger than Jack and Dino, which did not endear him to them or the other older detectives in the department who resented being told what to do by someone with far less experience. Neither of them, however, had ever applied for the sergeant's job. They preferred to work cases.

After being summoned, Dino and Jack trudged across the room, in no hurry to hear what the sergeant had to say. As they entered his office he got straight to the point. "What's the status of the Baylor skeleton?"

"He's dead, sir," Jack replied, attempting to add some levity to the situation. Dino glanced at Jack, hoping to signal him to be careful. Mendoza was a no-nonsense guy who did not appreciate wisecracks. Having worked his way through the ranks, he took his job seriously, too seriously at times. He did not, however, have a reputation for having a sense of humor.

"I'm not paying you to make jokes, detective. What's the status of your investigation?"

Dino replied, "We're making progress, sir. We've done some preliminary interviews and have a couple leads to check on. Jack is about to check with forensics. They've indicated they had something that might be useful for identifying the victim."

"What else?" Mendoza prompted.

Jack bristled and pushed back, "With all due respect, Sarge, without knowing the name of the victim, there's not much to go on. Our best guess is that the murder happened about fifteen years ago, so it's just another cold case. We've got a handle on who had the offices at the back of the chapel, but we don't know if any of them did it. The outside door was left open most nights, so anyone could've entered the building. It's gonna take some time to sort things out."

"I understand that," Mendoza acknowledged, "but it won't be long before I start catching hell from my bosses to get this case off the front page. Everyone starts getting real skittish when one of these town and gown issues comes up. If we can't show progress, they're going to start leaning on me to let it go. If they put pressure on me, you can bet I'm gonna do the same to you, and you know the old saying, crap runs downhill."

"It's taken fifteen years for the body to surface. We've had the case for less than fifteen days. Give us time to follow these leads and shake some trees. The process takes time."

"I doubt you'll get a lot of that. We're already short-staffed, so devoting time to tracking down a fifteen-year-old John Doe will not be seen as the best use of departmental resources. If you don't uncover something soon, I won't be able to justify the time. I'm giving you fair warning. Find something or put it on the back burner."

Jack started to say something, but the sergeant waved him off. "That's all. Dismissed." Before they left his office, however, Mendoza stopped Jack. "Farmer, I want you to type up the report you just gave me. If I start hearing from my bosses, I want something in writing to give them."

Once they were out of earshot, Jack let loose with several expletives. Dino tried to calm him down by taking a mollifying tack. "Good for us that he's the one feeling the pressure. He's gone from zero to sixty in no time since the last time he asked us about the case. I suspect he may already be getting heat. I have no interest in playing those political games. We'll just have to hope something comes from our leads."

20

Since Mendoza assigned Jack the task of writing up the report, Dino figured he had better make himself scarce. He told Jack he's going to track down Richard Danforth. He left the office and drove to Robinson tower at Baylor where the HR Department was located. Getting there was next to impossible, given all the roadwork going on downtown. The HR Department sits on the top floor of an eight-story office building on the other side of the interstate from the bulk of Baylor's campus. Named for a wealthy booster who donated the building to the university, it houses most of the administrative offices of the university. It allows Baylor to offer a kind of one-stop shop for all the administrative needs of students and staff.

Waco had become a tourist destination since Chip and Joanna Gaines set up their Magnolia empire downtown on a plot of land where grain used to be loaded onto railroad cars for transport. They refurbished two huge rusty silos to create the ultimate Magnolia shopping experience. Since then, however, the city of Waco had been racing to install sidewalks downtown to keep pedestrian visitors to the silos separated from the automobile traffic. At the same time, the Texas Department of Transportation decided to widen the stretch of I-35 that runs through Waco. As a result, the normally sedate traffic patterns have become an orange maze of detour signs that seemed to change daily. What should have been a ten-minute drive took Dino forty-five minutes to navigate. He then had to park in a lot that was too small to hold many visitors. He breathed a sigh of relief when he finally got into the elevator to ride it to the sixth floor. The glass at the back of the elevator looked out onto the city, offering a bird's eye view of the chaos below.

It took another twenty minutes for Dino to find someone in the HR Department who had the authority to look at the personnel files of

Baylor's faculty and staff, the vice president and chief human resources officer. Dino showed her his credentials and explained the situation. She dutifully expressed her sympathy regarding his request to see the employment history of Richard Danforth. Nevertheless, she politely but firmly explained to the detective that she could not grant him the access he was requesting without a court order.

Dino tried another approach. He asked her whether she could simply verify that Baylor had hired a person named Richard Danforth and when he worked for the university. She treated this more limited request as a matter of public record and agreed to look up the name. After several minutes and several dozen keystrokes, she nodded and told Dino that Richard Danforth had indeed worked for the Religion Department at Baylor University for the academic years 2005–2007. She refused, however, to provide him with any information regarding the circumstances of his departure. She simply repeated the HR mantra that personnel files are privileged and that he would need a court order if he wanted to see the contents of those files.

Dino explained to her again that this was a murder investigation, and that he was merely interested at this point in determining whether Richard Danforth was still alive. She nodded again understandingly but gestured that her hands were tied. Frustrated, Dino rose to leave but then turned around and asked whether he left any contact information when he departed. She admitted that the file does list a permanent contact number, but added that she has no way of knowing if it is still valid.

Dino was happy for any information he could get, so he asked her to give him the number. She was reluctant because the request falls into a gray area. Dino reiterated that he was there in an official capacity as part of a murder investigation and that sought information only. If he had to obtain a warrant, it would take days. If she gave him the number, it would only take minutes for him to place a call and see what he could learn. Finally, she acquiesced and gave him the phone number. Dino thanked her even though he did not feel a deep sense of gratitude. For him, the wheels of bureaucracy grind so slowly that they turn even the most mundane request into a painstaking ordeal. He decided to go back to the office to make the phone call.

It only took him thirty minutes to return to the office because he knew now where to anticipate the detours. When he arrived at his desk, he considered getting a cup of coffee since his HR consultation had really taken the wind out of his sails. Two things stopped him. First, he had reached a point in life where he would pay a price for having coffee after lunch, meaning he wouldn't sleep through the night if he had caffeine after lunch. Second, and probably more importantly, he remembered the last time he'd made the mistake of having coffee at the office. Calling it coffee was a stretch. It was more like black sludge.

He sat down, pulled out his notebook, and dialed the number he had recorded for Danforth. Someone answered on the fourth ring with a tentative hello. "May I speak with Richard Danforth?" Dino asked. When his question met with silence, Dino continued by identifying himself. "My name is Dean Piper. I'm a detective with the police department in Waco, Texas. Can you tell me if this phone number still belongs to Richard Danforth?"

"It does," came the reply. "This is he. Why are you calling me? I haven't been to Waco in a long time."

"So, you are the Richard Danforth who worked at Baylor University about fifteen years ago?"

"Yes, but may I ask why you want to know? I don't have any unpaid parking tickets. I've not been there since I left."

"It's a rather long story, Mr. Danforth. We are investigating the homicide of an unknown male who was killed about the time you left your position there, and all we've been able to determine was that the deceased had the initials R.D. When we learned that you suddenly departed under mysterious circumstances, we had to investigate."

"Mysterious circumstances? From my perspective, there was nothing mysterious about it at all. I took that position right out of graduate school, but I soon realized that I was not cut out for teaching. In my third semester, I finally admitted to myself that I was miserable. I fulfilled my contract for the year but decided not to return the next year. I finished the spring semester and came back to the west coast where I'm from. I took a job with my father, and I've been here ever since."

"Was your office in the back of the chapel the whole time?"

"Yes."

"Can I ask you what years you were there?"

"I taught at Baylor from 2003–2005."

"Do you remember who had those offices while you were there?"

"I'm not sure I remember. It's been too long ago. I'm not even sure they were full-time. They may have been adjuncts."

"Do you remember anything out of the ordinary that happened while you were there?"

"Like what?"

"People hanging around that shouldn't have been there. Students coming into the chapel at odd hours. Anything really."

"No, I don't remember anything like that. I was not around much late at night. I had early classes most semesters, but I did not come in much before class. I taught a lot of classes with a lot of students, and that kept me busy during the day. I didn't hang around if I didn't have to."

"Well, I have to say, I am glad you're alive, though it makes my job harder. We're no closer to figuring out the victim's identity than we were when we started."

"I would say I'm sorry I couldn't be more help, but that would be a lie. If I were the victim, you'd have an identity, but I'd be dead."

"Yeah, I can see where you're coming from."

Dino hung up the phone and sighed. Ironically, by finding someone still alive, he'd hit another dead end.

21

Since Jack had just about finished the report Mendoza assigned him, he told Dino he was just about ready to go to meet with the forensics team. Consequently, Dino decided to return to Baylor's main campus and see if he can learn more about graduate assistants from Marvin Peake. Fortunately, he found the professor in his office. Dino explained to him that they were getting pressure from above to make measurable progress of the investigation.

"Marvin, what can you tell me about the situation with undergraduates and graduate students who worked for the department about fifteen years ago?"

"Not sure I can remember that much. Seems like we may have three to five undergraduates on work-study every year, but I honestly couldn't tell you their names, especially from that far back. They are assigned on an as-needed basis, but apart from the occasional photocopying project, I didn't use them that much."

"What about graduate students? We were told that full-time faculty in the department were assigned someone to work for them each year."

"Yeah, that's right. Their productivity was really hit or miss, however. Some of them are outstanding, but with some it's like pulling teeth trying to get them to do the things you need done. Most of the time, I am satisfied if I can just get them to grade quizzes and exams for me."

"How come you didn't mention graduate students when I ask you about people who would've been around the offices?"

"That's easy. My graduate assistants were never around my office much. Those offices were too small to have a second person working in them, and the hallway wasn't big enough to have a desk for them to sit at. I typically talked to my graduate assistant before or after class, or else we'd meet in the conference room in the basement down the hall from the graduate student lounge."

"Do you remember any of their names?"

"Oh, gosh. Let me think. There would probably only be the one. When I got here in the fall of 2006, they hadn't yet instituted the two-year rule. Back then, I had the same graduate assistant for my first four years. He was quite good. His name was Dan Cotton. After that, it we made a rule that no faculty member would keep the same graduate assistant for more than two years."

"Where is this Dan Cotton now?"

"He teaches Old Testament at a small Baptist college in west Tennessee."

"What about the other faculty members who had those offices? Did they have graduate assistants as well? And did they come by the professors' offices more regularly than yours?"

"Actually, I think they did now that you mention it. Glen Cheatham liked the theatrics of having a graduate assistant. He had them meet at his office so they could 'walk and talk' as he called it. He'd make a bit of a show of it, telling his grad assistant what his goals for the day's class were. From what I could see, it was more of a monologue than a conversation. So, it was more like, we'll walk, and I'll talk."

"What about the others, specifically Pridwell and Fontenot?"

"Pridwell did, but I don't think Fontenot ever met her assistant up there. I suspect since most of the graduate students were male, Fontenot may not have wanted to do anything that would even give the appearance of impropriety."

"Do you remember their names?"

"Heavens no. They weren't Old Testament graduate students, so I didn't have much to do with them. If you're looking for names, the only person that might have that information would be the director of Graduate Studies, but I'm not sure their records go back that far."

"Who's the director?"

"That would be Jamie Felton, though she's fairly young and wasn't here that long ago."

"Well, it can't hurt to check. It's better to be thorough and methodical. I wouldn't want anyone to think I hadn't covered all my bases."

*   *   *

Dino had to check with Becky Long to get the office number for the director of Graduate Studies. He left Morrison Hall and crossed the quad to Alexander Hall where he had met the department chair previously. Once there, Becky told him that there was not enough room for all the administrators and their associates in the basement of Alexander Hall, so the director of Graduate Studies and her associate had to relocate to the fourth floor of Cashion Hall during the renovation. Cashion Hall, it turned out, is right next to Morrison, so Dino once again crossed the quad and made his way to Jamie Felton's office on the fourth floor.

The door to the big room on the fourth floor had a sign that simply stated, "Department of Religion." Once inside, the door to the Director of Graduate Studies office lay straight ahead. To the left, outside her office door, sat her administrative associate, Jocelyn Parker. Behind her desk was a cubicle farm, walls padded on three sides with a desk and filing drawers built into the walls of each module. It looked like a call center, except no one appeared to be occupying the stalls. Jocelyn Parker greeted him professionally and notified the director that Detective Piper of the Waco Police Department would like to see her. He sat down at the table across from Jamie Felton's desk as she joined him. He explained the problem and asked whether she might have records of who would have been assigned as graduate assistants to the three professors who had the offices in the chapel fifteen years ago. The director nodded but stipulated those dates preceded the time when either she or her administrative associate held these positions. She would have to check with Jocelyn Parker to see whether those records still existed. She asked him how far back he needed the data, and he told her it would be great if he had the assignments from 2004 through 2011. She stepped outside the door and spoke with her associate. In 2004, Dino remembered, the chapel offices were occupied by Larry Pridwell, Glen Cheatham, and Richard Danforth, all of whom they had already interviewed. It also covered the years that DelRae Fontenot had an office in the back of the chapel.

Jamie Felton returned to her office and sat down again. "Jocelyn is going to check and see what we have. Fortunately, she has folders on her computer from previous administrative associates who had this position, so she'll let us know in a few minutes what she's got, if anything."

"So, how long have you been in this position?"

"Only a few months, actually. I came to Baylor from the Boston area in 2012 as an associate professor and received tenure a year later when my second book was published."

"That's a long way to move. It must have been quite a culture shock. What brought you here?"

"The resources, the small teaching load, and the chance to teach doctoral students. Baylor's one of the few religion departments in the country that encourages their faculty to research and publish. By that I mean our research faculty only teach two courses a semester. In return, we are expected to publish on a regular basis. Since I really love research and writing, this job really had everything I wanted."

"Sounds like a good gig. Why did you take on this job as director? I imagine running this program has to eat into your time for research and writing."

"It does. I do get a course reduction each semester to help make up for that time. The short answer, though, is that my colleagues leaned on me to take it on. They convinced me that I had the skills and the temperament to do the work and still make progress on my own projects."

"Sounds like you are a worker bee."

"Excuse me? I don't follow."

"Sorry. Marvin Peake explained administrators to me using his typology of bees. He seemed to think that the best administrators were the ones who did all the work. They just keep their nose to the grindstone."

"Well, that's not surprising since Marvin was one of those who leaned on me the hardest. I've only given them a three-year commitment, so we'll see how it goes."

Jocelyn Parker knocked on the door. She had several sheets of paper in her hand. She told him, "I had to go back to my two predecessors' files, but they had spreadsheets for the years you asked about, so I went ahead and printed them for you."

"That's fantastic," Dino replied. "I can't believe you came up with this information so quickly."

"Well, that's par for the course with Jocelyn," Felton reported. "She's the real worker bee, not me. Truth be told, this department runs so smoothly not because of the directors and the chair, but because our administrative associates are top-notch. They're the ones to keep things running smoothly."

Ms. Parker nodded slightly in acknowledgment of the compliment and withdrew quietly.

"Mind if I look at this information here, just in case I have any questions?"

"Help yourself. I have to finish getting ready to teach my class. That's gonna take me a few minutes. At any rate, Jocelyn can probably answer your questions better than I could. Help yourself to one of the cubicles out in the big room."

"What's the deal with all the cubicles, anyway? The other faculty I met with had individual offices."

"Well, originally, the plan was to put the entire Religion Department in this room and the one next door while the Tidwell building was being renovated. COVID changed all that. They had to have enough room for social distancing, so they could only use half of the cubicles. The rest of the faculty are spread all over campus."

"So, this is temporary then?"

"Yes. Even still, the faculty are not happy. There's no room to keep your books in the cubicles. So now, instead of working in their offices, the faculty work on their writing projects at home. They only come in when they have class. And since summer classes are being taught remotely, that means no one really comes in here. No one will bother you."

Dino sat at the desk in one of the cubicles. Immediately, he felt somewhat claustrophobic. His own "office" was just a desk in a bullpen, but it didn't make him feel hemmed in like this cubicle did. He empathized with the faculty. Given the number of books he saw in Marvin Peake's office, he couldn't imagine how someone could write a book in this space.

He laid out the sheets that Jocelyn had given him. Each sheet represented one academic year. The sheets were conveniently printed with the name of the professor in the first column and the name of the graduate student in the second. There were also columns for contact information for graduate students. There had to be close to forty graduate students in all, and there were more graduate students in the later years than in the earlier ones. He remembered that the department chair had said that the program had grown, and he could see evidence of that.

Dino found the name Marvin Peake and confirmed that his graduate student was listed as Dan Cotton for four years just as Marvin had indicated. He had a different student in the fifth year. Glen Cheatham, by contrast, had a different student every year. Dino wonders why that was. Perhaps he wasn't the easiest person to work for. Or, it could simply be that he taught so many students each semester that no one wanted to work for him. DelRae Fontenot had the same student for three years, and then a different student for the next two. Larry Pridwell, however, was an anomaly. He had the same graduate student for the first two years, but then he had a different graduate student in years three and four. The student he had in year four continued to be his graduate assistant for the next three years. The student he had in year two, however, stayed with him only one year. Dino circled the name of that student to check on later, but as he did so, he paused. The name of that student was Bob Darden. Almost instantaneously, the thought popped into his head, "Bob has to be short for Robert. That means, this one has the initials R.D."

Robert Darden had the same initials as the victim, but Dino reminded himself that this could be a coincidence, just like Richard Danforth. Still, when he looked at the materials, he did not see Robert Darden listed in any of the other years. He needed more information, so he walked back up to Jocelyn's desk and asked, "Jocelyn, is there any way you could give me some more information about one of the students?"

"What kind of information do you need? We have files on everyone who's been admitted into the program, but we only keep certain things."

"Well, it looks like he was only in the program one year, but could you verify that? If so, will there be a note about why he left?"

"I may be able to figure out how long he was in the program, but I doubt there'll be anything in his file about why he left. Most of the time people just stop. They may plan on coming back but never do. Or, they may have been asked not to return if their grades indicated they shouldn't be in the program. All our students have an assessment at the end of the first year. It's rare, but if there are problems students can be dropped from the program."

"Anything you have is more than I've got right now. His name is Bob, or Robert, Darden.

"Let me pull up his file and see what we have on him. Give me just a second."

"If you wouldn't mind, go ahead and print out everything you've got. It might prove useful."

"Will do. Fortunately, we scanned all these files when we were getting ready to make the move. The offices in the new building have very little space for filing cabinets so we had to digitize everything. It took our student workers weeks to photocopy all the files and upload them to the cloud. In our old office we had five large filing cabinets full of records. Two of those were for former students. When they graduated, we would cull out everything but their final transcript, their dissertation approval form, and their application to enter the program."

"Any of that might be helpful."

"Here it is. Wait. That's odd."

"What is it?"

"He was a master's student, not a PhD student."

"Why is that unusual?"

"We don't typically admit master's students. Baylor has a seminary that offers several different types of master's degrees. The feeling is we shouldn't be competing with them for students at the master's level. Typically, to get into our program, an applicant must have a master's degree in religion already. Only occasionally have we even considered admitting a master's student. What's really odd, though, is that he was on the list of graduate assistants. We pay our graduate assistants competitively, considering they only work fifteen hours a week. On those occasions where we have made an offer to a master's student, we made it clear that they would not receive a stipend. The Graduate School is quite clear on this. They don't want us using stipend funding for master's students."

"Why would they have made an exception in this case?"

As she handed Dino the printout, Jocelyn remarked, "I can only guess that someone pleaded a special case for him. Maybe he didn't have money for school, or maybe he was deemed an exceptional student. It doesn't make sense to me."

"Interesting," Dino remarked aloud, but he was thinking, "somebody really thought this guy was something special. I wonder why."

Dino looked through the printout. "Jocelyn, his file doesn't have a final transcript. Does that mean he never graduated?"

"Let me see that. Well, all he's got in here is a tracking sheet that shows he only took classes for three semesters. His grades are not all that great. They are mostly B's with a couple that are B+ and even a B-. Getting a B+ in a graduate program as competitive as ours means that the student was not performing all that well and getting a B- means his performance was barely passable. His grade point average would've barely been above 3.0, which is the minimum score a student can make and keep receiving a stipend. That makes it even more strange that they gave him a stipend in the first place. If his GPA was so marginal, why would they have admitted him into the master's program? That's strange."

"Strange is not typically good in my line of work. There's got to be a story there I would imagine. Wait, am I reading this application correctly? It looks like he graduated from Baylor as an undergrad."

"That's what it says all right, but his transcript also indicates he never completed the master's program."

"I think we just found our victim."

Jamie Felton was just walking out of her office door. She stopped and looked surprised. "Really? You mean our files helped you make the identification?"

Dino replied, "I'll still need to track some stuff down to verify, but I'd bet dollars to donuts that Bob Darden is the name of our victim."

"That's impossible. I know Bob Darden. He preached at our church a couple months ago about the Black Gospel Music Restoration Project that he runs. I can assure you he was very much alive that day."

"Are you kidding me?"

"I am not. He teaches in the journalism department, so his office is in the Castlelaw building behind us at the far end of the Fountain Mall, to the left of the library. Jocelyn can get you his office number and call him to see if he's in his office. That might save you a trek across campus."

"Thanks. That would be great. I'd be grateful." Gratitude is not, however, the strongest emotion he was feeling at the moment. Silently he moaned, "I just can't seem to catch a break."

22

Just as Dino left to go to the Baylor Tower, Jack's cell phone rang, playing the opening bars of Claude Debussy's "Les Papillons," the ring tone Jack had assigned to Mariposa. She rarely called him during work hours. "*Ola mi querida*," he answered. "Is everything ok?" Mariposa apologized for the stereotypical nature of her call. She needed him to stop by a grocery store to pick up a few items on his way home that evening. "*Por supuesto*." Jack replied as he started down the hallway toward forensics. "*No problema*. It's always good to hear your voice, Mari *mi amor*. By the way, if everything goes as I think it will this afternoon, I should be home a little early. I may even beat the girls home from school. If you catch my drift."

"Now who's being stereotypical?" Mariposa chuckled.

"Hope springs eternal," Jack answered.

After Jack finished up the report, he realized he should include the information that the forensics team had for him. He'd put the final touches on the report after meeting with them. The forensics department was precisely what one might expect—a lab with all sorts of expensive-looking and intricate devices scattered around the various workstations. One of the technicians saw Jack at once and at once began telling Jack why they had summoned him. Pursuing the observation that the shoes found with the Baylor skeleton appeared to be high quality, technicians had disassembled them and rehydrated the dried leather with successive applications of Vaseline and lanolin. They were thereby able to raise on the inside of the tongue of the right shoe an embossed symbol and sequence of letters and numbers, a few still obscure ones could be either "1," "7," or a lower-case "l" and another could be either "3," "8" or upper-case "B."

The technician speculated that the symbol might identify the maker. If indeed the shoes were custom-made, the letter/number sequence might indicate something more—the year of manufacture, the style, even the customer. "The first lead with any promise we have gotten so far," Jack said appreciatively. "So, what did you find out about this symbol and these numbers?"

"Nothing. That's detective work. We restored the shoes. You have to chase down the details. Maybe you could start with Google."

Sighing, Jack foresaw an afternoon spent at the computer and on the phone, and probably not an early departure from the office, after all. "Thanks. Take care. I'll see you guys next major crime," Jack said and turned to go back to his desk.

*   *   *

Jack returned to his office where he began his effort to determine the significance of forensics' analysis of the shoes with a Google search for manufacturers of custom-made shoes who had been in business at the likely time of the murder. He found only half a dozen, but there was nothing on any of their websites about symbols or serial numbers. So, starting at the top of the list, he began making phone calls. He struck out with the first three, but hit a home run with the fourth call, to Schumer and Sons in Boston. When he identified himself and the purpose of his call, the receptionist connected him directly with a Mr. Weiss, the great-grandson of the founder of the firm. Mr. Weiss said that the description of what the police found inside the shoe sounded, indeed, like the identifying mark Schumer and Sons had always used. If the shoes were indeed Schumer and Sons products, the sequence of characters would indicate not only the style of the shoes, but also a customer number. He explained that they kept molds of their customers' feet. Customers could simply order shoes in their chosen style and color. The company then made the shoes based on the molds "on file," as it were. They retained all the information associated with customer numbers and molds going back as far as fifty years. It might take several minutes, Mr. Weiss said, but if Detective Farmer could email an image of the emblem and numbers, it should be possible to identify the customer. He would call Jack back with the outcome of the search, probably within the hour.

Jack emailed the .jpeg that forensics had already sent him, looked at his watch—hope springs eternal—and sat back to wait. Within fifteen minutes, Mr. Weiss called back confirming that Schumer and Sons had made the shoes. He promised to email him immediately a list of twenty-seven names, DOBs, and last known addresses that resulted from all the possible permutations of the obscure characters. Jack thanked him for his help and cooperation and opened his email to find the list already in his inbox.

The rest was easy. He first eliminated people who would have been too old to fit the age profile suggested by the autopsy report, cutting the list by two-thirds. Two of the remaining names stood out because of their initials: R(obert) D(arden) and B(ob) D(ouglas). Douglas's last known address was in Pennsylvania; Darden's was Texas! "Found him!" Jack exclaimed to no one in particular, texted the news to Dino, and glanced at his watch. He decided to send the report to Mendoza without the additional information from forensics because he wanted to leave for the weekend. If he wasted no time at the grocery. . .

23

About ten minutes after learning Bob Darden was in his office, Dino had made his way across campus to Darden's office. He knocked on the door and was happy to hear a voice inviting him to enter. When he walked in, he asked, "Are you Bob Darden?"

"That'd be me."

"So, you *are* alive. You can't be the Bob Darden I'm looking for, but maybe you can help me."

"What are you talking about, and who are you?"

"Sorry. My name is Detective Dean Piper with the Waco Police Department. I am trying to find the identity of the person whose skeleton was found in the back of the Tidwell Building during construction last week."

"Well, clearly it's not me," he chuckled.

"Clearly. This Bob, or Robert, Darden would only be in his early forties right now. He was a graduate student in the Religion Department at the time when someone placed the body in a storage crate behind the pipe organ about fifteen years ago, give or take."

"I guess my white hair gave it away that I'm not in my early forties."

"Pretty much, yeah. Sorry to have wasted your time."

"Not a problem. It's actually not the first time I've been killed."

"Okay. Now, I'm the one who's confused. What are you talking about?"

"You'd better come in. This'll take a minute. It's a long story."

Dino entered the room and sat down. Bob Darden put his feet up on the desk and leaned back. Dino took note of his very worn cowboy boots, and the thought struck him that this Bob Darden was not wearing custom shoes. It made him realize again how unusual it was that their skeleton man was wearing custom shoes. The dead man must have had a good deal of disposable income to have spent that kind of money on footwear.

Over the next twenty minutes, Darden told Dino a story that was almost as unbelievable as finding a fifteen-year-old skeleton behind the pipe organ in the Tidwell Building. Years ago, two film students taking a journalism class he taught came to him with an unusual request. They wanted to know if Darden would be willing to die on camera in a project that they were doing for a film course. They wanted to kill off a faculty member. They had already asked several other faculty members who declined. Darden, however, said he was happy to play the part and die on film.

"That's funny," Dino says.

"But that's not the end of the story. It turns out these two students went on to Hollywood, and became major producers, writers, and directors. Now, in nearly every TV show and movie they make, they kill off a character named Darden, usually Bob or Robert. They decided I was their lucky charm, so they kill me off as an homage in gratitude for helping them get their film careers started. As a result, they've killed me many times over."

"That's really cool. Did they write anything I would know?"

"Yeah, you've probably seen some of their shows. Their names are Derek Haas and Mike Brandt. They've written screen plays for some popular movies and TV shows, including the films *2 Fast 2 Furious*, *3:10 to Yuma*, and a few TV series, including the *Chicago Fire* series, *FBI*, and *FBI International*."

"Unbelievable."

"Oh, that's still not all. This story continues to grow. Other novelists and filmmakers have joined in the fun, including the mystery writer Laura Lippman and George Martin, the guy who writes the *Game of Throne* novels, as well as multiple video games! They've all killed me as well."

Dino chuckled and said, "Well, I'm certainly glad you are alive and well. I do think, however, that the person whose remains we found in the back of Tidwell was not so fortunate. I believe that his name was also Robert Darden, but we are still trying to confirm that. We know there was a graduate student in the Religion Department by that name who disappeared from Baylor. We still have to confirm that he's not living someplace else, but all the pieces fit. You wouldn't happen to remember him, would you?"

"Can't say I ever met him. I have a vague recollection of someone telling me years ago that there was another Robert Darden on campus, but in a university this size that's not surprising."

"Thanks for your time. Oh, and stay safe," he added with a twinkle in his eye.

"I'll try. But you know some things are just out of my control. If someone decides they want me dead again, I can't stop it."

As Dino left the building, he checked his phone and saw that he had a text from Jack. When he read the text, his pulse rate elevated. Jack had found the same name as Dino by tracking down the shoe manufacturer. That makes two independent pieces of evidence that led to the same name. If Bob Darden came from a wealthy family, and they could track down the family, they could tell Mendoza that the skeleton now has a name. Someone killed Robert Darden and hid him in the back of the building. Dino texted Jack excitedly, letting him know he'd come up with the same name. "This is real progress," he texted. "Our skeleton is no longer a John Doe. This will get the captain off our back. This cold case is now heating up."

Dino texted Jack back, asking him what they should do next. Jack said he was leaving work early. The text read, "One of the girls has a soccer game and one more weekend won't hurt. CU Monday."

24

Jack's text indicated he was leaving work early, so Dino decided he would swing by Marvin Peake's office again before he left campus to see if he could recall anything about Robert Darden. "Marvin," he asked, "you mind if I pick your brain?"

"As long as you don't pick too much of it. I need to keep as much of it as I can."

"I think you'll be fine. Something tells me you've got more brain cells than the average Joe off the street. I'm virtually certain that we've now identified the name of our victim. He was a graduate student in the Department of Religion from 2006 to 2007."

"You're kidding."

"Nope. His name was Robert Darden. Before you say anything, I know there's a Robert Darden teaching in the journalism department, but this is another person with the same name. He graduated Baylor in the spring of 2006, and he began his graduate program that fall. According to Jocelyn Parker, however, his entry into the program was unusual."

"How so? Wait, are you saying he graduated from the Religion Department or from the seminary?"

"From the Religion Department."

"That would be unusual for sure. He would've had to have started as an MA student, not a PhD student. We rarely admit a student into the MA program, because we tell them to go to Truett Seminary here on campus to get their master's degree."

"That's right. Jocelyn Parker gave me his application to the program. He applied for entry into the MA program and they accepted him. What's even more unusual, though, according to her, was that he worked as a graduate assistant for someone in the Religion Department."

"That is really weird. I was under the impression that we did not pay stipends to master's students."

"Apparently, someone made an exception for him. Any idea how that might've happened?"

"Hmm. Let me think. First, the area would have to recommend him for admission into the MA program. The admissions committee would then have to approve that request. Next, the Director of Graduate Studies would be the one who assigns stipends and sets up the payment. Back then, that would've been Dr. Williams. He is now the department chair. Before that becomes finalized, however, when they admit a student, the dean of the Graduate School has to sign off as well."

"Goodness gracious, I thought that police department bureaucracy was cumbersome. Sounds to me like university bureaucracy is even worse."

Dino looked at his watch and assumed that the department chair had left for the day. "I'll have to start with Dr. Williams, but I'll have to call him in the morning. It's getting late, and I really don't relish walking across campus one more time in this heat. Let me ask you one more question. You mentioned the first step was area approval. How would I find out what area he was in?"

"There's a couple ways, actually. We have four areas: Old Testament, New Testament, church history, and theology and ethics. You could look at his transcript and quickly figure it out by seeing whether he was taking mostly Bible seminars or history seminars, or theology and ethics."

"I may need to get some help with that. I'm not sure I could tell a theology course from a history course."

"The other options aren't that complicated either. If you have his application materials, he probably mentions his area of interest in his application letter. You can also tell him by looking at the professor for whom he worked as a graduate assistant. They try hard to match the graduate student with a professor in the area to which they applied, even if the professor is not on the graduate faculty.

"Yes. I'll definitely need to speak with Dr. Williams in the morning after I touch base with my partner. I also have Bob Darden's application materials back at the office, as well as the name of the professors with whom he worked. The body has waited this long. One more weekend won't hurt anything."

25

As usual, Dino arrived at the office before Jack. Dean figured that Jack had gotten tied up at breakfast with Mariposa, but that was just as well. It gave him time to sort out something that had bothered him overnight. The occupants of the three offices in the back of the chapel changed regularly during the time that Robert Darden had been associated with the Religion Department. It was difficult to keep straight who occupied which office during which year.

Dino decided to sort out specifics the best way he knew how, namely piece by piece. He pulled a whiteboard over beside the desks where he and Jack sat when they were in the office. He decided to make a grid that would help him understand visually who was in the offices during the time in question. As he began to draw the grid, however, it dawned on him that he still did not know a potentially vital piece of information. He needed to go through the information that Jocelyn Parker had given him to see who Robert Darden worked for as a graduate assistant during the year and a half that Darden was in the master's program. He knew that Robert Darden and Larry Pridwell had worked together extensively when Darden was an undergraduate, but he did not know whom Darden worked for when he was in the master's program.

Dino opened his case file and checked the annual assignments for graduate assistants. Interestingly, during his three semesters in the master's program he had worked one year for Glen Cheatham and one year for Pridwell. He went back to the whiteboard and drew a grid.

Office holders:	Years in office	03–4	04–5	05–6	06–7	07–8
Richard Danforth	2003–5		X	X		
Larry Pridwell	2004–7		X	X	X	
Glen Cheatham	2003–13	X	X	X	X	X
Marvin Peake	2006–12				X	X
Delrae Fontenot	2007–10					X
Robert Darden, MA	2006–7				X	1/2

As he created the chart, several items struck Dino as potentially relevant to the case at hand. First, Glen Cheatham had remained in his office for longer than any other person. The length of this difference correlated well with what they had learned about the difference between lecturers and research faculty. Nevertheless, other lecturers in the department joined the department after Cheatham who were never placed in the office behind the chapel. So, while the fact that Cheatham was a lecturer accounted for part of his lengthy tenure in the office, that wasn't the whole story. Dino thought that he would be more than a little bit pissed off if that happened to him, but given Cheatham's temper, he could well imagine that Cheatham had a few choice words to say on the matter. He was not clear, however, how exactly that might lead him to commit violence against Robert Darden.

Second, he looked at the files and learned that Darden had only worked for two professors during his time in the master's program, specifically Cheatham and Pridwell. According to Pridwell's testimony, however, which DelRae Fontenot had confirmed, Pridwell got one of the larger offices beginning in the fall of 2007. So, in the year Darden disappeared, he worked as a graduate student with Pridwell, but Pridwell had moved out of the chapel offices during that academic year. On the other hand, Pridwell had failed to mention that he had a graduate assistant disappear in the middle of the academic year. Dino would have to do some more digging before he could satisfy himself on whether either of these discrepancies is relevant.

Jack finally arrived at the office and sauntered up to the whiteboard where Dino was standing. "I see you've made another one of your charts. Why am I not surprised? Why couldn't you just be satisfied with a regular timeline like everybody else? Instead, you have to make a time chart."

"Well, aren't we sassy today? Awfully ballsy for a guy who's forty-five minutes late for work. Just because we figured out the victim's identity doesn't mean we've solved the case. And we need more physical evidence for confirmation"

"You're just jealous because Mariposa gave me something special for breakfast today. I couldn't just walk away."

"Yeah, right. We've just ID'd the vic, so you could have just had a piece of toast."

"I didn't say she made me breakfast. I said she gave me something special for breakfast. What I mean by that . . ."

"Stop. I know exactly what you mean. You got dessert for breakfast."

"No. I mean I got dessert instead of breakfast. I was late because I had to stop for a sausage biscuit. The drive through line was murder."

"Speaking of murder, despite your wisecrack, this chart is really important."

Dino then walked Jack through the observations he had made while drawing the chart. When he finished talking Jack through his observations, he summarized what the chart told him. "So, we still have unanswered questions about the same two people we both had questions about already. We can't yet rule out either Pridwell or Cheatham. We need more information about both of them, as well as our victim.

I want to call the chair of the Religion Department, or maybe Becky Long, and see if I can't get more of the story about Cheatham. Why was he kept in those offices so long? Is it possible Cheatham WANTED to remain in a chapel office? Why don't you see if you can find Robert Darden's next of kin? We need to let them know that we may have found his body. Maybe they can tell us more about who he was. Would he have ordered custom shoes? Did he have enemies? Did he have friends here in Waco that might know more about his personal life while he was in college than his parents would know?"

"Yeah, sounds good to me."

"That's it? No questions. No more snarky comments about my chart?"

"Well, like I said, I got dessert . . ."

At that very moment, Seargent Mendoza showed up at their desks. He did not appear to be in a particularly pleasant mood. "Well, detective, I'm happy to learn that you fed your face, but you are both behind in your paperwork. I need an update today, with no excuses. I'm getting pressure to move on from this cold case when the odds of solving it seem unlikely at best. We are already a man short in the department, and other cases need our attention, too. I'm not sure I can justify tying up our resources on this one case any longer."

Dino responded. "Sarge, we've had a significant break in the investigation. We think we have identified the name of the victim, but we need more forensic confirmation. We're no longer flying blind. I do think we can solve this case with hard work and determination."

Mendoza was not sold. "Well, good for you that you've identified the victim. You should contact his parents. I would hate for them to find out from someone else that we believe we've found his remains. They might have something of his we could send off for DNA confirmation. Contacting them doesn't really change the fact that this is an extraordinarily cold case, and we still have very little physical evidence that would tell us who killed the victim. The DA's office won't even come close to prosecuting this case without a hell of a lot more than we've got. You've got till the end of the day to give me a report that convinces me the case is worth pursuing. You'll need to make a strong case."

"Sarge," Dino says, "you know these things take time. We can't just rush out and manufacture evidence."

"I wasn't giving you a suggestion. My decision is not up for debate. Convince me that more time will prove helpful, or we have to move on. And I'm not just talking about getting your reports up to date on this case. You're both behind on your paperwork, and I expect it to you to catch up by end of day today."

Mendoza walked off and shut the door to his office, providing a physical exclamation point to emphasize that they'd been put on a very short leash. "Thanks a lot, Jack. I really could've used your help there. Instead, you just stood there. Where's the bulldog I used to have as a partner?"

"Well, like I said, I had dessert today. I guess I'm just super chill. Anyway, he'd already made up his mind. Nothing I could have said was going to change it. At least we have until the end of the day, so let's focus on what we can do."

Dino knew that Jack is right, but he hated the idea that the sergeant could shelve this case. He couldn't bring himself to apologize to Jack, so he simply said, "Let's get at it then. We need to make our calls first before we can write a convincing report to the sergeant. We better get started."

"I got you, bro. Chill out. We can do this."

Dino did not take much comfort in his partner's new-found optimism. He sat down at his desk and started looking up the phone number for Becky Long. He figured he'll start with her and see if he could find out more of the story about Cheatham's lengthy time in the back of the chapel.

26

The information that Jack had gotten from the shoe people included two addresses associated with Darden's account: a Waco apartment mailing address, presumably Darden's student residence, and another billing address in Richmond, Virginia for a certain William R. Darden. Unfortunately, the account information did not include telephone numbers. On a hunch that the billing address might belong to the victim's parents, Jack did a quick Google search for William R. Darden and quickly discovered a website for a Dr. William R. Darden, endocrinologist, in Richmond, Virginia, as well as an online obituary. A quick call to the endocrinology practice confirmed that Dr. Darden's only son, Robert, had disappeared some years ago. Moreover, by invoking police authority, he got the contact information for Mrs. Mary Louise Darden.

He thought that he should probably talk to Dino first about the step he was about to take. Besides, these are the kinds of interactions no police officer relished: informing a relative of the death of their loved one. Yet, the possibility of confirming that they had, in all probability, identified her son as the murder victim, and even more, of learning what the victim's mother knew about the circumstances of her son's disappearance provided him with the motivation to overcome his hesitancy on both counts.

Mary Louise Darden answered on the second ring. Jack explained who he was. He carefully gave her "just the facts," as he and Dino knew them, and delivered the line he'd been taught to say, "Mrs. Darden, we have located remains that could be those of your son."

Mrs. Darden initially reacted as one might expect, but she soon regained her composure. She insisted that Jack address her as Mary Louise and anticipated Jack by offering to answer any questions he might have. "My late husband, Bill, would want us to do whatever we can to help the police get to the bottom of this. We always knew that Robert would simply not go away without communicating with us. Bill and I were sure that something had happened to Robert. But finding him after all this time . . . Oh, this is simply horrible."

"Mary Louise, I am truly sorry to hear about your husband." Jack paused a moment in a show respect, then continued, "But if you're up to it, I'll take you up on the offer to answer some questions."

"If I can."

"Can you tell me how Robert felt about his studies? Was he enjoying them? Was he having any problems?"

"He was delighted to have gotten into the graduate program, and especially to study with one of the professors. I think he was even that professor's assistant for a time. I can't remember his name now if I ever knew it. "

"Cheatham? Pridwell? Peake?"

"All of those names sound familiar, but I can't be certain which one Robert spoke of."

"How about your son's personal life? Did he have any particularly close friends? Did he have a romantic interest?"

"I'm afraid I can't help there at all. Robert was a good son. He called regularly, for example, but he was also quite private about his personal life. He always was, even as a boy. Bill and I always joked that we would know that Robert had found a girl when he introduced her to us as his wife, but probably not before. No, I can't help there at all. I only know that, after he completed his undergraduate degree, he moved off campus and lived in an apartment with a roommate. We never met him, but they seemed to get along fine according to Robert."

"Do you remember his roommate's name?

"Give me a second. I sent him a Christmas card for a few years but never heard back. Wait, Whitson, that's it. His last name was Whitson, and his first name was . . . Andrew. I remember addressing the cards."

"Is there anything at all you might remember that could help us get an idea of what may have happened with Robert?"

"Well, I do still have a few boxes of his personal belongings. . .some papers, a few clothes, some jewelry, a few books, etc. Several months after Robert just flat out disappeared, we arranged to have his things from his apartment boxed up and shipped to us. They are in his bedroom closet. About a year before Bill passed, we went through it all and discarded some clothes, but we kept what we considered mementos. Once and while I still look through them and remember."

"Did your son like nice clothes. I got your name by tracking down the number of some custom-made leather shoes. Does that sound like something he would have worn?

"Oh, definitely. Robert loved wearing nice things."

"It really does sound like the body we found could be Robert's. Would you be willing to lend the box to us for a while? They may give us some clues. I can arrange for the Richmond Police Department to pick them up and send them to us. We will return them as soon as we can."

"I suppose I could do that. I would want them back. They are all I have left of Robert, and in a way, of Bill."

"I understand, and I promise that we will treat them with respect and return them as soon as we can."

"Alright, then."

"OK. Thank you. The police should stop by within the next 24 hours. I'll have them call ahead. I really appreciate your time, Mary Louise. And, again, I am sorry about Robert *and* Bill. Goodbye."

"Goodbye. And thank you. Please keep me informed about the progress your investigation."

"Certainly. Goodbye."

Jack, excited by this development, turned back to writing his report. 'That should satisfy Mendoza,' he judged as he included this latest information. He and Dino were making the kind of headway that the sergeant would have to appreciate.

27

Having found the name of Robert Darden's roommate from Darden's mother, Jack began searching to see if he could find Andrew Whitson. Another quick Google search revealed more than forty people by that name. They included Andrew Whitsons who were lawyers, accountants, CEOs, writers, politicians, and even a women's volleyball coach. None of these, however, lived in the Waco area. On a whim, Jack decided to check the police database. "Jackpot!" he yelled.

"What'd you find?"

"There's an Andrew Whitson with a rap sheet whose last known address is here in Waco. We gotta check him out."

"What's he done?"

"Mostly little things. Drug possession, small amounts though. Forged checks, and breaking and entering, got that pled down to a misdemeanor since he was caught before he could take anything."

"Sounds like he might not be the brightest bulb in the socket."

"Well, this is interesting. He was also cited for carrying an unregistered firearm. Small caliber. Yep, let's go talk to him."

"Jack, the sergeant's not gonna like that. If he finds out we've left the building without finishing our reports, he's gonna be pissed."

"Like I give a rat's ass. We're on a ticking clock, and this is an actual lead."

"Now there's the partner I know and love. Let's go."

They drove to the address, which turned out to be a townhome in the Beverly Hills section of Waco. Beverly Hills in Waco, for those unfamiliar with the area, conjures up images of wealth and luxury, homes of the stars. Ironically, however, in Waco it contains no mansions, no upscale businesses, and no famous personalities. One would classify the better housing in Beverly Hills as lower middle class, but most of the residences look seedy and dilapidated. Such was the case for the townhome that was the last known address for Andrew Whitson. Jack knocked, and after a few minutes a man opened the door. He was thin, bedraggled, wearing only a pair of shorts. His hair looked like he'd just gotten out of bed even though it was after ten o'clock in the morning.

"Why are you knocking on my door so freakin' early?"

"We are Detectives Farmer and Piper of the Waco PD. Are you Andrew Whitson?" Dino stated matter-of-factly.

He looked at them warily and went on the offensive, "I don't know what it is you think I've done, but it wasn't me."

"Sir, we're just here because we have some questions for Mr. Whitson. If that's you, may we come in? It shouldn't take too long."

"Yeah, I guess." He stepped aside so the detectives could enter. The living room had a sofa and a recliner. An old coffee table sat between the two, littered with beer cans and cigarette butts on a small plate overflowing with ashes.

"Looks like you had quite a party here last night. Sorry we disturbed your sleep," Jack quipped.

The sarcasm was not lost on Whitson. "Last I looked, there's nothing illegal about drinking beer. What exactly do you want?"

"Did you ever know a man named Robert Darden?" Dino continued in his "just the facts, ma'am" mode.

"Now there's a name I haven't heard in years. Let me guess. You found his body."

"What's left of it, yes. But how did you know that?"

"Robert and I were roommates. We shared an apartment together for three semesters. Then, he just disappeared. No call, no letter, no check for his half of the rent. He just vanished completely."

"Where was this apartment?"

"Not far from Baylor. There's a lot of apartments over there."

"So, you were a student at Baylor?" Jack asks with more than a hint of surprise in his voice.

"Yes, I was. Does that surprise you, detective?"

"A little, yes. You don't strike me as the typical Baylor graduate."

"I never said I graduated. My folks cut off my funding at the end of my freshman year because they said I was wasting their money partying with my frat brothers. Robert and I met at the end of his senior year, and we decided to share an apartment to save money. He was just starting his graduate program, but I was still an undergraduate. I managed to scrape together enough money to pay tuition for a while, but I didn't have enough money for the spring semester of the second year. Hell, when Robert left, I couldn't even afford to rent that apartment anymore."

"What year was that?" Dino interjected.

"End of the fall semester, 2007."

"When exactly did Robert Darden disappear? Do you happen to recall?"

"I do, actually. It was right after finals. At first, I just assumed he'd gone home for the holidays and forgot to tell me. Then, a few days later, I saw in the paper that he was listed as missing. After a week with no word, I figured something bad had happened to him. It wouldn't have been like him to just leave me stranded. Was I right?"

"Yes. Based upon where we found his remains, we are proceeding on the assumption that this was a homicide," Dino replied.

"So, where did you find his body?"

Dino looked at Jack, raising an eyebrow as if asking a question. Jack nodded, so Dino said, "In the back of the Tidwell Bible Building. I assume that's not far from your apartment at the time, correct?"

"Interesting. Wait, you can't possibly think I had something to do with his death, do you? I mean, I may be a bit of a screwup, but I wouldn't have killed Robert. We were good friends. We got along really well."

"We don't have any theories yet, but it would help us to know where you were at the time so we could eliminate you as a suspect." Dino's initial impression of Whitson was that he was much more than a "bit of a screwup." He wanted specifics.

"Gee whiz, guys. You've gotta be kidding me. There's no way I can say where I was at a certain time on some random day thirteen or fourteen years ago. I can take a guess, but I don't know if anybody can verify it. It was the end of the semester, so I was partying."

Impatiently, Dino pushed for more. "Do you remember the names of anybody who was at this party?"

"No way. Baylor didn't officially allow alcohol on campus, but somehow at the end of the semester coolers of beer and other libations found their way to the front yards of the houses around campus that people rented out. People just went out in the street and drank. We partied because the semester was over. I'm sure I was partying in the street just a couple blocks away from Tidwell. That's just what we did starting around noon and going well into the night."

"So, you don't recall any names of people who could vouch for you?" Dino asked, now with obvious impatience and disbelief.

"That's what I tried to tell you. The street was full of people. The campus cops would make a show of driving by every hour or so to make sure nothing got out of hand, but between the crowd and the booze I couldn't tell you who was there. Now, let me ask you a question. You said he was killed in the Tidwell Building, but how is it possible that you've only now come across the body? That's a big building, but people are in it every day."

"That's true," Jack conceded. "The body, however, was stashed in the back of the chapel, in a room behind the pipe organ. The room is seldom used, and the body had been placed in a wooden crate. It wouldn't have been visible to anyone who'd gone in there."

"Interesting. I mean that's terrible. Robert was a gentle soul. He was always trying to please people. Unlike me, he got good grades. He got into the master's program. He'd have made something of himself."

"Anything else you can tell us about him?" Jack asked. "Did he have any close friends? How did he spend his time when he wasn't in class?"

"Not really. I mean, no. When he wasn't in class or working, he was in the library or home studying."

Dino noticed a slight hesitation in his response. "What aren't you telling us?"

"Nothing, I swear. I'm just processing all of this. You'll have to excuse me. I really do need to grab a shower and get ready for work. So, if there's nothing else. . ."

"No, that'll do for now. Thank you for your time," Dino replied as he led Jack out the door.

When Dino and Jack got back in the car, Dino observed to his partner, "He knows more than he's saying. He seemed genuine and sincere when he was talking about Darden, but I could see the gears in his brain grinding away at something when we mentioned the chapel and asked about Darden's friends. He's holding something back, but I don't know what or why."

"Agreed. But at last, we have a definitive timeline. We can ask more questions and hopefully, come up with some more leads. Where do you think we should start?"

"Unfortunately, we're going to have to write those reports. Mendoza isn't going to wait for us to catch him up. Luckily, we've now got something considerably more substantive than we had this morning. Let's go see how quickly we can knock these things out."

28

Dino and Jack returned to the car, knowing they had to go back to the office to work on the reports that had been ignored because of the murder case. Sergeant Mendoza had made it clear that he expected the back-logged reports, along with a thorough sitrep on the cold case in order to justify the continued use of resources. Jack looked over at Dino and could tell he was focused on the murder. "What're you thinking, Dino?"

"What? Sorry. I just can't shake the feeling that Whitson knows more than he's saying, and that bothers me."

"Yeah, I thought that was darned obvious too. A couple times he answered it seemed like he was thinking about something else. He did, however, seem quite genuine when he talked about what a good guy Darden was. He really seemed to like him."

"Indeed. We did get one extremely useful piece of information. He gave us a lock on the precise day that Darden disappeared. His alibi is vague, but it could be true. There's just no way to prove that he was liter-ally partying in the street at the time when Darden was most likely killed. Given what he's done since he left Baylor, however, a big end of the se-mester party seems perfectly in keeping with what he would have done."

"So, what do we do now? Mendoza will have our butts if we don't get him those reports, and if we don't present a strong case that we're making progress on the murder, then he's going to shut us down."

"I think we've probably got enough already to justify continuing the cold case, but I'd feel better if we could get a little bit more. Not much doubt that Mendoza's getting pressure from the brass not to drag this case out. Now that we have a name and a definitive timeline, we should be able to do some digging into the case files from the middle of December 2007. With a little time, we can probably find someone at Baylor to tell us when finals ended that year. That would give us an exact date, and there has to be a record of the missing persons report that his parents filed—Whitson mentioned reading a missing person report in the paper. I'm sure we could track down a photograph of Darden as well. That might help jog the memories of some of the people we've spoken to."

"Only problem is, all that's gonna take some time to run down. I don't see how we can do all that and still get the reports done for Mendoza by the end of day. It's all but lunch time."

"You're right. *We* couldn't do both of those. I propose we split up. One of us can do the reports and the other can track down information about the murder."

"Why do I have a sneaking suspicion that I know which one you want me to do? You want me to do the paperwork, don't you?"

"Well, you do owe me one. I didn't tell Mendoza you were late because you were getting"—Dino paused, made air quotes, and continued melodramatically—"'dessert.' He'd have really busted your chops over that."

"Like I care. Besides, you're the better writer. Mendoza always wants to correct mine. Yours are always perfect."

"It's called proofreading, Jack. You should try it. Anyway, we just need to get the reports to him to get him off our back. We don't need a perfect essay. Come on Jack, I really want to do this."

"Okay. Okay. You win, but make no mistake, now you owe me."

Right then, they pulled into the parking lot of the police department. Before Jack could change his mind, Dino got out of the car and headed up to the office where he immediately began locating the number for the registrar's office at Baylor. With luck, he'd get an exact date that finals ended in the fall 2007. He could also search for the missing person report Darden's parents filed. If all went well, Dino thought, he would pop over to the library and read about the case in the paper. Perhaps he would find a clue in the article. Having the date of the final exams would let him search the paper more quickly to see if they reported the disappearance.

Dino found the registrar's number and started to call it. As he did, he heard a deep sigh from Jack as he sat down at his desk. The sigh was more like a moan, subtly underscoring, for Dino's benefit, what a sacrifice Jack thought he was making on Dino's behalf. Inwardly, Dino smiled as he finished punching in the numbers for the registrar's office, though he couldn't let on how happy he was for Jack to work on the reports for a change.

Dino reached one of the assistant registrars and asked whether she would have the date that finals ended in the fall 2007. She informed him that they didn't keep lists of dates going back that far. He was disappointed, but then she told him that she could help him figure it out because the dates for finals were controlled by the dates for graduation, which were in turn controlled by the date for the Christmas vacation in the fall.

She asked Dino to wait while she opened her calendar to December 2007. "Christmas was on a Tuesday that year. That means that graduation would have been on Saturday, December 15. Grades would have been due by noon on Wednesday for seniors, which means that Tuesday, December 11 would have been the last day of final exams."

Dino thanked her for her help and made notes. Next, armed with a specific date, he decided to go to the old files room. Digital records did not go back that far. He would have to find the old-fashioned way. Walking through long stacks of records sorted by date when the case was opened.

Dino succeeded in finding the missing person report without much difficulty and brought it back to his desk. On his way, he uttered a word of thanks to whatever clerk had filed it. It did not, however, contain much in the way of useful information other than to confirm that Robert Darden had spoken with his parents about coming home for the holidays after he finished grading exams. Dino looked at the chart on the whiteboard. In the fall 2007, Darden worked as a graduate assistant for Pridwell. It struck Dino as curious that Darden disappeared shortly after he graded exams, but that Pridwell did not mention that fact when asked if anything unusual had happened. Surely, having one's graduate assistant completely disappear after the fall semester would qualify as unusual. Yet by that time, Pridwell no longer occupied one of the offices behind the chapel. Rather, Pridwell's office that year was on the third floor at the other end of the building.

Dino looked through the case file to see whether it contained any evidence from interviews with the police department. He saw that the case had been assigned to a couple of senior detectives, but the file contained no notes regarding whom they might have interviewed or what those people told them. Dino remembered the detectives. Both were long gone from the department, one of them having died just prior to his retirement. The other moved to the Gulf Coast somewhere after he retired, maybe Houston or Corpus Christi. Dino did not know whether he was still alive.

"I can't believe they left no notes behind," he cursed under his breath. "Their sergeant should have made them leave a paper trail." Almost as soon as he thought this, the irony hit him. "Some things never change," he grinned glancing over at unhappy Jack busy at his desk. "No detective enjoys the paperwork that comes with the job. There's always somethingmore important going on, but that shouldn't mean you leave the file completely blank. At least Jack is taking care of our reports. Good for him. And better him than me." This time Dino smiled outwardly and nearly chuckled aloud, but he didn't want to stop and explain anything to Jack. No. He certainly didn't want to interrupt Jack's progress. Besides, he needed to go to the library to see if the newspaper printed anything about the case back in 2007.

*   *   *

Dino drove to the West Waco Library and Genealogical Center. They kept copies of the *Waco Tribune-Herald* on microfiche going back decades. It was a little further away than the downtown branch, but given the construction downtown, it would be faster to go there. There were also better options for grabbing lunch, so he figured he could kill two birds with one stone. He told Jack he'd bring lunch back. Jack stopped typing and made a request. "Since you will be in that part of town, why don't you stop at Schmaltz's Deli? I'll take a pastrami on a whole wheat bun, brown mustard, no mayo."

Dino went to the library and retrieved the microfiche that had the December 2007 issues of the *Waco Trib*. He inserted the microfiche into the machine, and searched until he found the issue from Friday, December 14. He scanned the pages quickly but found nothing about a missing person. The front page on December 15 had a big story about Baylor's impending graduation ceremonies. Some of them had already taken place on Friday, but the bulk of the graduates would receive their diplomas that Saturday. The story contained interviews with several graduates, but nothing in the story mentioned a missing person.

On page three, however, he found a one paragraph story that contained the barest essentials. Robert Darden, a graduate student in the Department of Religion had been reported missing. He was last seen on December 11. Anyone with any knowledge of his whereabouts was requested to call the tip line.

The Sunday paper devoted more space to local stories, and there was a larger article with several paragraphs with the headline, "Baylor Student Still Missing." Underneath the headline was a picture of Darden. The picture probably came from his ID photo. He looked like a kid, clean-cut and smiling. The picture struck a chord in Dino. He'd been driven to find answers about the skeleton, but something about seeing the person hit him even harder. "This kid deserves justice. No one deserves to be left like that."

Dino printed a copy of the article as he read through it on the screen. It quoted several students who had known Robert Darden. All of them mentioned what a sweet boy he was. Two of them mentioned that he was a stylish dresser who got along well with everyone. One of the police detectives had assured the reporter that every effort was being made to track Darden down. There was, however, no evidence of foul play, so this could be nothing more than a student who decided to leave school. It irritated Dino that the detective seemed to downplay the disappearance. He tried to be gracious to the detective, since the body had not been found, and would not be found for thirteen years. Still, deciding to leave school was one thing, but disappearing from his parents who were expecting him home for Christmas? That was another thing entirely.

Dino continued reading, noting that the detective reported that Darden had last been seen by a classroom full of students while proctoring an exam on the morning of Tuesday, December 11, and by Glen Cheatham who saw him grading papers in the chapel of the Tidwell Building. Dino's eyebrows arched. Again, Cheatham had left something out when he spoke with Jack. He never mentioned that he was perhaps the last person to ever see Darden alive.

29

Strangely, although younger than Dino, Jack did not like writing on a computer. He still preferred pen and paper; his thoughts flowed more fluidly when writing longhand. But given the time constraints, he realized that he didn't have time to write and then retype what he had written. So, he sat at his desktop and typed. Before turning to the cold murder case, Jack started on the backlog of other cases that Mendoza expected. These included three burglaries and a hit and run. The hit and run had not involved any injuries, but reports had to be filed for insurance purposes. A driver, presumably inebriated, sideswiped a car.

The three burglaries were each different. In one, someone broke into a suburban home. The second involved a robbery of a convenience store near downtown. The third case was the bicycle that had been stolen from the son of one of Mendoza's cronies. The convenience store had a camera system that captured a full view of the perpetrator as he committed the crime and as he left the store. The store owner recognized the man because he frequently bought gas at the store. He has been apprehended and charged with robbery. Jack smiled, "Not the brightest bulb in the box. Who decides to rob the convenience store where you buy your own gas?"

The home burglary had proven harder to solve. The homeowner had no security system. The thief made off with two TVs and two laptops. So far, none of the merchandise has surfaced, and while the investigation was ongoing, there were no leads. Jack was not optimistic that this case would be solved.

Finally, Jack wrote up the report about the missing bicycle. As he typed, he thought, "Dino would resent it if the sergeant won't let us stay on the case." The neighbors all mentioned that the son left the bike in the driveway most days. "Leaving an expensive bike out in the open like that was almost an invitation to take it," Jack thinks. He did note in the report that he and Dino checked several security cameras from businesses in the area, without success. He had to show Mendoza that they had made a good faith effort to find the boy's bike.

Dino was not back yet, so Jack decided to start on the report about the murder case. He first made a list of what they knew about the case that would demonstrate to Sergeant Mendoza that they were making significant progress. Surveying the list, he spotted something he had missed previously. Three people who had had close contact with Darden all seemed reluctant to talk about him.

When Dino arrived back at the office, he greeted Jack, "I've got lunch." He reached in the bag and handed Jack's pastrami sandwich to him. "Here's your pastrami on wheat and chips. I went with the Schmaltz. We can split them if you want." The deli's signature Schmaltz sandwich contained ham, salami, and three kinds of cheese, along with the vegetable filling to pack the sub.

"You read my mind, Dino. It's hard to choose just one sandwich. Let's go to the conference room. We can talk while we eat. I finished the four reports and was starting to take stock of where we are on the cold case. I think we're on to something. When I started listing out what we know, I was struck by the fact that three people do not want to be completely forthcoming about the victim."

"OK, let's lay out what we've got," Dino muttered in between bites.

"We've got a fifteen-year-old skeleton. We've managed to identify him as a young graduate student who had a troubled relationship with one faculty member and appears to be a favorite of another faculty member. Neither of these two professors claim to remember much of anything about him, and they act squirrelly when his name comes up. Then, we have his college roommate. After interviewing him, you and I both have a strong sense that he knows more than he cares to admit."

"Jack, when you put it like that, Mendoza will say it's all circumstantial. He'll say we can't arrest someone based on our feelings that someone is holding something back. We need a plan of attack."

"Right. You know me. I say we go into attack mode. We challenge Pridwell and Cheatham to explain the gaps in their stories."

"That's good, but we need some leverage. There have to be some buttons we can push, and we really need some actual evidence."

"Cheatham should be easy. He's volatile. We confront him with the fact that Darden worked for him again. He'll go ballistic."

"I think you're right about Cheatham. Pridwell, however, is a bit harder to read. He won't be so easy to rile. We do, however, know that he pulled some strings to get Darden into the graduate program. That information would not be something that would put him in a good light, I would think. That might be enough to throw him off his game and make him admit to knowing Darden. We can also go back and lean on Whitson some more. I bet we can get something else out of him."

"Sounds like a plan. Are you gonna eat your cookie?"

30

Jack and Dino entered the sergeant's office at the end of the day to plead their case. Jack told him that the reports are up-to-date, and the sergeant opens his computer. "Jack," he said as he read the first one, "The details are there, but there's too many spelling and grammar errors. Run the grammar and spell check before you paste the data into the system. Geez, you act like you've never used a word processor before."

Jack gave Dino a look that all but screamed, I told you so. Dino returned the glance with one of his own since he had advised Jack to proofread the document. Turning to Mendoza, Dino confidently asserted, "Sarge, you can see from the report on the murder case that we have made significant progress in the short time we've been on the case. We think we've got more than enough to keep working our leads, at least until we can see if they pan out."

"I'll grant you that you've made good progress, but it's still weak. You've identified the victim, but you don't have any hard evidence on a suspect. What do you think your next steps are going to be if I let you keep working the case?"

"Well, I think that the report makes that very clear."

"Give me the Cliff Notes version."

Dino resisted the urge to tell the sergeant to read the report again. It was clear he wasn't digesting the details. Instead, Dino laid out the plan for him.

"We have three additional lines of inquiry. We need to follow up with Pridwell, the provost, Cheatham, the ethics professor, and Whitson, the roommate of the deceased. Pridwell and Cheatham both have gaps in their statements. We need to figure out if those gaps are simply memory lapses or whether they have deliberately withheld information. Detective

Farmer and I both have the strong sense that the roommate, Whitson, also knows more than he's saying."

"Be that as it may, all three of those could be dead ends. You're basing your investigation on the theory that the murderer must be connected to one of those offices. That's an assumption, not a fact."

Dino intervened, "With all due respect, Sergeant, it's not an assumption. It's a line of inquiry, and one we need to resolve. For Christ's sake, the body is fifteen years old, so we had to start someplace. Starting with those who had knowledge of and access to the room behind the pipe organ is the logical place to begin. When we interviewed the four people who had those offices during the time in question, we eliminated two of the four. The other two, however, leave us both with unanswered questions. Once we identified the victim, we interviewed his roommate, and we're both convinced he knows something he's not telling us."

"I get all that, but you can't charge someone simply because they forgot something that happened fifteen years ago."

Jack got defensive as he heard the sergeant talk. "Sarge, you're missing the point. We're not at the point where were ready to charge anybody. We are, however, at the point where statements made by two people leave us with questions that we need to try to answer."

"Listen, I get it. This would be a big case if you broke it open. You'd get your name in the paper, and be quite the celebrities. But, I've got people above me who are telling me that the odds of solving this case are not good enough to justify keeping two detectives on it. I'm sure they've got people telling them it would be better for the university if this matter simply went away."

"That shouldn't matter," Dino insisted. "It has nothing to do with publicity. It's about justice. It's about following the evidence where it leads you. Right now, there's still a trail to follow."

"I'll give you one week to work this case. If you don't have something concrete by then we'll simply need to move on. I just can't keep two detectives following a trail that could lead nowhere for a long time."

"One week is not much," Dino complained.

"It's all I can spare, but there's a caveat. You know we're short staffed, so if something else major comes along I may not even be able to give you the week."

"We'll take it," Jack said and turned toward the door.

"And one more thing. I need you to go back and check on the stolen bike. Your report on that case is thin. I can't have my friend thinking we just went through the motions."

"You got it, Sarge."

Dino followed him but was less than pleased. When they got back to their desks, Dino confronted Jack. "Why did you do that? He was just giving us some bureaucratic mumbo-jumbo because he's getting some heat from above. We should have pushed harder for more time than just a week."

"Dino, for all I'm supposed to be the hothead, you've got to learn to choose your battles on some of these things. Especially with Mendoza. He'd made up his mind. You weren't gonna change it. The only thing you might have accomplished would have been to tick him off. Let's see where we are in a week. If we can catch a break, then we can ask for more time. I know the bureaucratic maze pisses you off. It always has. Sometimes, however, you just gotta take what you can get, and live to fight another day."

"Maybe so, but that doesn't mean I have to like it."

Jack smiled and said, "I never said you did. Let's get out of here. I'll see you in the morning."

"Aren't you forgetting something?"

"What?"

"You agreed to go check on the kid's bike."

"Crap. Can you do that? Mariposa's got a list of things for me to do. It's not too far out of your way." From the agitated look on Dino's face, Jack knew he'd gone too far. "Never mind. I'll do it on my way to work in the morning."

"Fine by me. I'm gonna swing by the Religion Department in the morning and do some follow-up."

31

DelRae Fontenot entered the provost's office and joined him at the circular table in front of his desk, where the provost was already seated. Coffee awaited them. Pridwell poured two cups as Fontenot took her seat.

"Thanks for meeting me on such short notice, DelRae," Pridwell began. "Something has come up that will take me away for several days early next week, and I'm going to count on you, as usual, to make sure things go smoothly in my absence."

Fontenot shifted slightly in her chair, bracing herself because she expected yet another in the long line of assignments Pridwell had given her to undergird his career and reputation. "Go on."

"This matter is personal and confidential, DelRae. I know that I can trust you to keep it so. I have just been contacted by a head-hunter firm regarding their interest in me for the presidency of an eastern university. I won't say where just yet. Especially since it is early days. I may not make the cut. Heck, I may not want the job when I learn all the details."

"Congratulations, Larry. You are certainly presidential material. I am not surprised by this news."

"Flattery will get you everywhere, DelRae. Anyway, here's the thing. I don't want the Baylor hierarchy to know about this just yet. It's much too contingent."

"Besides, you don't want people to get the idea that you are actively interested in moving on. I completely understand."

"They lose confidence in your commitment and your effectiveness diminishes. Exactly!"

"Well, I appreciate your trust in me to keep a confidence. Beyond that, though, how can I help?"

"I have already checked my calendar. . .and yours. There are several important matters while I am away that I should be involved in. I will have Mrs. Prescott forward you the dates and any files you will need to be prepared. I have every reason to believe that you can both represent me well *and* maintain my cover, as it were."

"Of course."

"By the way, I want to add that, although we don't have a tradition of naming our successors at Baylor, if this new opportunity should pan out for me, I will vaunt your virtues to my utmost on the way out the door."

"Thank you, sir. Anything else?"

"That covers it. Thank you."

Shortly after Fontenot left his office, he made a series of phone calls. First, to his wife, then to a travel agency. He took the unusual step of making his own travel arrangements. He was looking forward to being incommunicado for a few days.

32

Andrew Whitson had not thought about events surrounding the sudden and shocking disappearance of his roommate Bob Darden in years. He and Darden were comfortable roommates, but hardly confidants. Still, during the brief time that they shared a student apartment, Whitson noted Darden's habitual protectiveness of his personal life, although he could not practically mask every detail. Whitson had, for example, intuited his roommate's sexual orientation despite Darden's determined efforts to remain deeply in the closet.

Sitting across from a WPD detective and hearing that Darden had not just disappeared, but had been murdered, Whitson felt a resurgence of fragments of memory of his time sharing an apartment with the deceased. He had, for example, harbored suspicions that Darden's relationship with one of his professor's had far exceeded that of a grad assistant with his supervisor. Whitson is the kind of person that Marvin Peake would describe as a "wanna bee," always looking for shortcuts to success. Of course, Whitson would never be a college administrator, but most administrators are human, so the typology still works. Whitson's preferred pathways in life went around normal expectations rather than through them, like entering the garden by climbing over the back fence rather than going through the gate.

Almost immediately, he recognized another opportunity for reward by avoiding normal channels. He did not know for certain whether that professor had had anything to do with Darden's demise, but he knew enough about the relationship to know he could exploit the knowledge if he threatened to tell what he did know to the Waco police. Whether he would reveal what he knew would depend entirely on the professor's response. In the moment, he only hoped that his mannerisms had not betrayed any of his thinking to the detectives.

Whitson waited a couple of days after his interview with the WPD detectives to recover his memory more fully, making a mental list of all the observations and impressions that might interest the WPD—and the professor. It took him a day to recall the professor's name, and the better part of another day to see if the professor was still at Baylor. The name came to him when he drove by his old apartment near Baylor. As he drove down James Street, Whitson saw the Tidwell Building and he remembered that the professor's name rhymed with Tidwell—Pridwell. He drove back home and googled that name. He learned that Pridwell was not only still at Baylor, but that he was now some big wig administrator at the school. He rejected the idea of contacting Pridwell to ask for a meeting by e-mail or any other traceable means. He was, after all, contemplating both blackmail and withholding evidence in a murder investigation.

Instead, he called the office number listed on the website. He was told the provost is unavailable, so Whitson asked to leave a voice mail message. The message was cryptic, but not so cryptic that someone with a secret would fail to gather its significance. "We had a mutual acquaintance some years ago. I think it may benefit both of us to have a conversation about him. Oh, and I might add that, sadly, our mutual friend died over a decade ago now." Whitson left his number with instructions to return his call within twenty-four hours or face the consequences.

As he hung up, Whitson congratulated himself. That bit about the dead friend should be enough to set the bait. He thought any response from the professor would at least him gauge how significant a threat his knowledge posed. "The more fear, the more expensive his hush money demand could be," he thought. "Besides, this way, I haven't yet crossed any legal lines."

33

In the morning, Dino figured he would beat Jack to the office again, especially since Jack was going to check on the stolen bike, so decided to swing by the Religion Department at Baylor on his way to work. He needed to speak with someone about why Glen Cheatham kept the office behind Tidwell for so long. Dino wondered whether he might have been trying to hide something.

Becky Long sat at her desk when Dino makes his way into the small suite of basement offices where they had moved the Religion Department Administrators. Summer school was technically in session, but because of COVID all summer school courses were being taught online, so parking was not an issue.

Dino greeted Becky Long and asked whether Dr. Williams was available. She gave him a quizzical smile. "You must be kidding. He never arrives before ten unless he has a meeting, and he only schedules meetings on the days he has class. Otherwise, he works from home."

"Must be nice. Wish I had those hours."

"Well, he's usually writing in his home office, not sleeping the day away."

"Maybe you could help me then."

"I'll try. What do you need?"

"We've been speaking with faculty who had the offices in the back of Tidwell back at the time we think the person was murdered. Now that we know the name of the victim, we are trying to piece a few things together."

"Wait. You've found the name of the victim? Who was it?"

"His name was Robert Darden."

"I remember him."

"Not the journalism professor named Robert Darden."

"Obviously. The journalism professor's still alive and well, and he goes by Bob. No, I'm talking about Robert Darden, a Baylor student back in the mid-two-thousands. He went by Robert."

"What do you remember about him?"

"Well. He was super sweet. He worked as a student worker for our department. His parents must have been loaded because he always dressed really well. I'm talking fancy clothes, designer labels."

"That fits. We found his identity because my partner was able to track him down through a label on his custom shoes. His dad was an endocrinologist in Richmond . . ."

"Virginia. That's right, I remember. I didn't think of him earlier because I thought you were talking about an adult when you were here before. He was just a kid."

"Well, actually. He was probably twenty-three or twenty-four years old at the time he was killed, so technically, he was an adult."

"I guess I still think of him as the fresh-faced kid who came to interview for a job in the department when he was a freshman. He seemed so naïve and happy. He loved his studies and talked about them constantly."

"Didn't he stay at Baylor to do his masters?"

"That's my understanding. We found out that he went into the MA program with the Religion Department."

"Not the seminary?"

"No, and I understand that's unusual."

"Well, it used to happen more regularly before the seminary came into being."

"Actually, that's one of the reasons I want to speak with Dr. Williams. I believe he was the Director of Graduate Studies back then. We are hoping to figure out how that came about. We know that, as a graduate assistant, he worked for two professors, both of whom had offices in the back of the chapel. Drs. Pridwell and Cheatham."

"So, what's your question?"

"I'm wondering what you can tell me about why Glen Cheatham remained in the chapel office for so long. In making our timeline of who had those offices during the year of the murder, we realized he was there far longer than anyone else."

"Oh. I guess you'd have to say, I'm partially to blame for that."

"Really? How so?"

"Honestly, he just got on my nerves. Still does. He's always coming in here complaining about one thing or another. Also, he had two offices for a long time. He had an office in the Morrison Building where he taught for the Honors College, and he had one here. He basically just used the one in Tidwell for a storage closet for his books. He preferred hanging out with students and colleagues in the BIC, sorry, the Baylor Interdisciplinary Core program. I did not see why he needed a better office in our building when he just used it as a storage closet. To be fair, though, Dr. Williams agreed with me. As the Baylor faculty grew, they eventually stopped assigning multiple offices. Dr. Cheatham decided to keep his office here, so he wouldn't have to move all his books."

"So, it wasn't at his request that he stayed at the back of the chapel?"

"No."

"Do you remember whether he had a good relationship with Robert Darden? Apparently, he only had Robert as a graduate assistant for one year before he was assigned to Larry Pridwell."

"Actually, I don't know much about his relationship with Dr. Cheatham, but it would not surprise me if Robert asked to be reassigned to someone else. Dr. Cheatham can get very angry at little things. Robert was a very sweet person. He did not enjoy conflict. Dr. Cheatham seems to thrive on it."

"That tracks. My partner saw Dr. Cheatham's anger when he met with him."

"It would also make sense that he went to work for Dr. Pridwell in his second year."

"Why's that?"

"Robert worked for Dr. Pridwell quite a lot when he was an under-grad, especially during his junior and senior years. Dr. Pridwell requested his help specifically on projects he was working on."

"Thanks, Mrs. Long. I appreciate your help."

*   *   *

When Dino arrived at the office mid-morning, he was mildly surprised to see Jack coming out of sergeant Mendoza's office. Jack was supposed to do some additional legwork on the stolen bicycle. "Well done, Jack, and thanks for the update," he heard Mendoza congratulating Jack.

"Glad to help, sir."

Dino gives Jack a quizzical look. "What's the update, Jack?"

"Turns out I found the kid's bike."

"You what? Where?"

"Leaning up against the side of his house."

"That can't be true. We were there, and there was no bike leaning against the house."

"You're right. But apparently, someone took it and returned it. I'm guessing it was one of the neighbor kids. No need to make a federal case out of it. I told the sergeant he should tell his buddy to tell his son to put the bike in the garage. That way, we're done with it. The sergeant agreed."

"Not to mention, you get to be the one to tell Mendoza, so he can be the hero to his buddy."

"Hey, it could've been you. I offered to let you go check on it, but you didn't want to do it."

"Still don't. My time was better spent talking about Cheatham and Pridwell." He updated Jack on what he'd learned about Cheatham having the same office in the back of the chapel for so many years. Both agreed that since Cheatham did not choose to remain in the office, it was difficult to associate the length of time with a desire to hide something. Nevertheless, they decided to follow up on the initial interview because Cheatham was so angry. They also needed to figure out what Cheatham remembered about Robert Darden.

Dino summarized, "Turns out they both had more of a history with Robert Darden than they let on to us. We already know Darden worked for Cheatham, but he may have bullied Darden. At the very least, according to Ms. Long, Cheatham was known to have a temper, but Darden was a sweet kid who did not handle anger well. We'll definitely be able to lean on him about his relationship with Darden."

"So, what did you learn about Pridwell?"

"He definitely knew Darden better than he let on. Darden worked for Pridwell a lot for two years when he was an undergraduate. According to Mrs. Long, Pridwell specifically requested him, so she basically assigned Darden to work with Pridwell. Darden was also assigned to work for Pridwell when he was a graduate assistant. I have a hard time understanding how Pridwell could forget this guy. We'll want to push for an explanation."

34

FRIDAY, JUNE 26

Larry Pridwell checked his voice messages when he arrived at his office. The first two were from department chairs complaining about matters that department chairs always complain about. Pridwell determined he would reply to those by email later—dismissively, of course. The third voicemail belonged to Whitson.

It was troubling. It could be innocuous, of course, but Pridwell heard a threat in the tone of the message, its anonymity, its pointed reference to a death, and its implication that something of value is involved—something profitable to both the caller and himself. His first inclination was to ignore the message entirely. Larry Pridwell did not bend to pressure tactics. He usually found ways to make threats backfire on those who issued them. At any rate, his privacy instinct caused him to memorize the return phone number, to erase the voice message, and to end his work day after lunch.

On the drive home, Pridwell turned the problem over in his mind. While the messenger could represent only a nuisance, given recent events, Pridwell knew that the message must concern the skeletal victim found in the chapel. The caller, then, must be someone who linked Pridwell with Darden somehow. Was the link simply the fact that Pridwell is the provost? After all, this caller could be a prankster, or a political enemy of his father's or his brother's hoping to exploit a back-door weakness against the whole family. On the other hand, the whole situation could be more of a threat involving his personal relationship with Darden.

Just as he arrived home, Pridwell concluded preliminarily that he needed to work out an algorithm, a decision tree, for dealing with this messenger. If he gamed out all the possibilities in advance—anticipatory problem-solving as he likes to describe the process—he would be less likely to misstep in haste. This development could present a real difficulty. Obviously, he could not afford to ignore this caller the way he dismissed whiney department chairs. He first needed to find out who this guy is and what he thinks he knows. So, he decided to return the call the next day after all.

On his regular after-dinner walk in the park near his home, he returned to the problem. Supposing that the caller doesn't really know anything, Pridwell felt that he can probably deal with him by issuing his own threat, backed by the power of his office and his family name. If, however, he determined that there was even a slight chance that the caller had evidence of his personal interest in Darden, things could get more serious. Their relationship as professor and graduate assistant had been publicly known, of course. "Who would have, or think they have, information beyond this public knowledge?" Pridwell asked himself. "Wait! Didn't Darden have a roommate during the period just before his disappearance/demise? Whitehall? Whitestone? Whitson! Andrew Whitson!"

So, now, the options were clear. If the caller turned out to be Whitson, the response would have to be direct.He decided to arrange a meeting in Cameron Park on his way to the airport before dawn on Sunday morning—on the way to his presidential interview.

35

At 3:30 in the morning as Pridwell made his way down Cameron Park Drive beside the Brazos River. As he approached the bluff the road angled up the hill. He passed the zoo on his left and the Cameron Park Clubhouse on his right, a venue often used for weddings because of its scenic overview of the river below. He kept driving until he came to a narrow road on the right called Lovers Leap Road. The road twists down into a parking lot where he could meet with the caller in private. Though Whitson had never given Pridwell his name, Pridwell was almost certain he was the only one who could have known about his relationship with Darden.

Pridwell pulled his car into one of the parking spaces closest to the overlook where he had arranged to meet Whitson. He got out of his car and looked around to make certain he had arrived first. Next, he pulled out the tire jack and a crowbar and attached the jack to the frame of the car just in front of the rear tire on the driver's side. He loosened the spare tire in the trunk and pulled it forward until it leaned against the lip of the trunk where it was visible. Then he waited.

He had made it abundantly clear to Whitson that he was on a very tight time schedule and fortunately Whitson arrived only about ten minutes later. Whitson pulled into the parking space to the right of Pridwell and gets out of his car. Pridwell did not like Whitson just from the look of him. He appeared every bit as sleazy in person as he had sounded on the phone.

As he made his way over to Pridwell, Whitson stretched out his hand for Pridwell to shake. Pridwell could hardly imagine anyone treating this encounter as a social call. He shook off Whitson's offer: "Sorry. My hands are dirty. I must've hit a nail or a piece of glass on the way up here. My tire is low, and I have to change it if I'm going to make it to the airport on time. Go ahead and tell me what you came to say. I'll have to work on this while you talk."

Whitson began to speak, "Look, I know about your relationship with Robert Darden."

"I don't know what you think you know, but my relationship with Robert was strictly that of a professor and student."

"No. It most certainly was not. Robert was my roommate. He told me about your relationship. I know it started when he was an under-graduate and continued when he became a graduate student."

"You cannot possibly think that anyone will believe you and this cockamamie story."

"Maybe not everyone, but some will. More importantly, your secret will be out, and you will have no way to continue working at Baylor. If I go public, there will be an investigation. I would have to tell the police what I know. They won't be easily fooled."

Pridwell continued to fiddle with the tire jack and sneered, "So, I guess this is where you tell me how much it will cost me for you to keep your mouth shut."

"I think thirty thousand dollars sounds like a nice round number. I'm sure you can put your hands on that kind of money."

"Even if I could, what's to prevent you from coming back to me again? How do I know that this payment would be a one-time affair?"

"I guess you're just going to have to trust me on that. The way I see it, you don't have a choice."

"I'm not convinced that's true since no one will believe you. Anyway, I'm on my way out of town for three days. There's no way I can go to a bank at this time of day. I've got to leave to catch my 5:15 flight, so any decision I make will have to wait until I get back."

"I'll wait until you get back, but don't think you can get out of this. All I have to do is call the police detectives who interviewed me. They'll be more than happy to take my statement and talk to you about it. And things like that have a way of leaking to the press."

"I'll give it some thought. Meanwhile, can you hand me that tire from the trunk so I can change this thing?"

As Whitson turned to look at the back of the car, Pridwell moved quickly. He grabbed the crowbar in front of the tire jack just as Whitson was about to speak. With all his might, Pridwell swung the crowbar high in a wheelhouse motion. The crowbar came crashing down on the back of Whitson's skull. Pridwell heard it crack and watched as Whitson fell to the ground. He knew the blow had been solid.

Pridwell dropped the crowbar and moved over to the body. He turned Whitson over so he could grab his feet and drag him to the overlook. As he did, he heard Whitson moan and realized he was still alive. Pridwell jumped on his chest and put his hands around Whitson's neck. His adrenaline was pumping furiously, and he squeezed Whitson's neck more tightly than even he thought possible. He held his grip longer than he thought he needed to, but he had no choice.

Once he was certain that Whitson was dead, Pridwell rifled through his pockets. He removed Whitson's wallet, watch, and keys. He did not want to leave anything on him that might help someone identify the body. Quickly, he grabbed Whitson's feet and drug him to the edge of the overlook. He struggled to lift Whitson high enough to throw him over the stone railing, but he finally succeeded. The scenic overlook sits on a bluff more than three hundred and fifty feet above the Brazos River. Pridwell hoped that, with luck, the river would wash Whitson's body downstream and it would take days or weeks before what's left of it surfaced.

Pridwell made his way back to his car. He threw the tire jack back into the trunk. He realized that the crowbar had blood on it, so he took it back to the overlook and heaved it as far as he could throw it. He realized that Whitson's car would be a problem, but he had no way to move it. He briefly debated whether to remove the license plate to make it harder to identify the car as Whitson's, but he had not thought of bringing a screwdriver. He looked at his watch and realized he needed to leave for the airport if he was going to catch his flight. He opted to make sure all the car doors were locked, so it looked like someone had abandoned it there.

Pridwell got in his car and drove back out Lovers Leap Road, and headed in the opposite direction toward the airport. There was no traffic at this time of day, so he made good time. He pulled into the airport parking lot in time to make his flight, but barely. On the way into the terminal, he threw Whitson's wallet, watch, and keys into the trash bin on the sidewalk.

After checking in, he went strait to the gate since most other passengers had already boarded. Once on the plane, Pridwell contemplated, "It's not my fault. He brought it on himself. I was not going to pay him thirty thousand dollars, and I could certainly never trust him not to come back asking for more. He was right about one thing, though, if word got out,

I'd have been ruined. He was wrong, though, when he said I didn't have a choice. I had one. He just hadn't thought of it."

Pridwell smiled and congratulated himself, "If and when they find Whitson's body, I have an alibi. I'll be halfway across the country. There's no way they'll be able to prove that I was in town at the time of the murder." He admired his own ingenuity in coming up with his plan. He continued to grin smugly as he greeted the agent at the door and scanned his ticket.

36

MONDAY, JUNE 29

After catching up on paperwork from Friday, Jack and Dino left the office midmorning to drive to Baylor. They made their way to the Pat Neff building, where they entered the provost's suite. Dino asked the receptionist at the front to let them see the provost, but she told them that Provost Pridwell was not in the office today. He was, in fact, out of town for a couple of days. Jack turned to leave, but on a whim, Dino asked whether they could see Vice Provost Fontenot instead. The receptionist told them that she would check to see if Dr. Fontenot was available. Dino impressed upon her that they were on official police business, and it was important that they speak with her. The receptionist raised her eyebrows in mild surprise and dialed the four-digit extension and then spoke into the receiver in hushed tones.

After a couple of exchanges back and forth, the receptionist rose from her chair and stated in her official voice, "Dr. Fontenot will see you now." She led them back around the corner and knocked on the office door. After a few moments, the door opened and DelRae Fontenot invited them in. She asked whether the detectives would like something to drink. Jack declined. Dino, however, thought the gesture provided an opportunity to set a different tone for the conversation than the first time she spoke with Jack. "I'd love a cup of coffee, thank you. No cream. No sugar. Just plain coffee."

"I'll have the same, thank you," she told the receptionist. The vice provost motioned to the couch at the side of her desk. She invited them to sit, and they accepted. She then sat down in the armchair at one end of the sofa. Dino sat nearest to her while Jack gladly let Dino serve as the buffer between them after his initial encounter with her. In a matter of moments, the receptionist returned with two green mugs of black coffee. Gold lettering emblazoned the mugs with the words, "Office of the Provost." The letters arced around a copy of the university seal that Dino recognized from the class ring they found with the remains of Robert Darden.

Dino began politely. "We want to thank you for seeing us on short notice. And thank you for the coffee, too. It's quite good."

"I'm glad you like it. It's a special blend we serve here in the Pat Neff Building. The owners of Common Grounds make it special. That's the locally owned coffee shop at the edge of campus. The owners are alumni and friends of the university."

"Well, it really hits the spot after a morning of paperwork. It's a nice pick me up."

"Tell me about it. I spend half my time completing paperwork. Unfortunately, the other half of my time consists of sitting through endless meetings, which are the bane of every administrator's existence."

"We'll try not to keep you long, but we are asking some follow-up questions with the people who had the offices in the back of Tidwell. Now that we know the identity of the person victim, we're trying to piece together what may have been going on in his life."

"So, you have identified him?"

"Yes ma'am, we have. He was a graduate student in the Religion Department by the name of Robert Darden."

"I remember him, vaguely."

"What do you remember about him?"

"Mostly how nice he was. I was new. They had hired him to help me get my books in the office. The graduate studies director paid him for a couple hours of work to haul my book boxes and help me unpack them. He introduced me to Glen Cheatham with whom he had worked the previous year. After that, whenever I saw him, he always greeted me with a smile. I knew he was gone in the spring, but I had no idea he'd been murdered. I'm sure that Larry, Dr. Pridwell, will be quite sad to hear that the body was Robert's."

"Why is that?"

"Well, we talked as he was unloading the boxes. Robert Darden told me he was quite pleased to be working for Dr. Pridwell as his graduate assistant that year. You could tell that Robert thought the world of him."

"You mentioned that he introduced you to Glen Cheatham. What was their relationship like? We know that Robert worked for Dr.

Cheatham the previous year, but he was assigned to work for Dr. Pridwell starting in the fall of 2007. Was Dr. Cheatham upset about the change?"

"Not that I could tell. He had nothing but good things to say about the work that Robert had done for him the previous year."

"What about as the semester wore on? Did Robert still feel good about his time with Dr. Pridwell?"

"Well, we weren't that close that he would have confided in me. But, yes I would say he continued to enjoy his time with Dr. Pridwell. Whenever I saw the two of them together, Robert seemed to hang on his every word."

"Do you have any idea why Robert would have been up in the Tidwell offices behind the chapel? If he worked for Dr. Pridwell then, you'd think he would've spent more time at the other end of the building on the third floor where Dr. Pridwell's office was."

"I think that Robert thought of the chapel as a kind of sanctuary. I would often see him grading papers in the pews downstairs or sitting in one of the chairs outside the chapel offices while he was reading. I got the impression his roommate was something of a party animal, so finding a quiet place to study was important to him."

"That's helpful. Thanks. Switching gears if I may, do you happen to know when Dr. Pridwell will be back?"

"I believe he's out of town for two or three days."

Dino and Jack both noticed the instantaneous change in her demeanor. Where she had been relaxed and talkative while reminiscing about Robert Darden, her posture immediately stiffened when asked about Dr. Pridwell's absence. She glanced at her watch, which Dino took as his signal to end the conversation. He wanted to stay on good terms with her in case he needed to come back to talk about something else. He thanked her for the information about Robert, and he and Jack made their way back to the car.

"That was interesting," Jack observed. "She was nothing like that when I spoke with her."

"Yes, she was very forthcoming when we were talking about Robert Darden. But she was all business the moment I mentioned Larry Pridwell. I'm not sure what that's about. I'll have to chew on that a bit."

"Speaking of chewing, if we break now, we could beat the lunch crowd. You up for some soul food?"

"I could eat."

37

Mariposa was every bit as good a cook as her mama—Mexican and Tex-Mex mostly—and Jack loves their food. Sometimes, though, he "took a hankerin'" for the deep South cuisine of his youth, known as Soul Food outside the South. Jack always maintained that one of the perplexities of being southern was how blind white people, especially, were to the cultural commonalities that southern blacks and southern whites share. Food being chief among them.

A few months ago, Jack came across a diner on the edge of downtown named Sascees, the kind that still served blue plate specials. One day of the week, the special was what Texans call 'chicken-fried steak.' Jack could not distinguish it from what they call "country fried steak" back home, although Texans insist that their version is different somehow—and superior. Cube steak dredged in flour, seasoning, and sometimes herbs, fried until golden brown, served with gravy. The sides included fried green tomatoes, green beans, and mashed potatoes. Southern cooks from Texas to Georgia prepare green beans the same way, with fat back or bacon or some cut of cured pork, and sometimes diced onions, all boiled until well past *al dente*. In fact, they usually cook the beans to the point where all their nutritional value is probably lost. But, oh, Jack loved them, especially together on a fork with mashed potatoes, gravy, and a portion of ripe, red tomato. When they are in season, Jack always ordered fresh sliced tomatoes because he could eat good tomatoes prepared any way the cook chose to prepare them. And the diner makes their corn bread with fine ground white corn meal, not the coarse yellow stuff that produces corn bread with a consistency that reminded Jack of sand, and with buttermilk so that it holds together without being dense.

Usually, both Jack and Dino brought lunch from home or, sometimes, grabbed a deli sandwich or a taco at a fast-food establishment.

Detective salaries didn't encourage eating lunch at sit down restaurants. But once a month or so, by prearrangement, when country/chicken-fried steak was the blue plate for the day, Dino joined Jack at Sascees for lunch. Their rationale for the indulgence was that police work is hard and that sometimes you needed something more substantial than a turkey sandwich. Dino usually ordered fried chicken with sides of macaroni and coleslaw.

After lunching over fried steak and fried chicken, they returned to the office. Sergeant Mendoza had apparently been waiting for them. He emerged from his office immediately and approached Jack even before he could reach his desk.

"Where's your partner?" he asked in his typically gruff, down-to-business manner. Mendoza did not make small talk, especially with his detectives.

"In the john. I swear that man's watchwords are 'frequency' and 'urgency.'"

"He's reached that age. The time will come when you and I both are going to feel grateful for gravity, too, Jack."

"I don't quite follow you."

"It'll be our turn soon enough. Meanwhile, don't let him even sit down at his desk when he comes out. A hiker has found a body on the rocks below Lover's Leap in Cameron Park. Judging from the patrol officer's verbal report, the victim died very recently. You two get out there ASAP and take charge of the investigation. Hracek is taking a day off, but I'll send her out as soon as I can reach her."

As Dino walked into the room, Mendoza added, addressing both detectives, "Don't linger."

38

Jack and Dino went to the parking lot at Lovers Leap. Crime scene tape cordoned off the overlook. A uniformed officer stood in front of the tape. The detectives made their way over to him and Jack asks him what had happened.

"The body's down there," replied the officer as he tilted his head toward the stairway leading down to a hiking trail through the wooded section of the bluff to the right of the overlook. "A hiker was out for a walk with his dog. The dog wandered off the trail and up onto the rocks protruding from the base of the cliff. Apparently, the dog got curious because he could smell a dead body and went to check it out. The hiker had to go after him because he was off leash. That's when the hiker saw the body and called 911. My partner and I arrived at the scene about twenty minutes later. He's down at the bottom of the cliff with the body. I hope you brought some walking shoes because you'll need them."

"Thanks. The shoes I'm wearing have rubber soles, so I should be okay," Dino replied.

"Give me a minute," Jack sighed. "I keep a pair in the trunk. Won't take me but a minute."

Dino looked around the parking lot. He saw only one car that doesn't belong to a cop. He asked the patrolman, "Have you had that car checked out? Chances are it belongs to the vic. If he went over the edge of the overlook, he couldn't exactly have driven it away."

"I'll call it in. The vic didn't have any ID on him that we could find. The license plate may give us a line on him."

"You read my mind, officer."

Jack returned wearing his walking shoes. The detectives dipped under the crime scene tape and made their way to the stairs and start down. "Man, these things are steep. These are more like a ladder than a staircase."

"If you think it's steep now, wait till we have to go back up."

"Ugh. Didn't need you to tell me that."

When they reached the bottom of the stairs, they cut left at the outcropping of stone beneath the overlook. They soon reached the second patrol officer. He was standing about ten feet away from the body.

"So whatta we got here, officer?"

The officer responded to Jack, "I can't tell you much. He's very obviously dead, so I didn't want to disturb the body. Looks like a straight drop. If he committed suicide, I'd suspect he would've jumped out from the overlook. To me, it looks more like he just stepped off. Of course, I'm not the detective."

Dino and Jack looked up. Dino remarked, "Maybe not, but you got good instincts. Glad you didn't touch the body. Most suicide jumpers do just that. They jump off, not step off."

Jack made his way over to the body and bent down. "He's not wearing a watch."

"Maybe he just uses a cell phone and doesn't wear a watch."

"Don't think so. The guy's got a tan line where his watchband should be. He usually wore a watch. That doesn't mean he had it on him when he jumped. He could've taken it off and put it in his car."

"Still," Dino observed, "when you combine it with the straight drop, it starts to look suspicious. Does he have any ID on him? Can you check his pants pockets?"

Jack was already beginning to bend over to check for the victim's wallet, but he stopped and looked at Dino instead. "Don't need to."

"Jack, I know you don't want to disturb the body before Hracek gets here, but I think it'll make our job a lot easier if we know who this guy is."

"That's just it, we do know who he is. His face is bloody, but we interviewed him a couple days ago. This is Andrew Whitson."

"You've got to be kidding me."

At that moment, Dr. Hracek, the forensic pathologist, hailed the detectives. As she approached, Jack waved to her and joked, "Emily, we've got to stop meeting like this."

"You're probably right, but something tells me it's always going to be like this. So, what's the story?"

"We are hoping you can tell *us* something. The angle of his fall is almost completely vertical. He's missing a watch. I haven't had a chance to check his pockets yet, but Dino and I both recognize him. We inter-viewed him a couple days ago about the Baylor skeleton guy. Turns out, he was the roommate of the guy we found in the back of Tidwell when he disappeared back in 2007."

"Wow, that's quite a coincidence."

"Not sure I believe it's a coincidence. For me, that's too big a leap, no pun intended. Can you tell us whether he fell or was pushed?"

She walked over to the body and kneeled. She looked up to the top of the cliff and then back down at the body. "I'm not sure it was either. I'm almost certain he was dead before the fall." She turned the body over on its back and announced, "and that confirms it."

The detectives each gave her a quizzical look, so she continued, "You're right about the trajectory of the fall being too steep for someone who jumped. But also, even if he'd had stepped off, his head would've cleared the edge of the cliff. However, if you look closely at the back of his skull, you can see it's been fractured by a hard blow."

"Why couldn't that have happened from the fall when he landed on the rocks?"

"He would've had to have landed headfirst to fracture his skull, but if he did that the blow from the landing could have fractured the top of his skull, not the back right. The only way that could happen is if he were tumbling end over end as he was falling, but for that to happen he most likely would've had to jump headfirst, and that's not what jumpers typi-cally do. It might also happen if someone pushed him from behind, but again it's not likely. Somebody who's pushed off a ledge will try to right themselves so that they're going feetfirst. Also, the blow looks like it was delivered by something thin, like a pipe, not the jagged edges of the cliff."

"Meaning we're looking at a murder."

"Definitely, but here's the real kicker. The blow to the back of the head will likely not be the official cause of death. When you look at his eyes you can see he has petechial hemorrhaging which suggests that the guy was strangled. I would wager that the autopsy reveals a fractured hyoid bone, confirming my hunch."

"We'd better go back up then and secure a broader area."

"Good idea. I'm gonna call the office and have them send me a boat to load the body. There's no good way to get the body back up to the top of the cliff. The stairs are too steep and tall. You may want to have more forensics guys search the area for some kind of metal pipe or rod. The killer probably would not have wanted to take it with him."

"Thanks, doc. I imagine we'll see you back at the top."

"I may take the boat and have someone drive me back up to get my car. I don't need to climb those stairs if I don't have to."

"Yeah, tell me about it. Unfortunately, we have to."

39

Jack and Dino reached the top of the stairs and paused to catch their breath. Neither one of them considered themselves out of shape, but they were not accustomed to climbing stairs as steep as those connecting Lovers Leap to the bank below. Once he got his wind back, Dino told the officer stationed at the top of the overlook to cordon off the entire parking lot since the entire area was now the primary crime scene.

The two detectives instinctively moved across the parking lot to the car that they assumed belonged to Andrew Whitson, the deceased. Jack asked the patrolman whether he had gotten confirmation on the car. Officer Cramer stopped unrolling the caution tape long enough to tell Jack that the car was indeed registered to Whitson. Dino paused before he reached the car and crouched to look at a darkened spot on the pavement. "Jack, over here. I think this is blood. Bring some evidence markers."

Jack retrieved a handful of yellow, numbered placards from the trunk of their car. He ambled over to Dino who pointed to a spot about the size of a silver dollar, behind the parking spot next to Whitson's car. "It looks like blood alright, but the forensics guys will have to test it to be sure. There's not a lot of it, though."

"True, but if his skull was fractured, there would not be a lot of blood from that kind of injury."

Jack started toward the overlook, keeping his head down as he walked. Near the curb, he placed two more evidence markers a couple feet apart. "I've got a couple places here where the line of pebbles in the gutter looks like it's been disturbed. Could be where the killer dragged Whitson over to the lookout. Check it out, Dino."

Jack kept walking toward the lookout. When he reached the stone wall at the edge of the cliff, he squatted to examine the stones. "Here's another spot. My guess is that the killer propped him up against the wall so he could get a better grip. The wall's about four feet high, so the killer would have had to lift the body before he pushed him over the edge. This looks like it's about where we found the body down below."

"Maybe we'll get lucky, and the killer nicked himself on the rocks as he was trying to lift the body. It'd be great if this blood matched the killer and not the victim."

"Yeah, it'd be nice to catch a break."

Jack placed a marker on the ground beneath the blood spot on the stone. Dino suggested they go check out Whitson's car. Since the car is locked, however, they cannot rummage through the contents. They can see inside, and not surprisingly, the car is a mess. Several fast-food bags dotted the back seat and most of the floor. "Looks like he used his car as his dining room. The forensics guys will have to sort it out, but my guess is, it won't give us much."

Walking around the parking lot, they did not find any other signs of a struggle. There were no security cameras, unfortunately. There were no tire marks where someone peeled out while leaving the scene. A few scattered pieces of trash were laying around, but most of that looked like it has been there for days, not hours. Once the forensics team arrived, Jack and Dino drove back to the office. Most of the drive was quiet. Each thought about the dead man. Both thought this case related to the Tidwell murder somehow. Finally, Dino stated the obvious.

"We've got to get Mendoza to let us both work the two cases together, right?"

"Unless we can't. He's not gonna want to see the connection. You can tell from our last conversation that he sees a fresh dead body as a solution to his other problem. Assigning us to this case means the heat will be off him to let the Tidwell case die."

"Then we've got to make him see reason. We'll have to work this case to eliminate other reasons for Whitson's murder. We know Whitson knew something he wasn't telling us."

"Agreed, but Whitson was no saint. He could have gotten himself in trouble a bunch of other ways. Drugs, for instance. We'll have to eliminate other possibilities even as we continue to turn over rocks in the Tidwell case. Eventually, something will crawl out from underneath one of them."

40

Including the hike down to the body, the time they spent surveying the scene, and the hike back, Dino and Jack had spent the entire afternoon Monday at Lover's Leap. By the time they made it back to the station, Mendoza had gone for the day. He left the detectives a note saying that he expected to hear details first thing in the morning.

The next day, Mendoza was already in his office when Jack and Dino arrived. Both of them were actually several minutes early because they sensed the sergeant's urgency about the Lover's Leap murder.

"OK. Go over everything for me. I want it all," began the sergeant. Greetings were implicit.

Jack began. "Well, first, Hracek thinks that it is all but certain that this was a murder. Pockets empty, no ID of any kind on the victim, blunt force trauma to the back of the vic's head, although that injury was not fatal, in Hracek's judgment. Petechial hemorrhaging suggests murder. The blow may have been accidental or in the heat of an argument, but strangling the guy after knocking him out was clearly an intentional act."

"Second, there is no question as to the identity of the victim. Dino and I both recognized him immediately as Andrew Whitson because we questioned him recently in connection with the Darden case. Further, the plates of the abandoned car in the parking lot near Lover's Leap are registered to Whitson."

"Finally," Dino interjected, "we both think that Whitson's murder links somehow to the Darden case. We both feel that Whitson was holding something back when we questioned him, that he knew something he wasn't telling us. Our theory? Whitson knew something that could implicate Darden's killer. The killer knew or suspected that Whitson knew something and decided to eliminate the threat. Now, the details are yet to be determined, of course."

"Theories don't make indictments, Detective. Evidence does. I don't have to tell you that. I want you to put the Darden case on hold for now. We have a fresh murder here. Before it goes cold, I want it solved."

Dino paused a moment, seemingly collecting his thoughts. He and Jack exchanged knowing glances as if to say, we've been here before. "Sergeant Mendoza, with all due respect, we think that pursuing the Whitson case and pursuing the Darden case are virtually the same thing. Whitson was on our 'person of interest' list in the Darden case, and now he's been murdered."

"Coincidence," Mendoza muttered, dismissively.

"We don't believe in coincidence," Jack responded, supporting his partner, but seeking not to give the Mendoza reason to think that he and Dino were defying him. "How about, at least for now, we investigate the Whitson case with our eyes and ears open to possible connections to Darden. If they are connected, if we solve one, we'll solve the other."

Sergeant Mendoza looked from one of the detectives to the other as though he was measuring their attitudes. After a few moments, with a slight shrug of the shoulder, he assented. "Alright, that's the plan then. But remember, the Whitson murder is guiding this process." With that, he turned and headed down the hallway as if he had an errand to run.

41

After their conversation with sergeant Mendoza, Dino and Jack agreed to proceed by ruling out any possibilities other than that Whitson's murder linked to the Darden case. Hracek had not run the tox screen for drugs in his system when Jack and Dino left the crime scene, so they needed her preliminary report. Jack volunteered to pay her a visit.

"Are you hoping for more cherry kolaches?" Dino ribbed his partner.

"Lay off, Dino. I thought you'd rather talk to the forensics folks about the contents of Whitson's car. If they haven't already, ask them to check for any drug residue. The sooner we can rule out the possibility that someone murdered Whitson in a drug deal gone bad, the better. That is about the only scenario that would fit the evidence other than a Darden connection. Don't you think?"

Dino smiled knowingly and nodded in agreement. "Robbery is another possibility, I guess. But it's unlikely that Whitson had a chance encounter with a thief. Why would a thief troll Lover's Leap in a public park in the middle of the night? And if a robber had knocked Whitson unconscious while committing the robbery, why would he then strangle him? No. This has all the earmarks of a crime committed by someone Whitson knew. My guess is they had arranged a meeting. Look through the belongings Whiston had on him while you're at Hracek's office. Did he have anything valuable still on him that a thief would *not* have overlooked?"

"Good thinking. Meet back here by lunch?"

"Don't ruin your appetite with sweets." Dino couldn't resist another jab. But he was smiling, so Jack knew Dino was just giving him a hard time.

* * *

Jack found Emily Hracek in the morgue examining Whitson's body. "Oh, I'm glad you're here," she stated without looking up. "I am fifteen minutes or so into the preliminary exam of yesterday's victim. All I can confirm now is that a thin blunt object caused the non-fatal blow to the back of the head. It looks like a small pipe but beveled. He died of asphyxiation, though, strangling to be precise. His larynx was crushed."

"Would the blunt instrument be consistent with a crowbar? The crime scene guys found one in the river that does not look like it's been there long."

"It would. Bring it in and I can test it for prints, blood, and hair. The river probably washed away evidence, but I can at least tell you if it matches the head wound."

"Ok. Listen, Dino and I want to rule out a couple of possibilities. Any signs that the victim struggled with his assailant? Defensive wounds, that kind of thing?"

"None whatsoever. This was a surprise attack. The victim didn't expect it, probably didn't even see it coming. There are perimortem abrasions under both arms at the shoulder. I'd guess the murderer drug the decedent from the parking lot to the overlook."

"Yeah, we found scrape marks in the gravel that lead us to the same conclusion. We'd like to rule out another thing if we can. Have you found any traces of drugs on the body or his clothes? In his bloodstream?"

"I haven't gotten that far yet, but I'll make it a priority. I can do a snap drug screening for the most popular street drugs right now, if you'd like." She stepped over to a cabinet on the far wall, took a pre-packaged kit, and returned to the exam table. In a matter of minutes, she suctioned a small fluid sample from the body and injected it into a vial containing what Jack guessed was a reagent of some kind. She applied a drop of the mixture from the vial to a test strip using a dropper. "Negative. This man apparently has no illicit drugs in his system. Of course, they'll do a more thorough lab test in Dallas as part of the autopsy. And I'll ask forensics to look for residue in his clothing. I doubt that they'll find anything."

"How long will it take to get absolute confirmation either way?"

"Several days yet on the full autopsy results. I can get results from the clothes by this afternoon, if I put a rush on it."

"Great. Please do."

"Any other questions for me?"

"No, I think that covers it."

42

When Jack returned to the office, he updated Dino on what he had learned about Whitson's body from Emily Hracek. They decided to return to Baylor's campus to reinterview Pridwell and Cheatham. On the way to Baylor, they decided to check with Larry Pridwell first, since his office was closest to the parking lot.

When they arrived at the provost's office, however, they learned that Provost Pridwell was still out of town. His administrative associate could not say where he had gone. His calendar just indicated he is out of town. She suggested they check back again in two days.

As Jack and Dino exited the Pat Neff building, Dino mentioned to Jack, "Seems a little unusual, don't you think?"

"What's unusual?"

"Some bigwig leaves town without leaving word how he can be reached? Seems a bit strange to me."

"Maybe. Could also be he just wanted a vacation. We may as well interview Cheatham since we're here anyway."

Once they made their way across campus to Cheatham's office, they knocked on the door and a voice inside invited them in. When Cheatham recognized Jack, he immediately stood up behind his desk, and pointed to the door.

"I told you the last time you were here that I did not appreciate the tenor of your questions implying that I had something to do with someone's death. It's absurd. I already complained to the provost, and I will not stand for this harassment."

Jack replied, "Dr. Cheatham, as I tried to tell you earlier, my questions were not intended to be accusatory. At that time, we were trying to ascertain the identity of the person whose remains were found in the Tidwell Building. We now know his identity, but we are now trying to ascertain his whereabouts in the time leading up to his death. During our investigation, we've learned that he actually worked for you as a graduate assistant. We're interested in anything you might remember about him."

"A graduate assistant for me? Who was he?"

"His name was Robert Darden. He was an undergraduate religion major and then spent three semesters in the master's program, the first two of which he worked for you."

"His name's not ringing a bell to me. Not sure there's anything I can tell you."

Jack said, "You must remember something. He worked an entire year for you as your graduate assistant in the academic year 2006–2007."

"That's fourteen years ago, Detective. I hardly recall what I had for breakfast last week, much less fifteen years ago. Not to mention I've had fourteen graduate assistants since then, and I can't recall a single one of their names. I just don't get that close to them. They help me grade my exams and post the grades. That's a nice help for me, but I don't spend much time with them. Students fill in their guesses on Scantron cards, and the graduate assistant simply feeds them through the machine and then records the grades. It's not rocket science."

Dino pulled out a picture that he remembered to put in his pocket and handed it to Cheatham. "Here's a picture of Robert Darden. Maybe it will help you recall."

"Yes, he looks vaguely familiar now that I see the face, but I really can't say anything more than that."

Jack pushed him again, "Can't you remember anything? For instance, we know he was only your graduate assistant for one year, but we've also been told that most graduate assistants stay with a professor for two years. He left you to serve as a graduate assistant for Larry Pridwell. Did that create bad blood between you and Robert?"

"Detective, you have to understand. All of my graduate assistants typically stay with me for only a year. I teach four large classes every semester, and I ask them to grade assignments for those classes. They'd rather work with professors in their field, and I can't blame them for that. If you're asking whether it irritates me that I have to train a new graduate student every year, the answer is yes. But come on, how insane would I have to be to harbor a grudge against a graduate student so strongly that I would resort to violence. I suggest that you'd be better off speaking with Larry Pridwell about why he requested this particular student to work with him."

"So, you really don't remember anything else about him? If he requested the student, he must've found something about him that he liked."

"Is there anything you can remember about the fall 2007? Where were you on the last day of final exams?"

"If it's like most semesters, I was working on submitting grades. Since I teach four classes I have a busy final exam schedule. Because I teach so many students, that means I have to manually enter the grade for each student, then double check it to make sure I put the right grade with the right student. It takes hours to complete the process."

"So, you're saying," said Jack, "that you likely would've been in the Tidwell Building on that day?"

"I presume so, but if you're implying from that question that I had anything to do with this student's death, then you and I have a problem. I'll go back to the provost and complain to your superiors."

"Thanks for your time, professor," Dino replied. "We've taken up enough of your time, at least for now. If we have further questions, we'll come back."

When Dino and Jack got back to the car, Dino asked, "What are you thinking, Jack? Do you believe him that he really doesn't remember anything about this guy?"

"It's hard to say. He sounds plausible when he says he doesn't re-member the names of his graduate students. On the other hand, he got unbelievably angry and defensive when we forced him to admit he was in the Tidwell Building. Threatening to go to the provost and to call my boss for doing my job? I mean, who does that? He's either extraordinarily insecure, or he's deflecting, hoping to throw us off the scent."

They got back to the office, but before they could even seat them-selves, Sergeant Mendoza called out, "Piper. Farmer. My office, now."

43

Larry Pridwell took his first-class seat on the plane headed back to Waco via a layover in DFW. It was a late flight, and fortunately, the maze of checking luggage, negotiating airport security, and hiking to his gate had been routine. It was mid-week, so most passengers were business travelers going to or from their destinations. He had flown out to his meetings a day early because he wanted to be well-rested and in top form for his interviews, first with a couple of executives from the head-hunting firm that had identified him as the finalist for a university presidency, then with a committee of university trustees on the next day, and concluding with a short "de-briefing" with the head-hunter people again.

As he settled into his seat and the flight attendant brought him a cup of dark roast coffee with two raw sugars and a splash of half-n-half, he began reviewing events of the last couple of days. In all, the interviews had gone quite well, he thought. The only concern he had was how well he managed what he perceived to be a point of disagreement among the members of the trustee committee. One faction, it seemed to him, was wary that the Baylor provost might want to remake their university in the image of Baylor. One trustee had even cautioned Pridwell that the Texas way of doing things might not be well-received back East. Another group, in contrast, seemed interested in him precisely because they saw the future of their institution as becoming something like Baylor east of the Mississippi. They already had a strong academic reputation, but this group wanted a clearer acknowledgement of their religious heritage.

Pridwell had noticed this tension early in the interview. Had he walked the fine line that could unify both groups in favor of his candidacy? By the time he finished his coffee, he had convinced himself that he had been masterful. In any case, the trustee committee would put their recommendation to the full board—and inform him of their decision—early next week. He might try to pull a few more strings of influence remotely over the next day or so, he thought, but by-and-large, the matter was now out of his hands.

Pridwell finished his coffee just as the airplane reached cruising altitude, so he took his laptop from its case to make full use of the flight to Dallas. For now, he was still Baylor's provost, he reminded himself. He should check on things in Waco. He answered several emails, but most did not require action from him. He pulled up the online version of the *Waco Tribune-Herald* to catch up on local news. His mood changed immediately. On the equivalent of the front page was an article about the discovery of Andrew Whitson's body below Lover's Leap in Cameron Park, the very day Pridwell left for his interviews.

Pridwell scoured the article and then googled "Whitson murder Waco" in search of any information the article may have omitted. He found nothing indicating that the police had any leads in the case. The only obvious link to Baylor, and thus to Pridwell, was the fact that Whitson was once a Baylor student. "But that is true of half the population of Waco," he reminded himself, "so it's too early to become alarmed."

The first officer announced that the flight had begun its initial descent into DFW. Pridwell put his laptop away, returned the tray to its upright and locked position, and tried to relax for a few minutes before landing. His layover was short, so he needed to hustle to make the DFW to Waco flight.

44

While Jack checked on the prospects that Whitson's murder was gang-related, Dino decided to have another conversation with Marvin Peake. Between Cheatham's temper, Pridwell's pomposity, and DelRae Fontenot's reticence, Dino could not escape the nagging feeling that he was missing something. He called ahead to make sure that Marvin was in his office, then he drove to Baylor to speak with him. Marvin's office door was open when he arrived, and he greeted Dino with a warm handshake and a smile.

"So, you've come to interview me again. If this were a cop show, this would mean I'm still a suspect. Should I have a lawyer present?"

"Of course, you have a right to have an attorney present if you choose, but we don't think you are a suspect. I would, however, appreciate it if I could pick your brain regarding your impressions about a few of your colleagues."

"I'm happy to help in any way I can, but I'm not sure how much I can add."

"Well, here's the thing. I've spoken to three of your colleagues, but I feel like I've not gotten the whole story yet. Two of them, it seems to me, are holding something back, and the third one's reaction is so over-the-top that it is beyond all reason."

"Let me guess, Glen Cheatham is the one who has blown the whole thing out of proportion."

"You guessed right. How'd you know?"

"That's who he is. If he feels slighted or threatened, he goes from zero to sixty in a split second."

"Yes, but why would he feel threatened? These are routine questions, trying to ascertain the identity of our victim."

"I saw in the paper that you'd identified the victim as Robert Darden, one of our religion majors who'd gone on to do graduate work. That might have something to do with it."

"How do you mean?"

"Did you know they had a history?"

"I'm aware that Darden worked as Cheatham's graduate assistant for a year before changing over to work for Larry Pridwell if that's what you mean."

"Well, there's more to it than that. Robert Darden initiated a complaint against Glen Cheatham with the Graduate Studies Office. Darden accused Cheatham of unprofessional conduct and bullying. According to Darden, Cheatham tried to get him to do some yard work for him at home as part of the fifteen hours he was obligated to work as a graduate assistant."

"That doesn't sound kosher to me. What happened with the complaint?"

"Like most complaints at the university, it was dealt with quietly. This was the spring semester of 2007. Technically, the administration reassigned Darden's duties to another professor. They did not reprimand Cheatham publicly, but in the fall of 2007, the department's Graduate Studies Office created a list of acceptable assignments for graduate assistants. Needless to say, yardwork was not on the list."

"Interesting. I imagine there was bad blood between the two of them, then."

"Indeed. Especially on the part of Cheatham. He felt like they scapegoated him since other professors had previously assigned their graduate assistants to do things that were not academic in nature."

"Given what I've seen of Cheatham's temper, I can imagine he probably went ballistic."

"Most certainly. But then, when Darden didn't return to class in the spring of 2008, Cheatham felt vindicated. He told anyone who would listen that Darden clearly did not belong in the graduate program, and that once Darden himself realized that, he simply moved on."

"So, this bad blood between Darden and Cheatham goes to motive. Do you think Cheatham could've lashed out at Darden and struck him physically?"

"I couldn't really say for certain, but my gut says no. To be sure, Cheatham flies off the handle with almost no provocation, but his angry responses, as far as I've seen, are limited to verbal retorts."

"What can you tell me about Larry Pridwell? I have the distinct sense that he's holding something back. He claims not to recall anything unusual, but it turns out that Darden was his graduate assistant when he disappeared between the fall and spring semesters. Also, Pridwell appears to have gone to considerable lengths to get Darden admitted into the graduate program. I have a hard time believing him when he says it slipped his mind about his graduate student disappearing in the middle of an academic year."

"Not sure I can tell you much about him that you haven't already experienced. He comes across as a pompous . . . well, let's just say he is pompous. He has a very high opinion of himself and isn't afraid to tell you so. I'll admit, though, it's not like him to go out of his way to help someone else, especially a student. That's a bit surprising if you're right about him helping Darden get into the program. I can only guess that he thought the guy had potential, but Darden's grades don't indicate he was a stellar student. His grades in the graduate seminars he took were quite marginal."

"Sounds like he miscalculated." Dino pauses to record a comment in his notebook before continuing. "So, what's the story with DelRae Fontenot? My partner and I both have the impression there's something she's not telling us. I'm used to people who keep their cards close to the vest, but she's very difficult to read. She seems very protective of Larry Pridwell, but she also bristles at the idea that people think he's the only reason she's in the provost's office. And yet, she seems very reluctant to talk about herself at all."

"Ah. That may have something to do with her Boston marriage."

"Wait, I was under the impression that she was single. Are you telling me she's married to someone in Boston?"

"Sorry. A Boston marriage is a term that goes back to the late 1800s. I guess it's an obscure term. It refers to two women who share a house with one another. They may or may not be intimate with one another, but they do live together. No one asks whether they are partners or merely roommates. DelRae has shared a house with the same woman for the last twelve to fifteen years."

"So, you're saying that she's gay."

"Not openly gay, no. That would be a bridge too far for Baylor. Clearly, though, for all intents and purposes, she has a close relationship with the woman with whom she shares a house."

"I'm very surprised that Baylor might have someone in a leadership position who's gay."

"Dino, you sound like a lot of pastors I know. They recognize that a certain percentage of the population is gay, but they don't think any of that population belongs to their church. Do you honestly think there aren't gays on the Waco police force?"

"On the contrary. I know for a fact that there are. That has nothing to do with the fact that they do their jobs just like everybody else. I just assumed Baylor was different."

"It's complicated. Some gay faculty members still live in the closet, knowing that if they came out publicly, the university would likely terminate their employment. At the same time, we all know, or strongly suspect, that we have colleagues who are gay. Baylor also has students who are openly gay. For years they have petitioned the university to allow them to establish a student club, but so far, the administration has refused that request. Nevertheless, they keep petitioning the administration every year. The current generation of students is not like their parents or grandparents on this issue. Most of them have had high school friends who came out as gay in the seventh or eighth grade. I imagine at some point in the not-too-distant future, Baylor will finally allow gay students to form a university recognized club."

"When you put it like that, it makes sense. I'm old enough to have seen a lot of changes in society on this issue. I can see how DelRae Fontenot's situation would make her reluctant to speak about her personal life. Let me ask you this. Do you think Larry Pridwell knows about her situation?"

"Larry Pridwell is as pompous as anyone I've ever known, but he's not a neanderthal. He knows. He also knows DelRae Fontenot is a very gifted administrator. That's why he's hired her twice. She makes him look good. Everyone knows she's the reason the provost's office functions the way it does. He likes being the figurehead who presides over the meetings, but he doesn't do any of the day-to-day work of the office. He hires people to do that."

"Thanks, Marvin. You've given me a lot of insight. I appreciate it. I've got to get back to the office."

As Dino made his way back to the police station, he thought about what he had learned from his conversation with Marvin Peake. He felt like he had gained solid insight into DelRae Fontenot's guarded conversations. She was likely holding back something personal, but not something related to the case. On the other hand, Cheatham and Darden had a rancorous history, which adds some context that helps explain, perhaps, his volatile responses. If his temper got the better of him, Cheatham could have harmed Darden in a fit of anger. Marvin, however, believed Cheatham's outbursts were limited to verbal attacks. As for Pridwell, being pompous is not a crime. Still, as Dino had noted to himself, "Pridwell is hiding something. He advocated for Robert Darden's entry into the graduate program, even though Darden did not excel in the classroom. Intervening to help a marginal student is not typical of Pridwell's behavior. What made Robert Darden so special?"

45

When Jack found himself with a few minutes of free time, he decided to nose around the internet to see whether Whitson had any footprints there. If he had been involved in anything hinky, or if, for example, he was buying or selling online, Jack might find some trace. Perhaps his murder resulted from a transaction gone sour—not necessarily involving drugs, but possibly. An ambush with a monetary motive, perhaps. On the other hand, if, as Jack fully anticipated, he could not find evidence of risky behavior, the absence of information would be negative confirmation, limited but still useful, that would link the Whitson and Darden murders.

Minutes into his search, Dr. Emily Hracek breezed into the room and sat lightly in Dino's chair at the desk opposite Jack, plopping a file folder in front of him.

"To what do I owe this rare privilege?" Jack inquired, feigning polite officiousness.

"Kinda' surprised to find you here, Jack. In fact, I dropped by the office only because I know that you two are eager for these results."

"Oh, I thought for a second there that you're just being friendly. I guess I should've remembered that professionalism is your byword." Jack teased her because he knows her reputation in the building. Her trademark look (lab scientist meets 1940s librarian) and her well-known habit of working well into the evening seem designed, if anything, to reinforce the perception. "So, what's the word?"

"Well," Hracek replied, determined not to take the bait, "the autopsy confirms the cause and manner of death I surmised on my initial inspection of the body: a blow to the head stunned the victim who was subsequently strangled. Blood tests found no trace of drugs and I found no needle marks, not even between his toes. He was not a user. He had a small vitamin D deficiency and slightly elevated blood sugar. Probably pre-diabetic. Otherwise, *nada.*"

"Ok. *Muchas gracias por eso.* In this case, negative results may prove to have positive consequences. Dino and I are operating on the theory that this case and the Darden case are connected."

"Yeah. I gathered. I've been thinking along those lines, too."

"Maybe this info will help us convince the sergeant of that. He isn't of the same mind as us three. Thanks."

Although she did not react to Jack's taunt, she did not want to end the conversation without some sort of rejoinder. She remembered Jack's struggles with learning to dance and saw an opportunity. "At the risk of appearing overly friendly, how are your dancing lessons going? Do you need any tutoring? I did competitive ballroom when I was a kid. Besides, I'm a scientist. I might be able to help you get the hang of counting to three over and over without throwing in a fourth beat now and again."

Jack could not tell whether she was mocking him or teasing him. Both made him uncomfortable, but for different reasons. Realizing that she had turned the tables on him, he replied in his most professional tone, "I'm good. Thanks again for the information but no thanks for the offer. Now, I'm sure we both have things to do."

Hracek nodded with a mischievous smirk and stood up, but, unwilling to submit so readily to Jack's attempt to dismiss her, she remarked offhandedly. "Actually, I am on my way to lunch. Maybe you don't want to learn to dance, but how about joining me for lunch? I hate eating alone."

"Sure. Dino's interviewing one of the Baylor faculty, and I'm sure he'll pick something up on his way back. What'd you have in mind?"

"I would love some fried chicken over at Cajun Craft."

"Let's go."

*   *   *

As Jack drove back to the office after lunch, he licked his fingers, savoring the last vestiges of chicken flavor. He then thought about the morning. Nothing had come from his search for Whitson on Google or social media. Whitson had left virtually no trace whatsoever on the internet, and Jack found no affiliation with any known gang in Waco. Emily reported Whitson had no drugs in his system. "No gang affiliation. No drugs. No online presence," she had stated emphatically. Jack had spent the morning researching Whitson with nothing to show for his work. "At least I had a good lunch," he muttered under his breath.

46

After his interview with Marvin Peake, Dino stopped and picked up an order of Popeye's fried chicken for himself and took it back to the office. He got back shortly after noon. Jack was not at his desk, so Dino figured Jack was picking up his own lunch. Dino remembered that he had called in some favors from Jack earlier, so he sat down at his desk and started working on the case report he knew that Mendoza would expect from them.

About forty-five minutes later, Jack returned to the office where Dino sat munching on the last of his chicken. "Great minds think alike," mused Jack. "I went to lunch with Emily, and I got chicken as well, though we went to Cajun Craft."

"Mine came from Popeye's. Not bad for fast food, but not as good as Cajun Craft. You took Doctor Emily someplace fancy."

Dino cocked an eye and gave Jack a look. "Does Mariposa know you took another woman to lunch?"

"I did not say I took her to lunch, Dino. I said we had lunch together. I have absolutely no reason to tell Mariposa anything about who I have lunch with. You know I would never step out on Mariposa even if my life depended on it. That being said, don't you go blabbing your mouth to Mariposa about my having lunch with another woman. Knock it off, will ya. You're not funny."

"Right. Just let me point out one more thing, though. If Mariposa did find out about your lunch, your life just might depend upon it. She's got a bit of a jealous streak."

"You got that right, so let's just drop it. How did your conversation with Marvin Peake go?"

"It was illuminating. I learned some things, particularly about Cheatham and Fontenot. What I learned about Fontenot may help explain why she had such a strong reaction when you first met her, and why we think she's holding something back."

"How so?"

"Well, have you ever heard the term 'Boston marriage'?"

"Nope. Can't say that I have."

"Me neither, until today, but apparently, Fontenot is in one. It's a term that refers to two single women who share a house together. It may or may not mean that they share a bedroom, but, at least according to Marvin Peake, it probably does mean that in her case."

"Well, I'll be damned. I never saw that one coming. So, you're thinking she got spooked when I started asking questions that might have raised issues about the personal lives of her and her colleagues?"

"Yes, and Marvin thinks that Pridwell knows her secret as well, but that he hired her anyway because she's really good at what she does."

"And that also explains why she's so loyal to Pridwell."

"You got it. The unanswered question, though, is also important. Does that mean that Pridwell's evasiveness has something to do with him protecting her?"

"Maybe, but I'm not convinced. He's a pompous ass. He clearly thinks he's always the smartest person in the room, but he doesn't strike me as someone who would stick his neck out to help a colleague if there wasn't something in it for him."

"I agree. On top of that, I don't see any way that Fontenot would be strong enough to have cracked Darden's skull, strangled him, dragged him down the hallway, and lifted him up and put them in the box. No, I think we can eliminate her as a suspect."

"So, what'd you learn about Cheatham?"

"Well, that's where things get interesting. Marvin told me that Darden initiated a complaint about Cheatham. Darden claimed that Cheatham acted unprofessionally. Cheatham tried to force Darden into doing yard work for him, but Darden refused. Cheatham doubled down and tried to bully Darden into doing the work anyway. Darden then filed a formal complaint with the Graduate Studies office. The charges were serious enough that Darden's duties with Cheatham were reassigned in the spring of 2007."

"So, not only could Cheatham supposedly not recall the name of his graduate student, but he also conveniently forgot to tell us that Darden reported him for unprofessional behavior. He's been lying to us. I told you he had a temper. It's possible he and Darden got into an argument, and that that argument turned physical."

"I thought so too, but Marvin says that when Cheatham's temper flares up, it only results in verbal arguments. Marvin has never seen him physically lay a hand on anybody."

"I'm not sure I would agree. When he dressed down that student in his lecture, he was as angry as anybody I've ever seen. If there hadn't been a room full of witnesses, I could see where he might've lashed out physically. I say we keep him on our list of suspects."

"I'm with you. He had means, motive, and opportunity. We keep him on the list for the first murder for sure. I'm not sure how he's connected to Whitson, though. So, what did you learn from Doctor Emily?" he asked with a wry grin.

Ignoring the barb, Jack recounted what he had learned about Andrew Whitson's death. "I learned two things from Emily, I mean Dr. Hracek. First, the time of death for Andrew Whitson was somewhere between midnight and six in the morning. As far as we know, either of our two suspects could have driven up to the overlook and killed Whitson. We know Pridwell was out of town that day, but if we assume that Pridwell took the earliest flight out of Waco at 5 a.m., he still would've had time to get to Lover's Leap and to the airport."

"True enough, but we can't place either one of them there. It could've been them, or it could've been somebody else."

"Yes, but that's where the second thing I learned from Dr. Hracek becomes a factor. The preliminary tox screen that Dr. Hracek conducted did not show any evidence of drug use. While it doesn't prove conclusively that Whitson's death was not due to a drug deal gone bad, it mitigates the odds quite a bit. How many drug dealers do you know never touch the stuff?"

"I agree, but any good lawyer would just call that speculation. We need some kind of corroboration to place one of them at the scene. We first need to verify when Pridwell left the city. Assuming he flew, we should go out to the airport and find out which flight he took. We can also check out the security footage and see what time he arrived at the airport."

"Why don't you do that, Dino. Meanwhile, I'll check with the guys working narcotics and see if they've got any information regarding whether Whitson was dealing drugs. Then we can touch base and see where we are. Just because he was not taking drugs, that does not mean he could not be selling them. It'll take you longer to get to the airport and back, unless I find out Whitson was dealing. If I beat you back to the office, I'll start writing up the report for Mendoza. He's made it clear he wants to stay in the loop."

"I got that covered already. You told me I owed you one, so I went ahead and did that while I was waiting for you to get back from your lunch. All you'll need to do is fill in the information that Hracek gave you."

"Thanks, Dino. I'll find something to do till you get back."

"You can always check to see whether Dr. Emily wants you to bring her a cup of coffee."

"You're really not funny, man."

47

Dino left the office to drive out to the Waco airport. He needed to verify the accuracy of what Pridwell had told his administrative assistant and Vice Provost Fontenot, namely that he left the city on Wednesday morning, the day that Andrew Whitson was killed. Given Waco's proximity to large towns, Pridwell might have driven to Dallas or Austin. Those trips would have taken him two hours to the north or south respectively. Other than that, he would most likely fly out of Waco. As Dino approached the airport, he smiled as he always did, at the sign that reads "Waco Regional Airport." It sounds pretentious, as though Waco is some thriving metropolis that is so large you have to think of the greater Waco area. "Waco is just not that big," he thinks. "The airport has only one carrier that flies to Waco."

When Dino arrived, he showed his badge at the counter and explained that he needed to see the flight manifest from Monday to check where Pridwell was going, what time the flight departed, and whether he got on the plane. The attendant behind the counter told him, "I can give you the first two, but you'll have to speak to the TSA agent if you want to verify that he physically boarded the plane. They keep the security camera footage. What's the name of the passenger?"

"Last name Pridwell. Larry Pridwell."

"As in the provost at Baylor?"

"You know him?"

"Sure do. He flies out of here quite a bit on university business."

"You wouldn't happen to know if he flew out of here on Monday of this week, would you?"

"Sorry. I can't help you there. I was off that day. If you need it, I can give you the contact information for the person who was working the desk."

"First, let me know if he's in the system as having flown out of here or not."

With a few clicks on the keyboard, the ticket agent confirmed that Larry Pridwell was indeed booked on a flight to Raleigh, North Carolina, and that the flight left Sunday morning at 5 a.m., with a three-hour layover in DFW airport. He also told Dino that Provost Pridwell checked in for the flight but did not check a bag.

"Which means he could've left the building and driven to Dallas to catch his connecting flight from there. He would've had just enough time to drive back through Waco on the way to Dallas and still catch his flight. I'll need to see the flight manifest itself."

"You'll have to get that from the TSA agent. I don't have access to those records."

"Where is the TSA officer in charge?"

"His desk is in the office behind me, but you'll need to wait a few minutes. We only have three TSA agents working, and while the plane is boarding, the one who checks the baggage has to go outside to take the checked carry-on baggage down the steps to load it on the plane to Dallas. If you'll have a seat across from the security line, I'll let him know you're here."

"Waco Regional Airport, indeed," Dino laughed to himself. He could remember when Waco had two airlines, but now they only have one. Continental used to fly to Houston, where one could catch connecting flights. That kept the rates competitive. Now, however, only American flies into Waco, and they can charge what the market will bear. They also only have three flights a day, all of which go to DFW. The flight only takes twenty-five minutes, but flight schedules often mean that passengers can have a three-hour layover, or else have so little time before the next flight that they must literally run through the terminal to make it to the gate on time.

After several minutes, a TSA agent approached Dino. "I hear you need to check the flight manifests in the security footage for the provost at Baylor. I'll need to see your badge, and then I'll ask you to step into my office."

Dino held up his badge while the TSA agent checked it over. "It says special crimes. My colleague at the desk said you think that Baylor's provost was involved in a murder?"

"I'm sorry. I cannot comment on an ongoing investigation."

"Okay. I understand. Follow me to my office."

As it turned out, the agent's "office" was actually a desk in a room a little larger than a closet. "What's the provost's name again?"

"Pridwell. Larry Pridwell."

"Yep. Says here he boarded the five-a.m. flight."

"OK. I'd like to observe him from the time he entered the building until he boarded the plane. I need to watch his mannerisms before he gets on the plane."

"Sounds to me like you're saying he's a suspect."

"No comment. Just show me the sitting area outside the security gate starting about fifteen minutes before the security gates open for boarding."

The agent fast forwarded through the video until the timestamp read 4:15, then he slowed it down to run at normal speed. "He's not there. Can you speed it up a little bit see when he shows up?"

The agent nodded. Finally, just after 4:40, Larry Pridwell entered the front of the building. He was moving quickly because he had arrived very close to the time they would close the gate, and he still had to get through security. Dino watched as Pridwell made his way to the ticket counter. Fortunately for him, there was no one in either line. Before approaching the ticket counter, Pridwell stopped just long enough to look up and read the signs. Then he took two steps to the left and walked down the priority lane to the ticket counter, even though the same ticket agent was servicing both lanes. "How typical," Dino thought. "He thinks he's too good to go down the line for *normal* people. Isn't he special."

As Pridwell approached the counter to check-in, Dino saw him reach into his pocket to pull out a handkerchief to wipe his brow. Clearly, Pridwell had rushed from the parking lot and had started to sweat. When he put the handkerchief back in his pocket, he pulled something else out and looked at it. "Looks like he's checking his email," the TSA agent remarks. Right then, however, Pridwell went to the end of the ticket counter and dropped whatever was in his hand into the trashcan.

"I don't think so. Nobody throws their phone in the trash. I'm not sure what that was. Any chance that trash bag is still there?"

"Nope. They empty those things twice a day, and they clean out the dumpster every night. We use a lot of paper in this place."

Dino grunted his displeasure and watched as Pridwell went through security. He got through the line quickly because all the other passengers had already boarded. The agent at the gate began to reach for the microphone to issue the final boarding call, but just then she looked up and saw Pridwell coming to the gate, pulling his carry-on luggage behind him with one hand. He pulled out his cell phone with the other hand to call up his boarding pass. The gate agent smiled and waved. She spoke to Pridwell like she recognized him. As he approached the gate, he bypassed the general boarding lane again in favor of the priority lane. Dino shook his head and thought, "No doubt he sat in first class."

"I suppose you'll want a copy of the video, right?"

"Thank you. Here's my card. Please send it to the email address listed there."

"My God, he really is a suspect isn't he."

"I simply cannot comment on an ongoing investigation."

"Maybe not, but I can add two plus two."

"I'm happy that you have such highly advanced math skills. I still cannot comment on an ongoing investigation," remarked Dino, making a point to call attention to his best poker face.

The TSA agent whistled to himself as Dino left the building.

*   *   *

When Dino returned from the airport, he and Jack filled each other in on their respective conversations. The detectives realized they agreed on something important. Dino summarized, "Pridwell knows something he isn't telling us. He's hiding something, but why? Is he covering for someone, or is he the culprit? We need to interview him again."

"Listen, I'm tired of the arrogance of that pompous ass," Jack hissed. "Let's *not* do this interview in his office where he basks in his self-importance. It's time we straighten him out on the true lay of the land. We are the police. Provosts aren't above the law. Let's meet him somewhere off campus."

Dino nodded his assent. The partners agreed to "invite" Pridwell to coffee at Dichotomy, a local coffee and spirits bar near campus the next morning. They decided that Dino, as the senior partner, would issue the "invitation," accepting no excuses for delay or requests to change venue, making it clear that this is official police business. "I'll make sure he gets the message."

48

Jack and Dino met at the office the next morning and decided to ride together to Dichotomy. As they got in the car, Jack asked, "So, what'd you do last night?"

"Not much. Just worked on a little woodworking project I have been tinkering with." Dino still did not want to tell Jack about the jewelry box he was making for Jack's daughter's *quinceañera* this coming weekend. He wanted to surprise Jack as much as Sofia. He knew Jack would be touched.

Dino decided to change the topic. "How do you want to handle this?"

Jack reiterated his conviction that they need to "ruffle the peacock's feathers." Dino, although not as vehement about the matter as Jack, nodded in agreement.

"Do you want to be the good cop or the bad cop?" Dino asked. "Or need I ask?"

"You needn't. I want at this guy."

"OK, then. We have a plan."

Pridwell arrived over ten minutes late. He leisurely ordered coffee at the bar and added sugar and cream before joining the detectives in their booth. Jack did not waste a second before pouncing. He offered no pleasantries, no greeting whatsoever, in fact. "Pridwell, the citizens of Waco do not pay us to sit around waiting for someone. You should do us the simple courtesy of being on time."

Pridwell's eyes widened just far enough and for just long enough that both detectives noticed.

"Well," Dino thought, "Jack may be onto something here." Jack pressed on, "I'm going to be honest with you, Pridwell. We don't think that you've told us the truth. We want the truth, the whole truth. It's time to start."

Pridwell sat fully upright on his side of the table, clasped his hands together, then leaned forward slightly before replying, "I am unaccustomed to being accused of lying, detectives, and I do not appreciate your tone."

Jack did not miss a beat, "You see, that's the thing. We are accustomed to being lied to, which means that we know how to recognize it, and, as a matter of fact, your tone gives it away." Pridwell seemed genuinely surprised that his show of indignation had not cowered the detectives, at least a bit.

Dino quietly pushed the advantage. "We have several questions, but perhaps we can make up some of the time that you wasted for us by cutting to the chase. Explain to us, please, why we shouldn't conclude that you know something important about Whitson's murder. Heck, explain why we shouldn't consider you the prime suspect. We know that you two were in contact with one another recently."

"Okay, so that's a lie," Jack realized with some amusement, "but Pridwell doesn't know that. Let's see what falls from this shaken tree." As if by prearrangement, both detectives folded their arms and rocked back in their seats as if to say, "We are waiting."

Pridwell took a sip of his coffee and cleared his throat. "This is preposterous. I should think that police detectives would be familiar with the principles of logic. You're asking me to prove a negative!"

"In other words, you have no evidence of your non-involvement," Dino stated in his best quasi-academic tone. "Without such, we can only assume that we should dig deeper into your recent activities and whereabouts."

"Search warrants for your home, car. . . and office," Jack added.

The word "office" clearly startled Pridwell. After another sip of his coffee, he looked up to the left for a moment. When he returned his gaze to the detectives, he enunciated, in a controlled, evenly paced, almost monotone manner, "Would an alibi meet your criteria? It should not be necessary to remind you that I was out of town on personal business the day you say Whitson died. In fact, I left on the earliest flight out of Waco to DFW on Sunday. I did not retain my ticket or boarding pass, but the airline will have records confirming what I say."

"See, that wasn't so difficult now was it," Jack taunted. "Where, specifically, did you go. Who can corroborate your alibi?"

"That, sir, is none of your business. You speak of wasting your time," Pridwell jeered. "I consider this conversation to have been an imposition on mine. You may corroborate my alibi yourself. Now if there is nothing more, you'll have to excuse me." Without waiting for an answer, Pridwell stood up and strode decisively out of the coffee shop.

Jack turned to Dino. "Cage appropriately rattled, I would say."

"Yes, indeed. He doesn't know that we know he got on the plane, but there's no reason for him to fly off the handle like that. That suggests to me he's hiding something. Why doesn't he want us to know where he went? I still think there's more he can tell us."

"Oh, you bet. We just need a tidbit or two more to use on him. I think we can poke a permanent hole in that asshole's façade." Jack mockingly mimiced Pridwell's superior tone.

"Agreed." Changing the subject, Dino wondered how his partner is dealing with stresses at home. "You haven't updated me on the *quinceañera* preparations lately."

"Don't ruin what's started out as a profitable day. The whole family is driving me nuts with the preparations. Let's get to alibi checking."

49

Back at his desk after a solitary lunch in the faculty dining hall spent trying to settle his conflicting reactions to his coffee meeting with the detectives, Pridwell found it difficult to concentrate. On the one hand, he was offended, even indignant that these cops dare think that they can intimidate him. Since grade school, other boys had tried to manipulate or pressure him because he was different. He reacted instinctively to the detectives like the nerd among jocks he had been in those days. He defended himself then with his family status, and he had since perfected the art of throwing the weight of his economic and social status around, even in the face of threats that sometimes became physical.

On the other hand, he recognized the reality of the looming danger for the threat it is. Just having his name associated in any way with murder could seriously damage his reputation just when he is on the precipice of fulfilling a lifelong ambition. He desperately wanted to quash this police interest in him, or at least to evade their attention, or else misdirect them somehow. But how?

As life has a way of doing, the next few minutes pointed Pridwell's thinking in another direction. His phone rang. Katherine Doyle, his administrative associate, told him she had a Mr. Marshall on the line. She wanted to know whether the provost was available to take his call. Marshall chaired the search committee Pridwell had met with only two days ago. Of course he would take the call. "Yes, I will take his call, Mrs. Doyle."

Pridwell's heart raced. What to make of the rapid response? He would know soon enough.

"Hello, Mr. Marshall. It's good to hear from you," he stated politely when Ms. Doyle transferred the call. Pridwell struggled to keep his nervous excitement from sounding through in his voice. "What can I do for you?"

"Dr. Pridwell, we're both busy men. I hope that you won't mind if I get straight to the point." Marshall didn't pause to give the provost the opportunity to respond. "The search committee was impressed during our conversation with you earlier this week. We have voted to ask you to come to campus for a series of meetings with the full board and select members of the administration and academic leadership. Are you still interested?"

"Of course I am," Pridwell thought, but he also did not want to appear too eager. He needed to play a little hard to get to give himself leverage during salary negotiations. Again, he concentrated on speaking with measured confidence. "I am flattered, Mr. Marshall. I always say that it is important to pursue opportunities like this until it becomes clear to one or both parties whether this is a fit. So, I owe it both to your university and myself to take the next step."

"Excellent. Shall I have my secretary contact yours to make the arrangements?"

"No. I will manage that myself. You will understand that, until we reach an agreement, I would rather keep our conversations confidential. My secretary is not privy to my personal affairs."

"Oh. Of course. Expect an email soon, then."

"I will be looking forward to it as I will be looking forward to continuing the exploration."

"Goodbye then."

"Goodbye and thanks!"

50

Dino and Jack had driven back to the office after interviewing Pridwell at Dichotomy. Dino pondered what they had learned. Pridwell was telling the truth. He arrived at the airport in time to catch the five o'clock flight to Dallas. He had a long layover in Dallas before his flight to Raleigh, but Dino did not believe that he would have had enough time to drive back to Waco and still make his connecting flight from Dallas. To be thorough, Dino decided to check with someone at DFW to make sure Pridwell got on the plane there. Something told him, however, he very likely remained in Dallas until his flight left.

If he could verify that, Dino would know for certain that Pridwell did not drive back to Waco and kill Whitson. If Pridwell was the culprit, he would have killed Whitson before he got on the plane. It could be done, but the timeline was tight. Pridwell would have gotten to Dallas by six, meaning he could potentially have driven back to Waco and killed Whitson closer to seven-thirty or eight. The time was a little outside the six-hour window that Emily Hracek had given them, but she admitted her estimate was preliminary. Dino and Jack would need to locate any cameras between Pridwell's house and Lovers Leap where the murder took place. That would take time, however. Time that Mendoza would not give them. "That will have to wait. Boy, we really need to catch a break," Dino reflected to himself.

"Jack, why don't you track down Pridwell's address? While you're at it, find out what kind of car Pridwell drives. I'm gonna get someone in Dallas on the line to verify that Pridwell got on the plane from DFW to Raleigh. If he did, we're gonna have to start finding camera footage close to Pridwell's house."

Jack mused skeptically, "There's no way Mendoza will give us time to track Pridwell for the murder of Whitson unless we get some kind of concrete evidence. We need a break somehow."

One thing he saw on the airport video still troubled Dino. What had Pridwell pulled out of his pocket and thrown away? The TSA agent was right, the item looked like it was the size of a phone, but why would Pridwell have thrown it in the trash? Still, whatever it was, it didn't change the fact that Pridwell got on the plane in Waco.

Dino considered Pridwell the most likely suspect, but if it turned out Pridwell has a verifiable alibi, then that leaves Cheatham. "We can't yet rule him out yet," Dino reminded himself. "Someone killed Darden and Whitson. We need a plan."

True to form, Dino decided to approach the problem methodically. He decided to call DFW to verify that Pridwell boarded the flight to Raleigh he was scheduled to take. He would also have to talk with Jack to determine what evidence they might need from Cheatham that would either give him an iron-clad alibi or lead to something that might implicate him. Next, he and Jack together needed to study the video more closely. The TSA agent had probably emailed it by now.

When Dino arrived at the office, he laid out his plan to Jack. They agreed Dino would call DFW while Jack looked over Cheatam's file again. Then, they would watch the video together to see if they could figure out what Pridwell threw away. Dino checked his email and forwarded the video link to Jack. He then called the American Airlines ticket counter at DFW. He identified himself as a major crimes detective from the Waco Police Department. As usual, he had to explain the problem three times because each person transferred him up the chain of command. Each time, he was put on hold and forced to listen to a sickeningly upbeat commercial logging the merits of traveling through DFW. Finally, he reached the supervisor who could verify whether Pridwell went through security and boarded the flight to Raleigh. Of course, he put Dino on hold yet again while he searched the database. Surprisingly, instead of a commercial, Dino heard the slow, soothing sounds of instrumental music. Dino leaned back in his chair and let his mind relax while he waited.

As he sat listening, he did some relaxation exercises. 'Breathe in. Breathe out,' he repeated to himself. Breathing slowly, his mind stopped racing. Suddenly, a flash of insight broke him out of his Zen-like trance. He sat bolt upright. At that very moment, the supervisor came back on the line. "Thanks for waiting," he said.

"It *was* a phone."

"What'd you say? I thought you wanted me to confirm a passenger on a plane."

"It was a burner phone. He threw away a burner phone."

Without waiting for a response, Dino ended the call. The supervisor stared questioningly at the phone in his own hand. People often cussed him out for having to wait so long, like it was his fault. He was used to that. But this guy uttered some kind of nonsense about a burner phone. The supervisor just shook his head and recalled a billboard he'd seen recently while driving south on I-35. It read, "Things are wacko in Waco."

"That certainly must be true," he chuckled. "If that police detective is any indication. They certainly have some wacky cops in Waco."

Dino pulled up the call logs for Cheatham and Pridwell, going back to the days when he and Jack interviewed Cheatham, Pridwell, and Whitson. He wasn't quite sure what he was looking for, but hoped he might recognize something unusual. Dino thought it prudent to check both office phones since they had not yet eliminated Cheatham. "Maybe," he thought, "I'll recognize a suspicious number or a call one of them made around the time of the interviews."

He started with Cheatham, not really expecting to see anything. He noticed, however, that Cheatham's office number made an outgoing call to the provost's office shortly after the time Jack interviewed him. The call lasted nearly six minutes. "I wonder what that's about. It's certainly suspicious. Was he calling to inform the provost? Were they colluding about something? We definitely need to ask Pridwell and Cheatham about that call."

Nothing else looked unusual, so he turned to Pridwell's logs. He looked at the logs for the day when Cheatham called, and sure enough, he saw the call from Cheatham. Pridwell's private line, however, only showed the call lasting a little over two minutes. Dino smiled. He knew instinctively that Pridwell made Cheatham wait on hold before his administrative assistant transferred the call. "Pridwell," he smirked, "you are nothing if not consistent. You can't help but play your power games." Then, a random thought flashed through his brain. "I wonder what kind of music they play on Baylor's voicemail."

Another call jumped out at Dino. Or rather, a name stood out. The phone number belonged to Jack Pridwell. Dino knew he was the state senator and brother to the provost. The date of the call was the same day he and Jack interviewed Pridwell. It was also suspiciously close to the time that he and Jack were in Pridwell's office. Was Provost Pridwell calling his brother or the state senator? The call lasted over ten minutes.Dino deduced that the provost asked his brother, the senator, to make some calls on Baylor's behalf. The senator then likely called one of the higher ups in the WPD. Undoubtedly, those calls were the source of the pressure to close the investigation of the murder in the Tidwell Building.

Finally, Dino noticed a call from a number simply listed to "unknown caller." Dino knew instinctively that he had found the burner phone he was looking for. Given that assumption, he could now establish a direct link between Pridwell and Whitson. He had to connect the dots, but the trail was clear to him. The burner phone belonged to Whitson. He likely had it on him when he was murdered. Pridwell threw the burner phone into the trash at the airport before he got on the plane. Ergo, Pridwell had been at the murder scene. He must be the killer.

Dino had to tell Jack so they could figure out how to use this information, but when he looked up, Jack was not at his desk. He looked around and figured out he must be in the conference room. Jack would have told him if he had to leave the office. Dino printed out the relevant pages of the call logs and walked briskly into the conference room. He would explain the trail of the calls Jack. Excitedly, he reminded himself, "We still have to fill in the blanks to make the case stand up in court. The evidence is compelling to me. Whitson was trying to blackmail Pridwell. A defense lawyer will claim that it is purely circumstantial. But I know without a shadow of the doubt, we've got him now."

51

While Dino checked call logs for Pridwell and Cheatham, Jack got a call from forensics. The package containing Darden's personal belongings had arrived from Darden's mother. The forensics tech wanted Jack to be present when they opened it and began to catalog and review the contents.

Isabel Ortega, the forensics tech on duty when Jack walked through the door, was a relative newbie, eager, very serious about her work, but also very unseasoned. She handed Jack a pair of gloves and together she and Jack unsealed the shipping carton and began removing its contents, assigning each item an identifying label, listing the items individually in an evidence log, along with a brief description.

A few miscellaneous items of clothing were folded on top—a Baylor T-shirt, a pair of gym shorts, etc. Jack did not know if they will help, but he hoped for the possibility of recovering DNA to help confirm without a doubt that the remains belonged to Robert Darden. Of course, there was just a chance that forensics might also find other DNA from someone other than the owner of the clothing. Jack knew Dino would tell him not to get his hopes up, but he told Isabel to run DNA tests on the clothing.

"I will also be on the lookout for strands of hair, then" Isabel commented as much to herself as to Jack. "I'll also test for proteins. You know, just in case."

"Excellent. What's next?" She pulled out a layer of newsprint from under the clothing. A dozen or so items of jewelry lay below the newsprint, including a high school class ring, an expensive looking watch engraved simply with "to B from L always," and a handful of trinkets that a man might carry in his pants pockets and empty on the dresser or bedside table at night.

Jack and Isabel examined each item carefully. He told her, "The watch might turn out to be significant. We know it belonged to Darden, so we can assume that 'B' stood for "Bob." The word "always" conveys a sentimental or romantic message. "L" was probably the first initial of someone important in Darden's life.

"We want to find the model and make of this watch," Jack commented, "on the off chance that we might trace it to a point-of-sale and buyer. Be sure to look for a serial number."

Another layer of newsprint followed. "Mrs. Darden took great care in packing this stuff," Jack thought to himself. "But I'm not surprised. Keeping these token items shows how much she cherished them as memories of her son's life."

At the bottom of the box they found some assorted papers, none of which seemed at first blush to hold any evidentiary promise, except for a bound journal with dated entries, apparently in Darden's own hand. "I'll see what I can do about getting a sample of Darden's handwriting for comparison just to be sure," Isabel told Jack, as though anticipating his thoughts. She impressed Jack with her professionalism.

"Great. Now, as soon as we log this journal, I want to check it out and take it back to my desk. I need to read every word carefully."

"Sure thing," Isabel agreed, "I can go ahead and do that now."

"Thanks. Keep me posted on any trace evidence you find."

* * *

Jack returned to the office a few minutes later, but he saw Dino was on the phone, so Jack went to the conference room to start pouring over the journal. He counted eighty-three entries, usually a long paragraph, sometimes two. The entries contained full sentences of inelegant prose mixed with sentence fragments recording events, random thoughts, and feelings regarding Darden's daily life. The dates indicated that Darden had not made daily entries. Instead, he journaled two, maybe three, times a week.

The entries were replete with comments about Darden's college experience, but he was notably silent regarding people in his life. He had a habit of referring to them by a single initial. Jack quickly identifies the "C" who appeared frequently as "Cheatham" and "W" as "Whitson," but until he and Dino could reconstruct more of Darden's college life, the other individuals mentioned in the journal would have to remain anonymous. Besides, most of these references appeared as innocuous comments.

There was, however, a strand of brief comments referring to a certain "L." The "L" from the engraved watch perhaps? Read as a whole, this strand yielded evidence from the pronouns referring to "L" that "L" was male, and that Darden and "L" were in a torrid but increasingly troubled relationship. Darden feared "L" might leave him if he was promoted. Could this relationship have come to a sudden and violent end? Now, this was something Jack was eager for Dino to see.

52

After Jack showed Dino what was in the box that Darden's mother sent, both detectives knew they had independently found evidence that would now move the investigation forward. Jack read Darden's thoughts about his lover and realized that Darden was gay. Dino saw Pridwell toss what he now believed to be a burner phone into the trash at the airport. The call logs showed that Pridwell had received a phone call from an unknown number the day before Whitson was killed.

"The problem is," Dino observed, "everything we have is still circumstantial. It makes a compelling case to us, but the DA will tell us we need something concrete linking Pridwell to Whitson. The sergeant won't let us move forward with what we've got."

"You're right," Jack admitted while rubbing his chin. "And on top of that, there's no way we can prosecute Darden's killer without that link. We've still got two unsolved murders. We know in our guts that they're connected. It's too big a coincidence that the second victim was the roommate of the first victim, and that he ends up dead within days of our interviewing him."

"Okay, Jack, let's reason this out. We've got three phone calls that we need to explain. We've got a call from Cheatham to Pridwell, but we don't know what it was about. Around the same time, Pridwell calls his brother, the senator. If we're right, he got his brother to use his influence to end the investigation. Then, the day before Whitson's death, we have a call from a burner phone that probably went to voicemail. Man, what I wouldn't give to hear what was on that message."

"Email!" Jack almost shouted.

"No, Jack. I'm talking about the voicemail left by the burner phone."

"Yeah, I know, but I just remembered something. Before I met with DelRae Fontenot, I called to make an appointment. She was out of the office, so I left a voicemail. She was still out of her office, but she called me right back. Turns out Baylor has some super fancy voicemail system. When someone leaves a voicemail, the system sends a digital copy of the voicemail as an email attachment. The system also transcribes the voicemail and pastes into the email."

"You know what this means," Jack continuds excitedly. "We're gonna have to get a warrant to look at Pridwell's email messages. The sergeant's not gonna be happy about that."

Dino got a glint in his eye, and Jack knew that impish grin that follows meant he had come up with a plan. "So, we don't tell him. If we're right, he won't care. If we're wrong, he's got plausible deniability. It'll help him cover his you know what."

"If we're going to do this," Jack warned, "we'll need to be careful. Most of the judges in this town have strong connections to Baylor's law school and we are essentially telling the judge that we consider the provost of the university to be a suspect in two murders. And the provost's brother is a state senator who's already shown he's not afraid to use his influence to help Pridwell."

Dino continued to smile. "I'll start writing up the warrant. Why don't you get online and see if you can find a judge who either did not earn their law degree at Baylor or doesn't teach for them."

After searching for ten minutes, Jack found the name of one judge who didn't have deep Baylor connections, at least not the kind that would appear on a resume. "Dino, let's take the warrant to Judge Ivey. His degree is from Texas A&M, and everybody knows that Aggies don't like Baylor. More importantly, he's a friendly judge when it comes to issuing warrants for police investigations. He doesn't ask as many questions as some of them do."

"Sounds like a plan. I've typed up the form, so I just have to insert the judge's name and send it over. With luck, he'll get back to us quickly. Let's go grab a cup of coffee while we wait."

By the time they drank their coffee they had a response from Judge Ivey. He approved the warrant, but only for the two days in question. Jack and Dino headed over to the IT department at Baylor where they asked to speak to the person in charge. They were shown to the office of the IT Director who met them at the door when they knocked. They showed him the warrant and told them they need all of Larry Pridwell's emails sent and received on the day Jack and Dino interviewed him, and on the day that he received a message from the burner phone. The IT Director sat down at his desk and launched a program from his laptop. They watched as he keyed in the information. He pulled a thumb drive out of his desk and stuck it in the computer. "I'll save it on this so you can take it with you. I prefer not to print it out since the printer is in a common area and someone might see the contents."

"We appreciate that," Dino said. "It will also let us search the text."

"I assume you want any attachments as well."

"That would be helpful, yes."

After only a few minutes, the IT Director gave Dino the thumb drive. Dino turned and headed out the door, but Jack stood there a second longer before commenting to the IT Director, "It goes without saying that this request is confidential. It's part of an ongoing police investigation, and we expect you to keep it to yourself. I trust you understand."

"It's not my first rodeo, Detective. Discretion comes with the territory." Jack nodded once and followed Dino back to the car.

*   *   *

When they arrived back at the office, Jack pulled up a chair as Dino put the thumb drive into the slot on his own computer. The emails were sorted by date and time, so Dino began scrolling, looking at the heading of the emails as he did. One email quickly caught his eye, along with the subject line. It said you have a voicemail. It identified the sender as a phone number with a Baylor extension, and the subject line says, "voice mail."

"This has to be the transcript generated by the voicemail system," Dino excitedly uttered to Jack.

"What's it say?"

Dino began to read the transcription of the voicemail:

"Larry, I don't appreciate your games. You let me sit on hold for ten minutes before your secretary told me you were unavailable. I had her transfer me to your voicemail. I need to talk to you urgently. A police detective just questioned me about the skeleton found behind the chapel. You need to get them to back off. This is not good for Baylor, and I resent their intrusion. I'm coming to your office to talk about this in person."

"That's gotta be Cheatham. Sounds like you made quite an impression on the man, Jack."

Jack nodded and smiled. As Dino reached for a pile of papers on his desk, Jack's lips formed his own wry grin, "What can I say, Dino? I'm an impressive guy."

"Well, that's interesting," Dino said while pointing to another email. "Within minutes of this voicemail, Pridwell called his brother."

"What about the call from the burner?"

Dino ran his finger down the call log and found the time when the burner phone called Pridwell's office. Then Dino scrolled through the email transcript until he came to the one that corresponded to the time of the call. "We got him. Listen to this."

"Larry, we had a mutual acquaintance some years ago. I think it may benefit both of us to have a conversation about him. Oh, and I might add that, sadly, our mutual friend died over a decade ago now. Call me at this number within twenty-four hours or face the

the cons in trenches."

Jack and Dino looked at one another. "That's got to be Whitson," Jack stated emphatically. "The message is vague, but how many people would Pridwell know who died over a decade ago?"

"Who are the 'cons in trenches?'"

"Look, the email attachment has an MP3 file. It's gotta be a copy of the voicemail itself."

"Play it."

Dino found the attachment on the thumb drive and clicked on the file. The media player began to play the voicemail whose text they had read. Jack immediately repeated the end. "'Face the consequences' not 'cons in trenches.' It may be a technological marvel, but it's still only artificially intelligent. More importantly, that's Whitson's voice. I recognize his voice. We've got Pridwell. We've definitely got him now."

"Now there's only one problem," Dino added.

"What's that?"

"Now, we've got to tell the sergeant. We're going to have to think about how to present the case and make him understand that the two murders are linked. He's not gonna like that we've been working them together as much as we have."

"I'll give that some thought tonight, but now I need to leave early. We've got a birthday party tonight."

53

Jack left work early because it was Juanita's twelfth birthday, and Mariposa had planned a family dinner in her honor. Mariposa feared that all the attention that Juanita's older sister Sofia was getting over her *quinceañera* might be causing Juanita to feel left out. Jack agreed.

"You and Teri haven't forgotten tonight, I trust," Jack called out to Dino from the door to the hallway.

"Do you honestly think that there's a chance in Hades that Teri would forget her god-daughter's birthday? Or, and this is absolutely un-imaginable in my view, that I would miss out on a chance at some of your mother-in-law's cooking? All the double-murder confusion and the *quinceañera* pressure is messing with your thought processes, man." Dino could not turn down good food. He could not turn down an opportunity to rib Jack, either. Jack smirked and Dino softened the tone adding, "Seriously, can I lend a hand with the bike?"

"Thanks, but I had the bike shop take care of the 'some assembly required' part. I'm driving the SUV today so I can fit it in the back if I fold down the seats. With luck I'll be home well before the girls and can hide it in the garage. We'll see you two in a couple of hours."

Over Mariposa's objection that it was too expensive, Jack had decid-ed to give Juanita a new BMX bike. He and Juanita enjoyed spending time riding bikes together, but she really had outgrown her child's bike and had developed an interest in trail-biking. Of his two daughters, Juanita was the athlete and the outdoors lover. As Dino had just reminded him, *los suergos* will also be at the party, which means Jack may have to navi-gate critical comments from his mother-in-law directed at him. Maybe Teri will help deflect some of that. Maybe his *suegra* would appreciate Jack's grand gesture for her granddaughter.

As anticipated, Mariposa met Jack at the door with a list of last-minute chores in preparation for the celebration. Mariposa had already spent a couple of hours in the kitchen sous chefing for her mother. It seemed to Jack that her nerves were a bit frayed so he tackled the list cheerfully and industriously so as not to add to her frustration. *Abuelo* Sanchez will come separately. The party wasn't a surprise event, so when the girls got home from school, they both pitched in to help, which also seemed to relax their mother a bit. Sofia had always been a good big sister, and Juanita idolizes her. Both Jack and Mariposa were proud of their daughters' relationships with one another. They had friends whose children bickered regularly, but the Farmer household typically enjoyed harmony.

The Pipers arrived precisely at the appointed hour. "You can set your clock by Dino," Teri told Jack as she took the nachos she had made into the kitchen.

"Hey, Dino! *Bienvenido!*" Mariposa called out from the kitchen. "Get Jack to make you a drink. We just have a few finishing touches to add in here and we'll all join you."

When the girls heard their mother say Dino's name, they came running from somewhere in the interior of the house. They had known Uncle Dino and Aunt Teri their whole lives. They were born about the time the Piper's children left them with an empty nest, so, naturally, they developed a close relationship with the Farmer children. Dinner featured all of Juanita's favorites, special dishes her *abuelita* prepared, including *sopa de fides*, and for dessert, *buñuelos*. Even though the noodle soup is customarily served at lunch, and the sweet fried dough is traditionally a Christmas delight, her grandmother made these dishes because they were Juanita's favorite dishes.

Juanita squealed in delight when she saw her bike. Teri gave her a fancy new bike helmet and a colorful bicycling outfit to complement her parents' gift. "You'll be the most stylish biker on the track," Dino commented. Juanita giggled in delight. The festive mood even extended to Jack's interaction with his mother-in-law. She did not nag him once about his slow progress with the waltz.

After dinner finished, and Juanita opened all her gifts, Teri offered to help Mariposa tidy up as the girls get ready for bed. "Besides, we have some catching up to do," Teri insisted. "You men go find something useful to do."

A few minutes later, Mariposa sat down the pot she was rinsing. "Teri, do you ever worry that Dino can't put his work aside even for a moment, at his daughter's birthday, for example? Did you see Jack's jaw twitching during dinner? He clinches his teeth when something's on his mind."

"No, I didn't notice. I know Jack well, but I don't know him as well as you do, of course. Could it be that Juanita's twelfth birthday has him thinking about Sofia's fifteenth? The girls are growing up fast. I know what you're talking about with the work thing, though. Dino keeps note pads by his favorite chair in the den and in the nightstand on his side of the bed. He uses them regularly, too."

"I just worry that Jack will burn out or that the things he deals with—murder and the like. . ." Mariposa sighed as she trails off.

"I worry about these things, too, Mariposa," Teri sympathized. "I have been a cop's wife longer than you, so I can offer you a bit of consolation. First, if you are worried that this kind of thing can damage marriages, and I bet that you are, I can tell you that it can, but it hasn't damaged mine and I doubt it will damage yours. You have a beautiful family and, as far as I can see, a beautiful marriage. Second, if Jack follows Dino's trajectory, it will be at least a decade before Jack has had enough of police work."

"You sound like there's a definite timeline in the satisfaction-with-your job experience of police detectives."

"Don't tell Jack. Dino would be furious with me for telling you, but you need to hear it, I think. Dino is beginning to make noises about retiring soon. I don't think he's made up his mind yet. The case they're working on now. . ."

"Exactly!" Mariposa exclaimed. "Let's pact together to watch them closely. I can hardly wait for the *quinceañera* and that damned father-daughter dance to be behind us. And I want that case solved tomorrow."

After the Pipers had left and the girls had gone to bed, Jack sat for a few moments on the patio nursing a beer and reflecting on the evening, on how quickly his daughters were growing up, on how unusually well he and his in-laws got along with one another this evening, and on work. Despite the occasion, questions about how to make the Pridwell-Whitson connection clear to Mendoza had never been far from his thoughts. Even his mother-in-law noticed and expressed concern that Jack's emotional health and well-being would improve if he could leave work at the office. Now, alone with his beer, his thoughts returned to the case.

"Our interview prompted Whitson to contact Pridwell?" Jack summarized to himself. "Everything we learned about Whitson from the interview and the phone records suggests that Whitson lived by taking advantage of and manipulating others." So, he and Dino must get Mendoza to realize that Whitson had seen an opportunity to exploit Pridwell for what was going on fifteen years ago. "In turn," Jack's internal dialogue continued, "that arrogant, self-important, bombastic Pridwell could react angrily if anyone threatened his ambitions. His station and reputation mean everything to him." Jack's train of thought came up short.

As he finished his beer and started to bed himself, Jack uttered aloud the one word that summed up his internal dialogue: "Blackmail! That's the key. Mendoza will have to recognize that extortion is the key linking the two cases."

54

Jack and Dino sat down together to go over what they had learned. They realized they were at a crossroads. Things had fallen into place in the last twenty-four hours. They had documents, video, email, and logic as evidence. "We've got to lock this down," Jack mumbled uncharacteristically. "We know the two cases are linked, and we know the culprit. We've got to get the sergeant to understand."

Dino pulled out a pad of paper and clicked his pen. "I agree, but we're talking about arresting the provost at Baylor University for two murders. We need to lay out our case methodically and logically so the sergeant can't shut us down. Where should we start?"

"We start with the Whitson murder. That's where our evidence is stronger and the voicemail of Whitson blackmailing Pridwell creates the link to the earlier case."

"Okay, let's line it out. Step-by-step."

After about half an hour, they were satisfied with the order of their presentation. Jack rose, ready to head to Mendoza's office, but Dino stopped him. "Wait a minute, Jack. Are we sure about this? We need some context."

"What kind of context?"

"I've always had the impression that Baylor was a relatively progressive place. Would someone like Pridwell be so afraid of people finding out he was gay that he would knowingly murder two people?"

"Sounds like an argument for the defense attorneys. I'm sure they'll make that case. But I'm not terribly worried about it."

"Well, I'd feel better if we could connect the dots better between a possible motivation and potential consequences. Let me make a call to Reverend Haley, the former pastor of the Baptist Church across from Tidwell, to help us paint the picture more lucidly."

"Okay, Dino. I know what you're like when you're on the hunt. You call the reverend. While you do that, I'm gonna go and have a cup of coffee. I'll work on my Spanish while I'm waiting."

*   *   *

Dino reached Reverend Haley by phone a few minutes later. "Reverend, I'd like to use you as a background source if I could, but I need your word that you will keep our conversation in strictest confidence."

"Well, keeping secrets goes with the territory in my line of work, but color me intrigued that you think I could contribute. How can I help?"

"Well, we're still working on the case about the skeleton found in the Tidwell Building. The evidence has led us to believe that our suspect may have killed a young man to keep him from going public about their homosexual liaison. Since Baylor has a reputation for being somewhat tolerant on this issue, I'm wondering why our suspect would feel so threatened."

Reverend Haley cleared his throat. "I would say this about that. I agree that Baylor is quietly tolerant, to use your word, but also willfully ignorant. In other words, they are tolerant until they're not."

"I'm not sure I follow you. Are you saying they have a policy of don't ask, don't tell?"

"It's more complicated than that. Gay students can be fairly open about their sexuality, but employees would be terminated at the first hint that they identify as gay. If your suspect was a Baylor faculty member or administrator, especially fifteen years ago, and word of a homosexual relationship came out, that person's employment would have been finished almost immediately."

"That seems a little harsh. And, I must say it also seems a little hypocritical. It makes no sense to be silently tolerant in the abstract, but so callous in practice."

"Baylor doesn't see it as hypocritical. Their administrators consider themselves pragmatic. They know that they are situated in Texas, not in California. Central Texas is one of the most culturally conservative places in the country. When it comes to culture war issues like homosexuality, it's tough to have a reasonable debate in Texas. Most Baptists in Texas think homosexuality is a sin, even though Jesus never said a word about it. If Baylor took a different stance publicly, they would lose millions in donations, and they would have difficulty recruiting in Texas. They're not wrong, of course, but just because you're not wrong doesn't mean you're right."

"Explain please."

"As I said, the majority of Baylor's constituency takes a very conservative stance on this issue, but a significant minority think otherwise. Right here in Waco, we have Baptist churches and churches in other denominations that proclaim themselves to be welcoming and affirming to all people, including people who identify as LGBTQ."

"So, our suspect could go to one of these more open churches, but he would be fired if he did what his church said was okay."

"Even that is complicated. Those in leadership positions get scrutiny. They are quietly, but unmistakably, discouraged from attending those Baptist churches."

"That's all so convoluted. That must put people under considerable stress."

"So, let me ask you a question, detective. Is your suspect named Larry Pridwell?"

"How did you know that? I mean, I can't say because our suspect's part of an ongoing investigation. Why would you say his name?"

"As I said, detective, discretion goes with the territory in my line of work."

* * *

After Dino got off the phone with Reverend Haley, he walked down to the break room where Jack was finishing his coffee. Jack looked up from his seat and took off his headphones. "*Que pasó*, Dino?

"Is that all the Spanish you know, Jack? While I've been doing real detective work, you're sitting here sipping coffee and chewing on a biscotti."

"For your information, I'm chewing on a biscotto. Biscotti is plural in Italian. Biscotto is the singular, and I only ate one. So, did you get what you needed?"

"I did. Let's go see the sergeant."

Jack followed Dino back to the Mendoza's office. When they reached the sergeant's office, the door was open. Jack stepped inside and looked Mendoza in the eye, "Sarge, we need to talk. The two cases you've got us working are definitely linked, and we need to bring a suspect in for formal interrogation."

"Who?"

"Larry Pridwell, the provost."

"Holy crap. You'd better come in and lay it out for me. There's going to be a lot of stuff hitting the fan if we do this. I'm not putting my ass on the line if I'm not convinced."

Jack nodded to Dino, signaling him to go ahead. "Let's start with the most recent murder. According to the forensic evidence, someone killed Whitson between midnight and six in the morning. We have a video of Pridwell arriving at the airport just in time to catch his five-a.m. flight to Raleigh, North Carolina. That same video shows him tossing what we believe is a burner phone into the trashcan at the ticket counter."

"Unfortunately," Jack added, "the trash was emptied, so we don't have the phone itself. But we think the phone belonged to Whitson."

"Right. And we were able to search the phone logs for Pridwell which is where things get very interesting."

"How so?" Mendoza seemed, for the first time, genuinely intrigued.

"Well, the day before he left for North Carolina, Pridwell got a call from an unknown number."

"I get those all the time," Mendoza grunts. "Dad gum telemarketers."

"Except, this time the caller left a voicemail."

"How do you know that?"

"Well, Baylor has this fancy phone system. When someone leaves a voicemail, the computer system transcribes the voicemail and sends the transcription as an email to the person associated with that phone. We got a warrant to check Pridwell's email."

"You what? I didn't authorize that."

Jack interrupted. "Of course you didn't. We deliberately left you out of the loop, so you'd have plausible deniability if word got out."

"Oh. Thanks, I think. Not that it matters now if you're wanting to bring him in for questioning."

"But more to the point, we found the transcribed email and it had a digital recording of the email itself. Both Jack and I recognized Whitson's voice. The content of the voicemail contained a veiled, but clear threat. The caller demanded to meet with Pridwell concerning the death of their mutual friend."

"Are you sure the voice was Whitson's?"

"No doubt about it, Sarge," responded Jack confidently. "We both interviewed Whitson, and he had a very distinctive voice."

"And that's not all," inserted Dino. "The call logs also show two other interesting calls. We have another transcribed voicemail in which Cheatham left an angry message for Pridwell, also shortly after we interviewed Cheatham. From what we've gathered, Cheatham wasn't satisfied with leaving a voicemail. We know he went to Pridwell's office and confronted him in person shortly after leaving the voicemail."

"That sounds typical of Cheatham from what you've told me about him," Mendoza remarks.

"Finally, Pridwell also made an outgoing call shortly after our initial conversation with him. He called his brother, the state senator. We don't have a transcription of that call, but the timing is damning."

"How so? They're family. A defense attorney won't have any problem passing that call off as family business."

"That may be," intoned Jack, "but think about it. We interviewed Pridwell. He calls the state senator, who just happens to be his brother. Not long after that, you start getting pressure to shut down the investigation into the old murder. He killed the Darden kid."

"That sumbitch. He got his brother to do his dirty work. That makes sense, and it pisses me off, but how does this link back to Whitson?"

"Remember, Whitson shared an apartment with Darden at the time Darden disappeared. We figured out that Whitson knew something about a relationship between Darden and Pridwell."

Jack took over from there. "Darden's mother is still alive, living in Richmond, Virginia. She sent me a box of memorabilia that Darden kept. The box had two items of interest. First, there was an engraved watch. The engraving said, 'to B from L, always.' The second item of interest was Darden's diary. Among other things, the diary contained numerous entries about a romantic relationship that Darden had, one that he never told his parents about. He referred to his lover simply as 'L.'"

"So, you're saying. . ."

"That's exactly what were saying," Jack continued. "The L stands for Larry, as in Larry Pridwell, and he was romantically involved with Darden, one of his students."

Mendoza whistled. "This stuff really is going to hit the fan if you're right."

Dino summarized the case, "It all starts to make sense when you see the connections. Pridwell went to extraordinary lengths to get Darden a spot in the graduate program. Darden didn't have the grades to get in, and he didn't perform well in those classes. Nevertheless, Pridwell requested him as his graduate assistant after Darden's first year had gone badly with Cheatham."

"Didn't anybody suspect they had a relationship?"

"No. Well, that's not quite true. The former pastor of Seventh and James suspected, or was told in confidence, but he's the only one we know of. If you think about the timeline, the relationship probably started when Darden was an undergraduate. The offices in the back of the chapel gave the two of them unfettered privacy. When Pridwell moved to a larger office in another part of the building, Darden still had access to Cheatham's office in his first year of graduate school, so they could continue meeting at night when no one else was around."

"But what about the second year? By then, Darden was working for Pridwell, not Cheatham."

"True, but both Darden and Pridwell had keys. If you remember, by this time almost everyone was getting master keys because they lost track of the individual keys to the offices over the years."

"So, if they were in such a cozy relationship, what changed? How and why would Pridwell murder him?"

"Ambition, pure and simple," Jack explained. "Pridwell had just learned he was being promoted to the Dean's office. It only makes sense that he decided to break off the relationship with Darden because he'd have to move out of Tidwell."

"Can't imagine that went over well with Darden," continued Dino. "He probably threatened to go public, and that's when Pridwell attacked him. It was probably a spur of the moment thing. If someone backed Pridwell into a corner, he'd do anything to keep his job. Look what he did to Whitson when Whitson tried to blackmail him."

"Even before that, Pridwell worked hard to shut down the investigation. He instigated his brother, the state senator, to kill the investigation 'for the good of the university.'"

"And I'm the one who paid the price for that," Mendoza grumbled through clenched teeth. "I'm the one who got told to stop the investigation." Jack and Dino refrained from looking at one another, but each of them had the same thought. "The command may have come to you, but you pushed it on to us with absolute conviction."

Mendoza made a steeple with his fingers. "You make a compelling case, but let me get this straight. You're saying that Pridwell committed both murders. He murdered Whitson because Whitson was trying to blackmail him because Pridwell had a homosexual liaison with a student, and then he killed that student."

"Yes sir. That's about the size of it," Jack answered while nodding. "Whitson put the pieces together that Pridwell was romantically involved with Darden. Whitson tried to blackmail Pridwell, not realizing how dangerous he was."

"And Pridwell killed Darden to keep him from going public about their relationship?"

"It's the most logical explanation," Jack remarked.

"And you're proposing we bring him in for questioning as a formal person of interest?"

"Yes. We think we should bring him in Monday. Naturally, he'll bring his lawyer with him."

"Naturally. But we would be negligent if we did not bring him in for a formal conversation, and it should be done here. Now, let me ask you one other thing."

"What's that?"

"How certain are you about Pridwell trying to shut down the investigation?"

Dino replied, "Some might say the evidence is circumstantial, but we don't think so. The time between our interview with Pridwell and his call to his brother is too tight to be coincidental. We think Pridwell got his brother to put pressure on the higher-ups at the police department for Baylor's sake."

"And in turn, those higher-ups put pressure on me. I don't like being used, and I don't like my department being treated as a pawn."

"No sir. I wouldn't think you would."

"Well, I might just have trick or two up my sleeve to make Pridwell feel some pressure himself. Have him here Monday at nine o'clock for the interview. Don't take no for an answer. We'll give him the courtesy of coming here on his own accord, but make sure he knows that we'll come get him if he's not here."

"Will do, Sergeant. We'll go take care of it right now."

After the detectives left his office, Mendoza shut the door behind them. He returned to his desk and did a quick Google search. He dialed the number for the *Waco Tribune-Herald*.

When a human finally answered, he said, "This is sergeant George Mendoza of the Waco Police Department. I need to speak to a reporter on the crime beat."

He smiled to himself as he waited for someone to come on the line. "It'll be good for Pridwell to get a taste of his own medicine. Let's see how he likes the pressure."

55

The detectives left their meeting with Sergeant Mendoza and went directly to their desks to place the call to Pridwell. Both of them were on the call. Katherine Doyle, Pridwell's executive assistant, answered and gave the typical gatekeeper's response to their request to speak with the provost, who, it seemed, was about to leave for an important meeting and could not be detained. Could they call at another time?

"Listen, I know that you are only doing your job," Dino stated calmly but firmly, "but this is an urgent, official police matter." He spoke the last four words slowly, separating each word distinctly, with a slightly elevated volume. "Now, please put the provost on the phone."

"Please hold the line."

Jack commented that he could well imagine the conversation going on between the two principals on the other end. After a few moments Pridwell came on the line. He wasted no time and effort in asserting his superiority.

"Tell me, detectives, why I shouldn't consider this police harassment and contact my lawyer—to initiate a civil action against you, the Waco Police Department, and the city of Waco. As you may or may not know my brother is also a state senator. I've already told you everything that I know about both Darden and Whitson." Pridwell sounded angry and defensive.

"Actually," Dino countered, "we have good reason to believe that statement to be false, which is why we're calling."

"To come to the point," Jack intruded, "we need you to come to the station Monday morning for a formal interview. You can bring your lawyer/brother/senator along if you'd like. In fact, it might be advisable. We have set aside time at nine o'clock for an interview. Don't be late."

Jack matched Dino's measured emphases but conveyed a stronger sense of urgency.

"I have no intention of coming to the police department Monday morning or ever, for that matter, unless it were to lodge a formal complaint against both of you," Pridwell exclaimed, his voice loaded with indignation and arrogance. "I repeat, I have nothing more to tell you. You're skating on thin ice here."

Dino was tired of Pridwell's bluster, so he decided to drop a couple of bombs. "First, Dr. Pridwell, perhaps you should consider the fact that, among other interesting items, we have transcripts of your email messages for the period prior to Whitson's murder. Please don't continue to insult us with your claims not to know more than you've told us. And, second, we are not issuing an invitation to chat over coffee. We are summoning you, as we told your assistant, on urgent, official police business."

Jack jumped in. "In other words, if we don't see you walking through the door of the station by 9 a.m. Monday, we will send uniformed officers to arrest you. I mean promptly, 9 a.m. Do you understand? We are doing you the courtesy of appearing on your own volition."

"I'll follow the advice of counsel. Now goodbye."

Dino made a wise crack about Pridwell's haughtiness. "He thinks he's playing chess while we're playing checkers. But come Monday, we'll put him in check. Maybe not checkmate yet, but check for sure."

*　*　*

After virtually hanging up on the detectives, Pridwell sat at his desk fidgeting and brooding. He had hoped to back the detectives down with his threat to begin legal proceedings, to raise the stakes, as it were, but they had called his hand. Now, to keep from seeming to have been bluffing, he really needed a lawyer. He called his brother.

To the provost's surprise, the senator answered the phone almost immediately. "Hello, Larry. I've been wondering whether I might be hearing from you soon. Rumors about murder and some Baylor involvement have been flying around among Baylor Law School alumni for a couple of days now. Give me the scoop."

"I'm fine thanks for asking. And how is your family?" The elder Pridwell replied sarcastically. After a pause, half for effect, and waiting for the smartass rejoinder typical of his brother, he turned to the topic at hand. "A couple of WPD detectives are harassing me. By pure coincidence, the poor unfortunate whose skeleton was discovered on campus some time ago had been my TA once. Also, again purely by coincidence, his roommate, the Whitson fellow who was found dead recently contacted me. I wasn't able to determine what he wanted because I had to go out of town. When I got back, however, he was already dead."

His brother interrupted. "And the detectives suspect that what you are really calling coincidences are in fact circumstantial evidence that you were somehow involved. Am I right?"

"Exactly! And I just thought that you might be able to get them off my back. Threaten them with a harassment lawsuit, maybe. Especially since they have just summoned me for an interview at police headquarters Monday morning."

"Larry, this is beginning to sound serious. Tell me straight, have you any reason to be worried?"

"Absolutely not. . . Well, . . . appearances and timing could be a problem for my career. I planned not to say anything about this to family and friends until it became certain, but I am up for a university presidency. Let's just say in the East. I expect an offer soon. This whole thing could jinx my chances."

"Well, that may be, but you need to get your priorities straight. Deal with the police and clearing your name first. The harassment suit is a nonstarter. From what you are telling me, they must have evidence and want to look into your association with the dead guys. You need a lawyer alright—and before you ask—it can't be me."

"But I thought that. . ."

"No. First, I'm not even sure that it would be possible under the senate's ethics rules. Second, it would smell of influence peddling and that would boomerang on both of us."

"So, no help at all for your big brother?"

"I can recommend a firm in Waco. They have a good reputation and good record. I'll email you the particulars when we get off the phone. Call their office immediately and arrange for representation on Monday in your meeting with the police. You can mention my name. Be advised, though, on such short notice they'll probably send a junior member of the firm."

"Thanks for that much, at least."

"Listen, Larry, don't try any of your condescending gamesmanship on these cops and don't be thinking that you're smarter than your lawyer, even if he or she is a relative newbie. These people know police work and the law. Do what your lawyer says. Dutifully. Alright?"

"Yes sir," Larry acquiesced cheekily, but, if his brother had meant to rattle him, it had worked.

56

MONDAY, JULY 5, 8:30 A.M.

For once, Jack was already at his desk when Dino arrived. Dino had gotten up early to put the finishing touches on his gift for Jack's daughter's *quinceañera*, which delayed his departure for work. Before Dino sat down, Jack looked up from his computer and asked, "Have you seen yesterday's paper?"

"Nope. Anything interesting?" Dino assumed the paper may have covered yesterday's Fourth of July parade and fireworks.

"Our case is on the front page."

"What do you mean?"

Jack turned his computer monitor so Dino could see the screen. The line at the top of the page read, "Baylor Provost Named Person of Interest in Two Murders." Dino continued reading the first paragraph,

Baylor provost Lawrence Pridwell will be interrogated Monday at the police station regarding his involvement in two murders. According to sources close to the investigation, police have linked Pridwell to the murder of Andrew Whitson last week. A hiker discovered Whitson's body at the foot of Lovers Leap. Allegedly, Whitson attempted to black-mail Pridwell concerning his role in the disappearance of Robert Darden fifteen years ago. Construction workers found Darden's skeleton while renovating the Tidwell Building earlier this month. The skeleton had remained hidden since Darden's disappearance in 2007. Police sources allege that Pridwell had been romantically involved with Darden and that a lover's quarrel had led to the death of Darden. Details remain sketchy, but the police believe they have evidence linking the two crimes to Pridwell.

Dino sat in his chair and asked Jack, "Did you speak to a reporter?"

"I'll not even dignify that question with an answer. I assume you're also not 'sources close to the investigation,' but this will complicate our questioning of Pridwell today."

"Does the sergeant know?"

"He's not been in yet, so I don't know. He's not going to be happy when he does find out."

"Speak of the devil," Dino whispers. "He just walked into his office."

"We'd better go give him a heads up."

As they got to the door of Mendoza's office, they heard whistling coming from inside. "Doesn't sound like he's heard yet," noted Jack. "Looks like we get to be the ones to tell him. I hope he doesn't shoot the messenger."

"Sergeant, can we come in?" Dino asks.

"Come on in, boys. I've just been having a moment. I went out to breakfast and took a little extra time to read the paper this morning."

"So, you've seen today's paper?"

"I did. Isn't it a beautiful morning?"

Jack and Dino look at one another. "Then, you saw the headline about Pridwell?"

"Couldn't have happened to a nicer guy."

"Sergeant," Jack comments gently, "Dino and I are not the sources of that story."

"Never thought you were. Anything else?"

"No, we just came by to give you a heads up about the newspaper story."

"Well, you better go get ready for your big interview. That little pissant will be here in about half an hour. I trust you two can handle the interrogation. I'll be listening from the observation room. He's going to have to answer some uncomfortable questions. I imagine your morning's going better than his."

"What just happened in there?" Jack wondered aloud as they walked back to their desks.

"Don't you know? We just spoke with 'sources close to the investigation,'" Dino replied using air quotes.

"Yeah, we did. I gotta say, the sergeant's got balls. I didn't think he had it in him. You gotta respect that."

"I don't know," Dino remarks with some consternation. "If you or I had done that, we'd be writing parking tickets by this afternoon. It's another case of him misusing his authority. That kind of thing that drives me crazy. Those are the same kinds of power games that Pridwell likes to play."

"Yeah, but the game's more fun when you get to be the spectator."

57

Pridwell hadspent the weekend nervously plotting. He determined that the situation warranted striking an aggressive tone in the interview. He vowed not to allow his nerves to show. At her request, Pridwell met his lawyer in the parking lot of police headquarters at 8:45 to confer quickly about the approach they would take in the upcoming interview. Pridwell judged Anne Jackson to be in her late twenties or early thirties. She dressed to emphasize her professionalism and sobriety. She wore a two-piece navy business suit with a long-sleeved notched lapel blazer, matching pencil skirt, and a cream, long-collared silk blouse open at the neck. And of course, a black leather briefcase. Except for her youth, which his brother had warned him about, Pridwell was pleased. Appearance mattered to him, which was why he also chose power professional attire for this morning—a solid black summer weight Merino wool trim-fitting suit. He also wore a crisply starched white shirt with a tennis collar and French cuffs, and a cardinal red bow tie crisscrossed by a pattern of fine silver threads. They agreed that Pridwell would answer any reasonable question simply and honestly, but that he would not volunteer information or editorialize.

Inside police headquarters, a uniformed officer met them and showed them to an interview room, asking them to take seats on one side of a rectangular table. A recording device sat in the middle of the table. Two chairs faced them on the other side, and a display board covered almost the entirety of one wall behind the empty chairs. Cameras mounted in the upper corners of the room perched diagonally across from one another to provide views from two angles. The officer told them that they were early but that the detectives would be along shortly. Pridwell interlaced the fingers of his two hands and placed them on the table. He sat erect and closed his eyes.

After only a few minutes, which seemed interminable to Pridwell, the detectives entered the room, led by Jack holding several file folders. He placed them on the table as he and Dino took their seats. Dino started the recording device and described the purpose of the interview for the record, including its date and time, and a list of those present. He also elicited Pridwell's acknowledgement that he is aware that they are recording the interview, and that, while he is not under arrest, Miranda rules still apply.

Ms. Jackson immediately objected. "My client, I understand, has already told you everything that he knows about this affair. He contends that that you have nothing to gain through this interview unless it is to harass him."

Jack opened the file folder on top and removed the first document. He then stood and pinned it to the display board with pushpins. "This is a list of the commonalities between the murders of Robert Darden and Andrew Whitson. You'll notice that the item at the bottom of this list is simply the name Larry Pridwell. Darden was your graduate assistant in the period just before he died, Dr. Pridwell. Whitson was Darden's roommate. Although, as far as we can tell and according to your statements, you did not know Whitson personally, he still reached out to you as soon as the identity of the remains discovered on campus became publicly known. These connections alone make it difficult for us to believe that you do not know more than you have told us."

"Coincidence. Simply coincidence," Pridwell stated flatly.

Dino reached over to the folder and handed Jack several pages stapled together. As Jack pinned them to the board, Dino stretched his hands out flat on the table sliding them toward Pridwell. "Hmmm," Dino sighed, or better, grunted. "Jack is pinning up transcripts of your email from the period between the discovery of the skeleton and Whitson's murder. The packet also contains a log of calls to your office phone and from your cellphone. In one email, Whitson called you and left a voice mail. In another, your cell phone called Whitson's number. I don't have to tell you the contents of the voice mail, but I encourage you to offer an explanation beyond mere coincidence."

"You haven't asked a question, Detective Piper," Ms. Jackson interjected.

For the first time since sitting at the table, Pridwell unclasped his hands and shifted in his chair. Dino, who was watching Pridwell closely, noted the change in posture and saw perspiration beginning to accumulate on Pridwell's upper lip. "Was his respiration also quickening?"

Jack removed another set of pages from the folder, including a photograph. "How about we turn our attention to Darden for a moment."

Pridwell straightened his bowtie as Jack continued. "You are fully aware of the contents of the call and email logs. You don't know about the contents of a box of Darden's personal effects we obtained from his mother." Pridwell startled, then immediately painted a look of nonchalance on his face.

Jack posted a photograph of Darden's watch. "This very expensive watch was among Darden's things. You can see that it bears the inscription 'to B from L always.' We reckon that 'B' is, of course, 'Bob.' Who do you reckon the 'L' is? Or do you know firsthand? Could it be 'Larry'?'

"This is outrageous speculation!" Pridwell barked.

"I must concur," Ms. Jackson added. "Speculation like this won't sustain an arrest warrant, let alone obtain a conviction. Are we about through here?"

Jack persisted. "These are copies of pages from Darden's journal. Did you know that he kept a journal, Dr. Pridwell?" Pridwell looked toward Ms. Jackson as though she should speak up, but Jack spoke first. "Do you know that the journal apparently refers to this same 'L'?"

"Really, Detective Farmer," Ms. Jackson scolds Jack, "'L' could refer to almost anyone. My partner's name is Lisa. Are you going to interrogate her as well?"

Suddenly, Pridwell's cellphone emitted an alert tone. Pridwell took it out of his inner coat pocket and saw the caller's name, Winston Marshall. He was the chair of the presidential search committee from North Carolina. "Excuse me gentlemen. I really must take this call," he blustered as he walked to the far end of the room.

Pridwell held the phone to his ear and spoke softly. "Mr. Marshall, to what do I owe the pleasure?"

Marshall responded directly. "I won't beat around the bush, Dr. Pridwell. We must rescind the offer to bring you to campus. It would not be prudent to interview you now."

Pridwell stammered back, "I don't understand. Nothing has changed on my end. Why are you pulling the offer?"

"It's because of the newspaper article, Dr. Pridwell. I am sure you, of all people, understand that the article makes it impossible for us to continue our conversations. I do hope you understand, and I wish you well."

"Wait. Is it because the article said I'm gay?"

"No, Dr. Pridwell. That would actually work in your favor at our institution because we value diversity of all kinds. We would welcome an administrator with your experience who is gay."

"But . . . Then I do not understand. Why are you shutting down the conversations?"

"Dr. Pridwell, it's because of the murders. We cannot interview someone who is under suspicion of two murders. I am sorry." The phone went silent, and Pridwell's face turned white.

When Pridwell sat back down, he was noticeably shaking and subdued. Dino and Jack both saw it, but it was Jack who leaned forward, like a cougar moving in for the kill, forcing Pridwell to look directly into his eyes.

"Do you know that he describes a rather sizzling love affair with 'L'?" Jack continued as though the interruption had not happened. Clearly, Jack was pushing for an advantage. "Unfortunately, in the few entries dating to just before Darden's death, he indicated that the affair was souring. Do you think that a love affair gone wrong could have motivated his murderer? Did 'L' kill 'B'? What do you think, Larry? Or do you know full well?"

The use of Pridwell's proper name, in its shortened familiar form, struck the provost as a provocation, if not an insult. "You're asking me to cooperate in this guessing game? I hope you are soon coming to the end of this amusement of yours. 'L' could be 'Lucy' or 'Lisa,' for all any of us know. Ms. Jackson, let's leave."

"Oh, but I forgot to mention that Darden always refers to 'L' using masculine pronouns, so that rules out Lucy and Lisa. Darden was your graduate assistant. Did you know that he was gay? Didn't he ever mention a love interest?" Jack prodded, knowing that Dino was about to spring the trap involving a fabrication that they had planned. Now, Pridwell was exhibiting overt signs of agitation. His hands trembled, and pushed back from the table as though he was about to stand.

Dino continued the conversation. "Did you know that the serial number on that watch has enabled us to do much more than speculate, Larry? We traced it to the point of sale. We know who bought it. You do, too."

Without warning, Pridwell lunged across the table. He grabbed Dino by the throat and screamed at him. "Of course, I know, you moron. I'm the one who gave it to him."

58

As soon as Pridwell lunged at Dino, Jack jumped from his seat and bull rushed Pridwell into the wall behind him. The move caught Pridwell by surprise and knocked the air out of him. Jack flipped him around and put handcuffs around Pridwell's wrists behind his back before Pridwell could get air back in his lungs. Jack sat him back in the chair, allowing him to catch his breath. Pridwell's shoulders slouched, and he looked defeated. "It really doesn't matter now," he lamented.

Jack responded in a milder tone, "Larry Pridwell, I am placing you under arrest for assaulting a police officer and for the murders of Robert Darden and Andrew Whitson. You have the right to remain silent. Anything you say can and will be used against you in a court of law. Do you understand these rights as I read them to?"

Pridwell nodded and replied with little energy, "Yes. I understand, but there's no point in denying it anymore. I killed them both. I really regret killing Robert Darden. He was a nice boy. He shouldn't have had to die."

"Then why did you do it?" inquired Dino.

"I had to. He threatened me. When I was asked to join the Dean's office, I knew I had to end our relationship. We were able to keep the relationship a secret when we were in the Tidwell Building, but once I moved to the Dean's office, I would not have had any private space where we could meet, and I couldn't have made excuses to visit Tidwell on a regular basis. It just had to stop."

"That doesn't sound like much of a threat, Provost Tidwell. You could've just ended the relationship."

"That's what I tried to do, but he threatened to go public with it. I'd have lost my job. I was destined to lead, but I would've been terminated if word got out about our relationship."

"So, what'd you do?"

"I just pushed him. I didn't mean to kill him. He hit his head on the concrete wall and down he went."

"Then you must've hit him kinda hard though, huh?"

"You saw how my temper got the better of me a few minutes ago. When I get angry, sometimes I don't even know how strong I am. I am sorry he died, though. I can't say the same for that Whitson fella. He tried to blackmail me. The little shit had the audacity to try to shake me down for thirty thousand dollars. Again, my anger got the better of me. I was changing a flat tire while he was trying to extort me for money, a lot of money. I got angry. I hit him with a tire iron. It happened on the spur of the moment. Okay, it wasn't accident in his case, but it wasn't premeditated."

"See, now, that's where you start to lose us. Your story doesn't line up with the facts in either case. Yes, Robert Darden experienced a significant blow to the head. It was enough to knock him out, but not enough to kill him. Our forensics person found evidence he'd been strangled. That's shows intent to commit murder. You chose to hold your hands around someone's neck so tight he could not breathe for several minutes."

"No, I didn't mean to do it."

"Oh, but you did. You may have lashed out without thinking when you pushed him against the wall, but you chose to strangle him. That's murder in the first degree."

"That's it," interrupted Pridwell's lawyer. "My client will not be answering any further questions. You cannot force him to do so."

"No, we can't," Jack admitted, "but we can tell you the rest of the story. You didn't hit Andrew Whitson with a tire iron. You hit him with a crowbar, a big, heavy, metal crowbar. We found it in the river where you threw it. No one uses a crowbar to change a tire. You also strangled him. He had bruising on his neck from where your hands wrapped around it. His hyoid bone was broken, just like Robert Darden's. Unlike Robert Darden's death, however, you planned this one in advance. You brought the crowbar with you to smash his head. When that didn't work as you had hoped, you strangled him too. Do you have anything to say about my version of the story?"

"He does not," said the lawyer as Pridwell just glared at Jack.

"In that case, please stand up. An officer will book you, make sure you get a new suit of prison clothes, and escort you to your cell, where you will stay until you are formally arraigned on three felony counts, including two counts of first-degree murder."

Dino opened the door and handed Pridwell over to the officer who was waiting outside. "In a way, he's kinda lucky, you know," Dino said to Jack after Pridwell and his lawyer left.

"How do you figure that?"

"Well, instead of that nice fancy black suit he's wearing, he'll be getting a nice orange jumpsuit. That's a real upgrade."

"What are you talking about, Dino? In what world is a prison jumpsuit an improvement over a custom-made Italian suit?"

"Haven't you heard? Orange is the new black."

"My friend, you have the strangest sense of humor."

59

From his vantage point near one end of the head table, Dino enjoyed watching the pageantry of Sofia's *quinceañera* unfold before him and, especially, watching Jack. The celebration had begun with the private mass attended by the honoree, her court, and her family—which included Dino, her *padrino*, his wife Teri, and Jack's parents, Bill and Linda Farmer who had flown from Georgia for the occasion. When the entire group arrived at the Cameron Park Clubhouse, they made a procession into the hall where the guests were awaiting them. Everyone took their seats, and Jack stood to offer a welcome and make his opening toast.

Dino had never seen Jack Farmer dressed this way. Dino had seen Jack many times in a loose sports coat or wearing an Atlanta Braves baseball cap, almost always in loafers. Jack's two button black western style tuxedo gave him the air of old Texas money, with its black western string bowtie, pale burgundy vest matching Mariposa's dress, and a paisley pattern stitched in shiny silver thread. Dino marveled at the courage it must have taken Jack to wear the black dress western boots with a high heel, not just because they were so out of character, but because Dino couldn't see how Jack could possibly waltz in them.

Then came Jack's toast. Dino knew that Jack had been working hard on it and was as nervous about the toast as he was about the father-daughter dance yet to come. Jack began,

"Querida familia y queridos amigos,

Hoy estamos aquí reunidos para celebrar un momento único en la vida de mi hija, Sofia, un día lleno de significado y emoción: su quinceañera."

Dino took the insert from his program which contained an English translation of Jack's toast provided for folks like Dino. It read,

"My daughter, there are no words sufficient for expressing how proud I am of you. Seeing you grow and transform into this beautiful young woman, strong and full of courage, fills me with happiness and hope. Every day you show that you carry in you the strength and grace of the extraordinary women in our family: your mother and your grandmothers.

With her love and dedication, your mother has shown me what it means to be a capable and courageous woman. With their wisdom and perseverance, your grandmothers are the perfect example of what it means to confront life with dignity and strength. And you, my daughter, are the reflection of all this and more.

Today we raise our glasses to celebrate not only your fifteenth birthday but also the marvelous future that you have before you. I know that you will succeed in everything that you propose to do because you have the strength of your heritage and the determination of your spirit."

Just as Dino finished reading the English version, Jack finished the toast.

"*Por ti, mi hija, por tu presente, tu futura, y por las increíbles mujeres que te inspiran. ¡Salud!*"

Honestly, Jack outdid himself, doing the whole thing in what sounded fluent to Dino, who spoke only meager Spanish. Okay, so Jack paused a few times as he spoke, but it wasn't clear to Dino whether that was because he had trouble with the Spanish or because Jack was struggling with his emotions, another thing Dino didn't recognize about Jack tonight.

The meal that followed was lavish—*birria*, vegetarian enchiladas for the non-carnivores, with traditional sides of refried beans, Spanish rice, and a bean pot, an assortment of beverages including *horchata*, *agua fresca*, peach and watermelon spritzers, fruit punch, and soda, and a magnificent multi-tiered cake with fondant icing topped with a figurine meant to represent Sofia. Dino knew that Jack could not afford this extravagance on his detective's salary and speculated that Mariposa's parents were probably footing the bill. After all, the whole affair was clearly as much for their sake as for Sofia's. The vast majority of attendees were friends of Mariposa's family and not from Jack's family or circle of acquaintances. Dino noticed that Jack's parents, who had no experience to compare with this, were sticking as close to Juanita as possible, obviously relying on her to navigate them through events. Mostly, though, Dino marveled at the patience Jack consistently displayed with his in-laws.

Indeed, Dino took impish delight watching Jack interact with guests who approached the head table periodically to congratulate him and Mariposa. Dino could overhear them. Several of them, he noted particularly, began in Spanish before switching to English as if to suggest that Jack's Spanish wasn't so good after all. Dino recognized the signs on Jack's face that he was extremely uncomfortable. The whole spectacle was a study in human behavior for Detective Dino.

After dinner, at Jack's invitation, everyone moved to the ballroom, decorated, it seemed to Dino, as though for a high-class high school prom. There, Sofia went through the ritual exchanging of her flats for high heels. Mariposa explained to Dino in a whisper that this act symbolized her transition to young womanhood. Then, came the moment Dino had been waiting for and Jack had been dreading. By that time, Emily Hracek had joined Dino, Teri, and Jack's parents Bill and Linda. They all stood among those gathered in a grand circle, leaving an open area for the opening father-daughter waltz.

"Do you think the lessons are going to have paid off?" Linda whispered to Dino.

"Well, I know that he was still nervous as recently as yesterday. And I don't know whether he's been practicing in those boots, so. . ."

Teri took Dino's arm and added her own thoughts. "The Jack I know will have worked as hard as necessary to rise to the challenge. It seems to me that he has suffered enough indignity for his daughter. I, for one, hope and believe that we will witness the amazing debut of Jack Astaire."

"I know I should express confidence in my son, but I have to second Dino," Bill chuckled, "especially since I remember that he broke up with girlfriends in high school so he wouldn't have to take them to homecoming dances and proms and such."

The five of them laughed good-heartedly just as the live mariachi band struck up a medium tempo waltz that Dino did not recognize. No DJ would be good enough for the granddaughter of Alejandro and Inez Sanchez, Jack's in-laws. Jack did fine for a good two minutes before Alejandro tapped in and finished the waltz with his granddaughter. He clearly knew his way around the dance floor.

Looking relieved, Jack went over to Mariposa, kissed her, and confidently led her out onto the dance floor. Just as the waltz came to its end, Jack's mother-in-law tapped in to dance with Jack for the last few measures. Jack's face showed the same look of surprise that came over

Dino's at the same moment. As they began to dance, she whispered simply, "*Gracias, mijo.*"

Something caught in the back of Jack's throat, but he managed to smile and nod. The waltz ended, and Jack left the dance floor. His body language seemed to say he had left it permanently, and he found Mariposa again. He led her over to where his parents, Dino, Teri, and Emily were standing.

"I told Dino and your dad that you would do yourself proud, Jack. They were both skeptical, but you did great!" Teri greeted Jack and Mariposa.

"Dad, you didn't have any more faith in me than Dino did. I'm disappointed. I didn't notice you tapping Alejandro out, by the way," Jack ribbed his father. Jack was clearly relieved that the whole dance thing was over.

"Son," Linda joined in, "your dad hasn't admitted that his doubts about your dancing ability have mostly to do with his confidence in genetics!"

Bill blushed and everyone snickered.

"Well, partner, as surprised as I am, I have to agree with Teri. Congratulations!" Dino admitted.

"And even without my tutelage," Emily joked, "but Bill, I can give you a pointer or two," she said as she virtually compelled the other Mr. Farmer onto the dance floor.

*　*　*

About forty-five minutes later, Dino had made his way outside to the patio, where he looked out across the river basin, lost in thought. Someone tapped him on the shoulder from behind. He turned around and saw Jack's daughter Sofia. In her hand, she held the jewelry box that Dino had made for her. "It's beautiful," she exclaimed. "I absolutely love it."

"I'm glad you like it. I truly enjoyed making it. I hope you'll think of me sometimes when you use it."

"Always," she said as she gave him a big hug. "I love you, *Tio Dino.*"

With that, she was gone. Only then did Dino notice Jack standing where she had been. "It really is gorgeous," Jack affirmed. "I can't imagine how much time you spent on that."

"You should be proud of her, and Juanita as well. You and Mariposa have done a great job."

"It's been quite the week, hasn't it?" Jack changed the topic. Clearly, the emotion of the evening made him feel uneasy. "I'm glad we wrapped up that case before this evening's festivities."

"You and me both. It's hard to fathom how much sorrow and pain one person can both inflict and endure. Pridwell will pay for what he did. He's going to be in jail for a long time. To think, he was days away from being named president of a university."

"I can't help but feel a little sorry for him, though," Jack empathized. "Can you imagine what it must've been like for him, having to hide who he was for so long. And now he's going to be spending the rest of his life behind prison bars."

Dino noticed a change in Jack's face. The lines around his eyes highlighted that impish grin he always gets just before he says something he is proud of. "Yeah, I feel sorry for him, but you gotta look on the bright side."

"The bright side?"

"Yeah. He may be locked in a prison cell, but at least he's out of the closet."

Dino rolled his eyes. Then he took a deep breath and begins speaking very slowly, "Jack, I need to tell you something."

"Sounds serious."

"It's important. Come the end of the year, I'll have put in enough time to qualify for my pension. At that point, I'm going to retire."

"No way. You're too young. You'll go stir crazy. I know you. You won't be happy if you're not trying to solve the puzzles we call cases."

"I can't keep doing that, though, not with this police department. Working through the bureaucratic maze and with a sergeant who thinks he knows it all. That will kill me faster than retirement. I simply cannot stand being jerked around anymore, not to mention filing the paperwork so other people get all the credit. I do have a plan, though, to keep my hand in some cases. But cases of my own. With my pension, Teri and I can get by since she's still working full time. What I'm going to do, though, is open my own small detective agency. I'll just take on a few cases a month, and only those that interest me."

"Man, Dino. You're serious. I can't believe you've given it this much thought without even mentioning it to me. It won't be the same without you. Who else is going to help me make life miserable for Mendoza?"

"I'll still be around. You can't get rid of me that easily. Besides, you'll probably handle Mendoza better without me than with me. He doesn't push your buttons like he does mine."

"Yeah, but that's because you write most of the reports. I'm gonna go crazy if I have to start writing them all myself."

"Don't worry. Mendoza will probably give you some greenhorn that he'll expect you to train. You'll just have to make sure you give them a long probationary period so they can learn to write reports properly."

"I can't talk about this anymore tonight. I appreciate you giving me a heads up, but now I need something to drink that's got a little kick. You want to join me?"

"Can't think of anything I'd rather do."

60

Just over a year later, Dino sat nursing a leisurely cup of coffee with breakfast, at home with his wife, Teri. He left the police department in January and was enjoying a life of semi-retirement. He qualified for his pension and got his private detective's license, expediting that process because of his years on the police force. He hung out his shingle, so to speak, by building a she-shed for his wife in the backyard and using half of the shed to create a small office space for his new business. He set up a website and opened accounts on Twitter and Instagram advertising his services as a private eye. He took on a few cases a month, but, as he had explained to Jack, only those that interested him. More importantly, he completed those he accepted. He no longer had to deal with a supervisor who was always chasing the next case that will bring him the most acclaim or curry the most favor.

Dino kicked back in his recliner and pulled out his laptop. He opened the day's edition of the *Waco Tribune-Herald*. On Tuesdays, in addition to local and national stories, they print a column by a local reporter, Mike Copeland, regarding happenings in the local business scene. A month earlier, the reporter had interviewed Dino about his new business, Dean Piper Detective Agency. The exposure generated three or four solid inquiries, as well as a number of congratulatory emails from people in the community. He liked this low-key approach to marketing. Usually, Dino read Copeland's business column first. If nothing else, it allowed him to keep up with new restaurants that were opening or closing in Waco. He and Teri enjoyed going out once or twice a week. That day, however, the lead story concerned the public celebration of the reopening of the newly remodeled Tidwell Building.

"You're working today, right?" he asked Teri.

"Yes, you don't have to rub it in. I still work for a living. Why do you ask?"

"They've reopened the Tidwell Building. I'm in between cases right now, so maybe I'll pop over to Baylor and take a look at what they did with the place."

"Just don't go digging up any more bodies."

*   *   *

The fall semester had begun already, so finding a parking space was difficult. Plus, Dino was no longer on official police business, so he had to settle for visitor parking a couple blocks away from the Tidwell Building. Just as he was about to give up, a spot opened. He walked to Tidwell, but this time he approached from the front of the building. He immediately saw the improvements. The building now had only one door instead of three, and it was made of glass. The entryway gave the building a modern vibe, contrasting beautifully with the original art deco and neo-classical design. Previously, there had been three solid metal doors and casements, which had made the entryway look stodgy from the outside and blocked the natural light from entering the inside. As Dino entered the foyer, he could not help but notice how much brighter it was inside. The new glass entryway allowed natural light to enter the foyer, unlike before the renovation. Straight ahead, another glass doorway opened into a suite of offices. Cursive lettering emblazoned on the glass to the left of the door identified the suite of offices inside as the Department of Religion. The entire area had a sleek, modern vibe to it. Dino entered the reception area of the Religion Department, but there was no one seated at the front desk. A massive relief covered the left side of the back wall depicting what looked like a huge bird with human feet and hands. 'I wonder what that is.'

"How do you like our icon, Detective Piper?" Dino turned around and was surprised to see that the voice belonged to Marvin Peake.

"Looks like a couple ferocious beasts or some kind of foreign god or king," Dino replied. "What is it exactly?"

"It's an ancient Assyrian king named Ashurnasirpal II and his attendant deities. It's a relief that was carved and hung on the wall of his royal palace in the ninth century BCE. One of our archaeologists was on the dig that uncovered it years ago. Baylor purchased a full-size replica of the wall. It used to hang on the back wall of a classroom in the basement, but now it hangs here and makes quite the statement."

"So, Baylor promoted a pagan king from the basement to the reception area of the Religion Department. It just goes to show you, things and people in this building are not always what they seem to be. And it continues the theme of blending the old with the new. The Grecian urns and the neo-gothic architecture outside contrast nicely with the modern glass and sleek lines of the reception area inside."

"You've got quite the eye for architecture, Detective. Maybe you missed your calling."

"Maybe I did. By the way, it's just Dean or Dino now. I retired from the police force in January. How are you, Marvin?"

"Good. Can't complain too much. I'm surprised, though. You look much too young to be retired."

"Maybe. But I'm too old to put up with crap anymore. Once I qualified for my pension, I took it."

"Funny, you struck me as someone who really liked your job. You and your partner seemed like a good team."

"Both those things are true. But the bureaucracy and the politics just got to be too much. I had to deal with sergeants who wanted to be lieutenants, lieutenants who wanted to be captains, and captains who wanted . . . Well, you get my point. Let's just say the supervisor to whom I reported was a real piece of work."

"I hear you. Things have certainly improved around here since we got new leadership."

"Yeah, not so much in my department," Dino remarked. "After we closed the Tidwell case, our sergeant took all the credit. He held several press conferences and kept going on about how we, we, we solved the case; how *we* figured out that the two cases were related, and how *we* got Pridwell to confess. I didn't want the publicity for just doing my job, and it was a team effort. I was, however, quite peeved with him taking the credit when he was not a real integral part of the team. He tried to take Jack and me off the case just as we were starting to make real progress. We, that is Jack and I, had to split up just to keep working the cold case, and we had to fight like crazy to get him to agree to do that. It was purely coincidental that Jack and I figured out the two cases were related. So, naturally, my narcissistic sergeant claimed that his actions were what helped connect the two murders."

"Well, if you've got a minute, why don't you come on down to my cubbyhole so we can catch up? I'll grab us a cup of coffee on the way."

"Sure, I'd like that," Dino said as he started following Marvin down the hallway to the right. Dino paused to look at the five two-story stained-glass windows that lined the hallways of the first and second floor offices while Marvin ducked into the kitchenette to grab the coffees. The two-story suite of offices looked stunning with the light streaming in through the stained-glass windows.

"Wow, this building looks amazing," Dino exclaimed as Marvin arrived with his arm extended to present Dino with coffee. Dino takes the coffee, so Marvin can open the door to his office. Dino takes a sip and says, "Man, this is a lot better than the swill they serve at the police department."

"It ought to be, given the twenty million bucks they spent renovating this building."

Dino followed Marvin into the office. Marvin went first so he could sit at the chair in front of the computer, leaving Dino to choose one of the two chairs placed in front of the peninsula jutting out from the right-hand side of the computer desk. The office was clean, uncluttered, and sleek. As Marvin walked to his desk, the office lights came on automatically, obviously controlled by motion detectors.

"I have to say, Marvin, when you said cubbyhole, I was expecting something considerably smaller. You've got a computer desk, a writing surface with filing cabinets underneath. You've got a couple of book-shelves, a whiteboard, and all new furniture that matches. And those motion detectors that turn the light on when you enter the room, that's just fancy."

"Like I said, I can't complain, or at least I shouldn't complain. You gotta understand, though, before the renovation my office was twice this size. It had beautiful, wooden, built-in bookshelves from floor-to-ceiling on three of the four walls. I had all my books in my office, and I have a lot of books. I've never used a whiteboard in my office before now, and I doubt I'll ever use one in the future. I had to renovate my home, essentially adding a new wing with a home office just to accommodate my library. When I come to the office, I feel like I've entered a corporate office park, not my department. I used to be in my office from eight to five every day, teaching and working on my writing projects. Students and colleagues stopped by frequently. Now, I just come to this sterile space just to teach my classes. Right after class, I go home to work on my writing projects. I used to feel like I was part of a department of colleagues, but now I feel like a lone wolf."

"I get that. I felt like I had to leave the police department for my own mental stability. I miss being around the guys, though, especially working with Jack every day. We still keep up socially, but it's not the same."

"How about your partner? I imagine he's bummed about having to train a new partner."

"Not as much as you'd think, actually. It turns out one of our really good people in forensics got tired of just working with the technical stuff, so she took the detective's exam and passed it just as I was leaving the department. The lieutenant hired her as my replacement. He's been under pressure to diversify the police force, and she was a great candidate. She's bright and even our sergeant, who is usually very quick to condemn DEI initiatives, said not one word about the lieutenant hiring her. She's got medical training, and that combined with her knowledge of forensics, will make her a real asset out in the field. Besides that, she and Jack already got along very well, so he ended up with another partner that he can work with quite well."

"And how do you like your new job as a private investigator?"

"For the most part, it's great. Financially, I can live on my pension, especially since my wife still works full time. It's not easy building a business from the ground up, even if I only get two or three clients a month, the extra income helps. I don't have to rent an office because I work from home, but it cost me a lot to make that happen. Like you, I had to lay out big bucks to redecorate my house. I built a she-shed that I share with my wife. She keeps her gardening supplies in one half, and I use the other half as an office and to meet with clients. That meant, though, I had to run electricity and air conditioning, but it's got Wi-Fi and a place to work on my computer. So, overall, I'm better off, but I did have to compromise on some things."

"How about you? I imagine you're liking your new office."

"Well, on my good days, I describe the new situation as a glass half-full kind of thing. Other days, I'd say it's a glass half empty. It's not really an improvement, but it's not terrible. Some things about it are downright funny though."

"Like what?"

"Well, they're still working the kinks out of the building itself, and that's created some interesting moments. They've got this new key card system to enter the building. No more master keys. You can only enter the office space if your ID card has access. On the day they turned on the system for the first time, alarms started going off left and right. No one could figure out why. It took two of our intrepid administrative associates to solve the problem. They got out the fancy monitoring software used to program the alarm system so they could figure out which alarm was being set off. When they went to the offending door, there was nothing there."

"You mean the alarm lights weren't flashing red?"

"No, I mean there was literally nothing there. No card reader. No door. Just a blank wall. Turns out there was a last-minute change in the construction orders. There used to be a door at the back of the old chapel that led into the smaller chapel. They rightly decided that door looked out of place in the new space, so they covered it over with drywall. Nobody thought about the fact that the wiring for the alarms had already been installed in the doorframe. So, they had to turn the big fancy alarm system off for several days while they cut through the wall to fix the problem."

"That's hilarious."

"Yep. And then there's the motion detectors. When they installed them, they only aimed about half of them at the doors, so there was no movement to detect. Mine's still not working correctly. It points at the door, so the lights come on when I enter the room, but the sensor only covers about a third of the office. It does not detect movement when I'm at my computer keyboard. So, I'll be sitting here between classes answering email, and suddenly, the lights just cut off, and the room goes completely black. I have to stand up in the dark, back up three steps, and wave my hands like I'm in a Pentecostal worship service."

Dino could not help but chuckle out loud. He took another sip of his coffee and said, "So, you mentioned the change in leadership. It sounds like that's gone better."

"It has. The administration appointed DelRae Fontenot interim provost and named a search committee to find Pridwell's replacement. They ran a national search, but in this case, they really didn't need to bother. Everybody could immediately tell the difference in the provost's office. She's collaborative. She works through committee structures, so everyone feels heard on issues affecting them. She leads like a colleague, not a queen. Not surprisingly, they appointed her provost on a permanent basis. Almost everyone is thrilled."

"That's a little surprising. Not that she did such a good job, but you indicated she's known to be in a Boston marriage. I'm surprised they'd appoint her to such a high-level position. Pridwell felt like he had to make a choice between his sexuality and his job. His ambition made the choice for him, and that led him down a very dark path. It is beyond ironic that his replacement might also be gay."

"Actually, she's even beginning to lead Baylor forward on that issue a little more proactively. Our younger students have grown up around LGBTQ people. They don't see them as sinful. Our younger faculty think Baylor's policy on homosexuality is antiquated, and they'd like to see it changed. DelRae has managed to restart conversations with the Regents about recognizing a gay and lesbian group on campus like almost every other university in the country. They've rewritten the policy statement on the web site so that it doesn't sound so accusatory. Don't get me wrong, nothing substantive will happen overnight. Baylor's constituency, at least the most vocal among them, will slow the progress. But at least it's starting to head in the right direction."

At just that moment, the lights in Marvin's office went out, and the room went completely dark. "Hold on," Marvin said. He swiveled in his chair, stood up in the darkness, and began to wave his hands above his head. Right then, the lights came back on like magic. Marvin stood there with his hands above his head and just shrugged his shoulders.

"I guess that's a sign," Dino observed. "The gods are telling me that I've taken up enough of your time for today, Marvin. I really enjoyed catching up with you. I still remember your typology of bees. It sounds like Provost Fontenot fits into the category of a 'hasta bee.' I told Jack about your typology. When the case was over and we arrested Pridwell, Jack said we should tell you that there's another category to add to your typology."

"Really? I thought it was rather comprehensive."

"Turns out, according to Jack, you left one out. He realized that Pridwell was a 'killer bee.'"

www.ingramcontent.com/pod-product-compliance
Lightning Source LLC
Chambersburg PA
CBHW061441030726
47503CB00005B/1515